On a Wing and a Dare

CW01497708

Linda Ulleseit

San Jose, California
2013

ISBN-13: 978-0615749204 (Flying Horse Books)
ISBN-10: 0615749208

Flying Horse Books
San Jose, California

Email: **lindaulleseit@sbcglobal.net**

Website: **http://flyinghorsebooks.wordpress.com**

Cover design by Tirzah Goodwin
http://acleverwhatever.blogspot.com/

For my students,
who always inspire…

Gwynned

Yr Wydda   Afon Dyfi

Tremeirchson

Merionneth

Cardigan
Bay

Wales

4

Village of
Tremeirchson

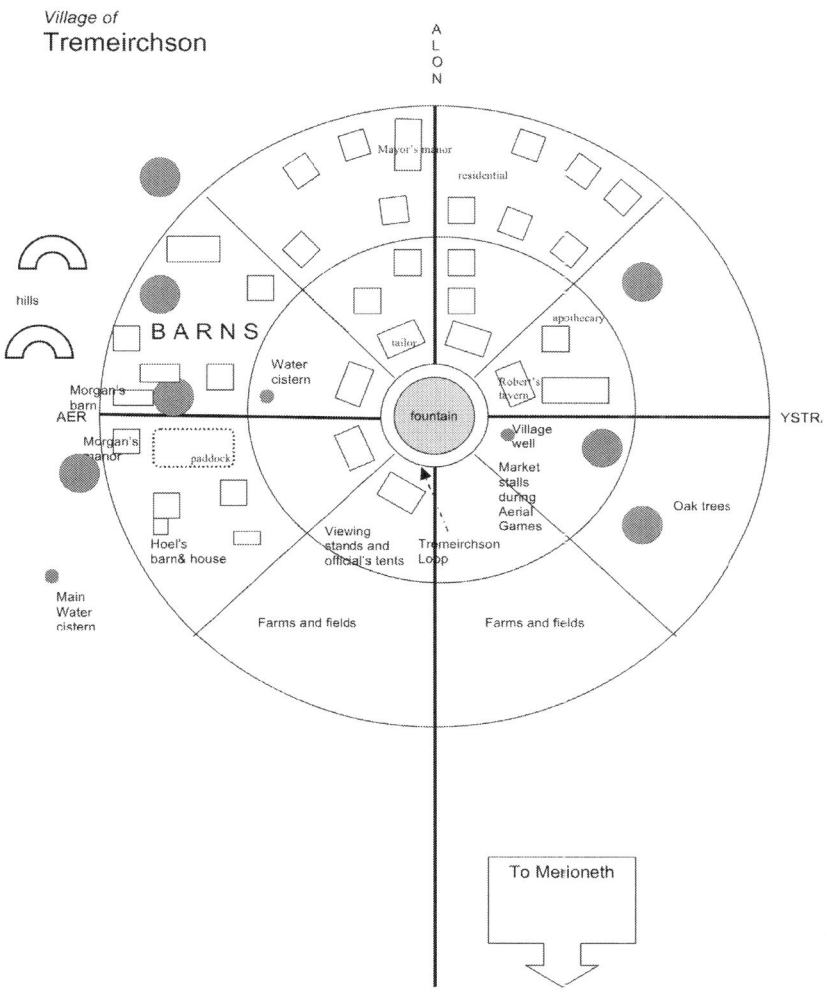

A L O N

hills

BARNS

Water cistern

Mayor's manor

residential

tailor

apothecary

Morgan's barn

AER

Morgan's manor

paddock

fountain

Robert's tavern

Village well

Market stalls during Aerial Games

YSTR.

Oak trees

Hoel's barn & house

Viewing stands and official's tents

Tremeirchson Loop

Main Water cistern

Farms and fields

Farms and fields

To Merioneth

Chapter 1: Fanfare

"Rhys is listless, not eating…" Mum's voice trailed off as the winged colt collapsed like an empty burlap sack.

Emma dropped to the floor, heedless of her skirts, and cradled Rhys's head. The glow of early dawn helped the flickering lantern illuminate the stall.

"Mum?" she asked. "What's wrong with him?"

"He's fevered. Try giving him some water."

"*Iawn, del,*" Emma murmured in Welsh as she dribbled a handful of liquid into Rhys's mouth. She wrinkled her nose at the smell of the water and turned to ask her mother about it, but Neste was preoccupied, thinking out loud.

Water balances fever, but it's not strong enough. Maybe the mare's…" Mum broke off. "Emma, don't risk angering your father

today of all days. I'll care for Rhys. Go."

"Da won't notice I'm not there."

"*Cariad,* you're sixteen. Time to take over your

7

responsibilities to the barn and the family."

Emma reluctantly laid the colt's head on the straw and rose. "Send a groom if you need me." Her mother nodded, reaching to fold the colt's stubby wings.

Outside the sanctuary of Rhys's stall, the rest of the barn came alive as the sun rose and the winged horses began taking flight. Riders and grooms scurried forth clad in blue and silver barn colors. For her father it was all about the glory of the barn, and to Rhiannon's Fire with everything else. Da cared more about winning the Aerial Games than about sick colts or his daughter. Emma couldn't deal with him right now. She slipped away from the barn and headed for her best friends, Davyd and Evan, the sons of Da's biggest rival.

Davyd paced the room, moving from the fireplace with its banked coals to the window in the stone wall. His boots thunked on the wooden floor. It had only been minutes since his father, Morgan, had left. It seemed like hours. He'd promised to wait for Mum, and she was taking longer than usual. Anxious to join his father and brother before the opening ceremonies of the Aerial Games, he stared at the curtain that hid his parents' small bedroom from the living area where he and his brother had beds by the fire.

"Mum? Ready yet?" he called, pushing the curtain aside.

"I can't ride Wynne in the Dance of Welcome today." She sat stiffly on the edge of the bed, her face contorted in pain.

Davyd lowered his eyes, afraid of what was

coming.

"Please, *cariad*," his mother begged, as if the Welsh endearment would convince him. "Please cover for me. Wynne will hate being left alone in the barn when the other horses are flying. And her absence will ruin the formation. She knows what to do. You just have to hang on and wave to the crowd."

His heart froze. Considering how to say no, Davyd went to the bed and sat next to her. He licked his lips and swallowed. She pushed an errant brown curl out of his eyes. He hated it when she did that. With a shake of his head, the curl came back, along with others.

She started to smile before a back spasm gripped her, tensing her body and erasing the humor.

Who could refuse an injured mother?

He managed to give her a reassuring smile. Terror dissipated it, though, as he went downstairs, footsteps echoing as he crossed the Great Hall and left the two-story stone manor. Shaded by ancient oak trees, the structure faced the barn across a wide cobblestone courtyard. Davyd, his brother Evan, and their parents lived upstairs. The kitchen, Great Hall, and some rooms for riders were downstairs.

The barn bustled with activity. Ten stalls faced a covered wooden walkway that paralleled the road. Riders in green and gold tunics called greetings to each other, and grooms led horses blanketed in the same green and gold. The horses stretched their wings, and the enormous feathers glinted in the spring sun.

Davyd crossed the courtyard, his brow already sweating. He entered Wynne's stall with his heart galloping. The white mare tossed her head and rustled her wing feathers. Davyd leaned his forehead against her satiny neck and closed his eyes. Butterflies spun around the frozen ball in his stomach as he imagined the steep spirals and loops of the performance he was about to undertake. Today his secret would come out, and that frightened him even more.

Someone entered Wynne's stall behind him. "*Bore da,* Davyd. Why are you hiding in here? Where's your mum?"

Emma had a knack for showing up whenever he needed a friend.

"She hurt her back and wants me to ride Wynne in the Dance of Welcome." He tried to grin at her, but the smile wavered and he busied himself saddling the mare.

"So what's wrong? You can fly alone for the first time! I'm *so* jealous!"

His shoulders slumped and he turned to face her. She stood with her hands on her hips, her face full of confusion. Her blue dress was clean and neat, but her boots showed how much time she spent in the barn. The lighter streaks in her long chestnut hair blazed in the fingers of sun reaching into the stall. Emma would never hesitate to ride. She was always about independence and fire.

"I'm sorry about your mum being hurt," she said, "but why aren't you thrilled about this?"

"I can't. I just can't."

And like the true friend she'd always been, she eyed his clammy hands and damp hairline. Understanding blossomed on her face. "You're afraid? Oh, in Rhiannon's name, since when?"

He just shook his head and buried his face in the

horse's mane.

"You must get past this," she told him desperately.

"I'm really trying, but I thought I had until summer. I'm not ready."

She hesitated for a moment. "Give me the cloak. I'll ride for you."

"*Na*," he protested, "your father... It's not traditional. It's not right." Hoel would be furious. Her father and his had been enemies longer than he and Emma had been alive. But his agony threatened to engulf him and she was offering to save him.

Helpless to deny it any longer, Davyd put the woolen riding cloak in Emma's outstretched hand. He found a divided riding skirt of his mother's hanging forgotten in the tack room. He gave it to Emma and handed her a green and gold leather helmet. She clapped it on her head and tucked her long hair out of sight as he sagged weakly against the mare in relief.

As she fastened the leather strap of the helmet, Emma felt a moment of doubt. Her father would disapprove. And her mother might need help with Rhys. But Davyd had been a friend forever, and he needed her. She shooed him out of the stall so she could slip on the divided skirt with its unfamiliar green and gold pattern.

Turning to Wynne, she stroked the mare's nose and talked to her, watching the ears twist to catch the words. "This is going to go well, Wynne. I know it is." She knew the mare but had never been alone with her. She knew how to ride, but had never done so alone. "My father won't ever know. It's not your fault, Wynne, *del*. My father just doesn't understand how I long for the sky, or how much I want to be a real part of the barn. He wants a serf, not a daughter." Continuing to pet the horse, Emma moved around her, admiring the snowy mane and silver-tipped wings in a soothing tone. Wynne ignored her. "We can do this, girl, together."

Shouts from the courtyard told Emma time was running out. Morgan's barn was preparing to take flight. She took a deep breath, muttered a hasty invocation to Rhiannon, and led Wynne from the stall. Ten horses in various stages of being mounted milled about the yard. It was easy to find her place and swing up into the saddle like she'd done it a thousand times. Trying not to draw Morgan's gaze, she kept her head down and fiddled with her reins.

"Cutting it pretty close, Elen. Everything all right?" a rider asked.

Emma grinned. He'd mistaken her for Wynne's regular rider! She nodded and waved to him, pretending to adjust something on the saddle so that she could turn her back instead of answering.

A trumpet sounded, and the horse beneath her tensed. Emma gathered the reins and gripped Wynne with her legs. For an instant her heart fluttered, then they were galloping to liftoff, then gliding above the ground. As Wynne stroked powerful wings to gain altitude, Emma's heart sang.

The clear spring sky and towering mountains made a perfect backdrop for the Aerial Games. Spectators thronged the cobblestone streets, their eyes on winged horses leaping skyward from Tremeirchson's nine barns. Against the purplish mountains dominated by the peak of Yr Wydda, black and gold and brown horses soared to the familiar trumpet fanfare that announced the opening of each year's Games. Davyd craned his neck and shaded his eyes. Above him, his father's brown stallion led the herd. Emma followed on Wynne, then came the eight others, including Evan, his brother, older by two years.

The ten horses hovered at the correct height for their opening dance. Davyd admired how tightly they tucked their legs under their bodies, and how their wings beat in unison. They made it look easy, but he knew how hard they worked to master a complicated dance. Two horses led the rest into a large circle, and Davyd could see their chest muscles working.

His father's riders wore green and gold helmets and cloaks. Sitting between the massive feathered pinions, legs tucked behind, the riders were completely hidden on every upstroke. Davyd's eyes followed Wynne. He anxiously scrutinized the mare and decided only a family member could tell today's rider wasn't his mother.

He relaxed, enjoying the spring sun that highlighted the darker horsehide colors and made the lighter feathered wings sparkle. Wynne flew well. The stranger on her back didn't seem to affect her ability to execute the maneuvers she'd been taught.

Among the graceful soaring turns, however, Davyd sensed trouble a split second before it happened. A black stallion, draped in the blue and silver of Hoel's barn, swerved too close to Wynne. She tossed her head and shied away. Davyd gulped short breaths of air as his fear of heights manifested itself before him.

A shadow distracted Emma. On the outside of the formation, a black horse flew perilously close. She recognized the stallion from her father's barn a split second before her eyes met the dark familiar eyes of the rider.

"Tristan! What in Rhiannon's name are you doing?" Emma knew he couldn't hear her shout.

Wynne shied away from the big black stallion. The unexpected movement startled Emma, and she clutched at the reins. Wynne threw her head up and flapped her wings, driving her away from Morgan's grouping. The other riders in Morgan's formation jerked their mounts up short, transforming the elegant Dance of Welcome into a chaotic scramble to stay airborne.

A shrill whinny made Emma lurch to one side. She paled when she realized it was Wynne who was screaming. Emma leaned forward over the mare's neck, desperate to see past the upswept wings. On the downstroke, her breath caught. A bay horse from her father's barn appeared just off Wynne's wingtip, the reddish tints in its coat sparking like fire in the sun. This was an unpredictable mare, beautiful and talented, but capricious. Emma tensed as the bay flew right into Wynne's shoulder, colliding with a dull thud. The world spun as Wynne plummeted from the sky.

The headlong rush for the ground streamed tears out of Emma's eyes and back toward her ears. Somehow the bay mare's black wings tangled around Wynne's white ones. The two horses spiraled out of control. The green grass became sky and the blue sky stretched under Wynne's hooves. Emma's stomach clenched in fear then roiled with dizziness. Black and white wings rasped as they scraped each other and tangled with slashing legs.

Wynne stretched her neck toward the bay, teeth bared and ears back. The other horse panicked, thrashing wings and legs and head as if she was drowning in the air. The whites of both horses' eyes flashed amongst tossing heads. The other rider sawed frantically on the bay's reins. Wynne struggled to stay aloft, with Emma desperate to avoid entangling the other horse.

After what seemed like hours, but was surely mere seconds, Wynne extended her massive white wings and with a powerful beat flew clear. Once more gliding upright, Emma fought to control her shaking hands. The bay tried to gain altitude only to shy violently away from the black stallion that had caused the chaos. With wings held too tightly for the powerful strokes needed to save herself, the bay mare fell to earth, horse and rider both screaming.

Emma shut her eyes until the screaming stopped. The shaking continued, and spread to her arms, then her legs. When she opened her eyes, it was as if the floodgates were loosed. Tears flowed down her face. She gulped air and turned Wynne back toward Morgan's barn. Some riders had landed, but others struggled to control crazed horses still in the air. Emma felt all eyes on her as Wynne landed in Morgan's courtyard.

For a long moment Emma sat atop the horse, not trusting her limbs to support her if she dismounted. She forced her thoughts away from the falling red horse and rider she'd known her entire life. Odd, she couldn't even recall their names at this moment. Dazed, Emma realized people were running toward her from all directions.

Their arms waved and their mouths moved, but she couldn't hear anything but her screaming thoughts. She shook her head and noise rushed in. It took another minute to make sense of it.

Weakly, she stood up in the left stirrup and swung her right leg over the mare's back. Sliding along the horse's body next to the folded wing, Emma managed to get both feet on the ground. She took a shaky step away from the horse and waited for chaos to swallow her.

Davyd had gaped in horror as riders jerked their mounts out of formation. He couldn't watch, but he couldn't look away. Visions remained of Wynne plummeting from the sky, spiraling around a russet bay horse from Hoel's barn; of black and white wings fluttered uselessly around the massive bodies. Cold pearls of sweat dotted Davyd's forehead.

Shocked into momentary silence, the crowd watched as riders still aloft controlled their animals. Then they came alive with excited conversations and loud exclamations punctuated movement as people converged on the barns. Men in expensive fine linen strode forward, followed by lesser-dressed men and beautifully gowned women. They were outsiders, necessary but apart. Davyd tried to nod politely as he raced to the center of the courtyard, his attention on his father and Emma.

His father had leaped from the brown stallion's back as soon as its hooves touched the ground and stormed toward Wynne, who threw her head and lifted her tail.

Davyd reached Emma first, swallowing hard when

Linda Ulleseit

he saw her tear-streaked face and shaking hands. "Are you okay?"

What a stupid question. Of course she wasn't okay. His mouth set in a grim line, he helped her remove the green and gold helmet.

As Davyd removed her helmet, Emma's first impression was of cool breeze across her sweaty head as her chestnut hair fell free to her waist. Morgan approached and stood with his legs apart, shoulders squared, eyes drilling Emma as grooms and riders and spectators swarmed toward them. He waved one arm above his head. "Evan, get those patrons out of here," he snapped.

"Barn Leader Morgan," Emma said in a shaky voice.

Emma focused on gripping the helmet so that her hands wouldn't shake as she let the terror of the ride dissipate.

"Emma *verch* Hoel. Where's my wife?"

Of course he was angry. She took a deep breath and locked her knees so she wouldn't crumple to the ground. Before she could answer, Davyd stepped up.

"Mum hurt her back but she wanted Wynne to fly today." His voice was rushed and anxious, but he was on her side.

"So she asked Emma to ride?" Morgan's glare never left her face.

"Not exactly..." Davyd lowered his eyes to the ground.

"It's my fault, *syr*," Emma interrupted. "Davyd was

17

going to ride Wynne, but I begged him to let me do it. I'm sorry."

The grooms arrived and led the horses to their stalls. Wynne pranced, clearly recovered, and nosed her groom's pockets for a molasses treat.

A rider wearing Hoel's blue and silver approached. Emma gritted her teeth as she recognized Tristan, the rider of the black horse and her father's favorite rider. She wanted to ask after the bay mare and her rider, but she was in too much trouble herself.

"You out of your mind up there, Tristan?" Davyd's brother returned in time to challenge the rider.

"Evan, stop." Morgan's glare turned from his son to the other young man. "Return to your barn, Tristan."

"I thought Wynne's rider seemed familiar. She looked good up there." Tristan nodded at her, and Emma blushed, embarrassed and furious.

"Until you tried to tie her in knots," Evan spat.

Before Morgan could say anything, another man stormed up and Emma swallowed nervously. The tall, wiry rider had grayed early, and long hours in the sun had weathered his skin to leather. His dark eyes burned with anger.

"What's the meaning of this?" he demanded.

"Barn Leader Hoel," Morgan began.

"Da. . ." Emma blurted out at the same time.

Hoel was not to be put off. "Why is my daughter riding in your wing?"

"I didn't give permission," Morgan stated. "But that's not the issue here. Wynne would've been fine if your rider hadn't strayed. So would your rider."

Hoel and Morgan glared at each other.

"Da, *mae'n ddrwg gen i."* Emma whispered, hoping the apology sounded better in Welsh.

"It was an accident," Davyd said to Morgan.

"My horse and rider both have broken legs," Hoel snarled. "The mare's being put down, and the rider will be out of commission for weeks."

"Although I am sorry for the loss of a fine animal, I can't condone a barn where riders don't take responsibility for their mistakes," Morgan said.

"And I can't respect a barn leader who lets an untried girl fly someone else's horse," Hoel responded.

"Da, I'm fine," Emma said, grabbing his arm and pulling her father toward their barn. Hoel resisted.

An imposing woman barreled toward them from the main street of Tremeirchson. Dressed in a green and gold gown and surrounded by fluttering stewards dressed in silk and velvet, she had to be Morgan's patroness. Emma allowed herself a deep calming breath since the focus would now shift from her to this woman.

"Morgan. How is the mare?" The woman's tone commanded. She was used to respect.

Davyd's father nodded his head. "Lady Margery. Wynne appears to be fine. Her groom is checking her over now."

The ice queen raked Emma with cold eyes. "And you are?"

Hoel stepped in front of his daughter. "My daughter."

Lady Margery did not step back. "And you are?" she repeated.

The barn leader flushed. "Barn Leader Hoel. This is my daughter, Emma."

"I see," Lady Margery said thoughtfully. "Then the horse and rider that caused this incident are yours. As are the pair that fell."

Hoel reached to rub the back of his neck. Davyd grimaced at Emma and brushed his hair out of his eyes with both hands. Morgan stood respectfully at Lady Margery's side, his face impassive. Evan, two years older than Davyd and Emma, paced angrily in back of the patroness, his boots stamping his fury into the cobblestones. Tristan shot furious glares at Evan. Emma suddenly remembered the rider's name. Catrin. And her red mare was Bronwyn. What had her father said? Bronwyn was being destroyed? An anguished moan escaped her.

Her father gave her a quizzical glance before answering the patroness. "The champion Bronwyn has broken a leg. She's been put down."

He said nothing about Catrin to the patroness, nor about Tristan, the rider who caused it all. Lady Margery would be concerned with the bloodstock, not the people.

"It's hard to lose a champion," Lady Margery said, but her tone held no compassion.

Morgan stepped forward. "I think we're done here, Hoel."

"Come on, Da." Emma pulled harder on her father's arm. This time, he followed.

To Emma's dismay, Tristan did too. Her breathing had returned to normal, but she was unable to block out images of Catrin and Bronwyn falling from the sky.

"So whatever possessed you to ride Wynne, really?" Tristan sneered.

She ground her teeth and made an effort to stand

up straighter before answering. "Davyd needed my help."

Her father snorted in disbelief as the trio walked down a dirt lane between barns. "This accident will have repercussions, Emma," he said. "You are responsible for the loss of a champion. Our patron will be irate."

"Me?" Emma glared at Tristan, who smirked back at her.

The golden boy could do no wrong, and the daughter could do no right.

On a Wing and a Dare

Chapter 2: It Begins

"Well, let's go see how much your mother saw of this," Morgan told his sons as he watched them walk away, Emma miserable, Tristan smug, and Hoel straight-backed with anger.

"I'll be right up, Da," Davyd said. "I want to check on Wynne."

Morgan nodded, and he and Evan crossed the empty courtyard to the manor. Davyd let out a breath he hadn't been aware he was holding. His cowardice had almost caused the death of his closest friend.

The humid warmth of the barn, with its familiar horsey smell and soft rustling noises, was no comfort. Wynne snorted into his hair, sending brown curls flying as he stroked her snowy muzzle. She shook her wings and snuffled his body.

"You flew well today, Wynne, *del*, my darling." Wynne moved to drink some water, leaving a cold void next to Davyd.

In June, barn leaders would invite young men and women to become riders to the two-year-olds in their barns. His father expected him to become a rider. Davyd

On a Wing and a Dare

had ridden before, of course, with one parent or the other. As a child, he remembered clutching fistfuls of Wynne's mane as he sat snuggled in front of his mother. The feeling then was more about the security of her arms than the height above the ground. Later he'd ridden behind his father on Deryn, and his heart was introduced to his throat for the first time. Since then he'd avoided riding while managing to be verbally enthusiastic about it. He assumed he'd grow out of his fear, but he hadn't. Now he was expected to fly solo. The mere notion made him sick.

Emma, however, longed to be a rider. The same vicious fate that made him afraid to fly had attached Emma to a favored colt in his father's barn. It wasn't unusual for barn leaders to trade promising colts to improve bloodlines, but never this colt and never to Hoel. Emma would have to come to Morgan's barn. Today's events wouldn't help her accomplish that at all.

Sixteen, and hiding in the stall of his mother's mare! Davyd dredged righteous indignation from deep inside himself. Five more weeks to accustom himself to the duty that would be laid before him like an honor. Might as well start now.

In front of Hoel's barn, riders stood talking in small groups that fell silent as they passed. The big barn doors stood ajar, and Emma's mother stood waiting. Neste was an older, softer version of her daughter. Emma could see the gray streaks in her mother's hair, cut shorter than the glorious thick locks Emma refused to put a cap on. Mum's face was grim, her shoulders slumped as if

24

heavily weighed down. Guilt twisted Emma's heart.

"Neste?" Hoel asked. His tone implied a thousand questions. How is Catrin's leg? Are the riders coping? Is Bronwyn gone?

The shadows under Mum's eyes told more than her words.

Her father, standing in the stall doorway, broke the crushing silence. "Emma, we need to talk."

He turned and walked down the center of the barn. She could hear his bootsteps stop, waiting for her.

Neste gripped Emma's hand. "Go. There's no need to make him angrier."

Emma stood up and brushed her skirt, dismayed to find she still wore the green and gold divided riding skirt that belonged to Elen. "Mum? Do you have an apron?"

"It won't matter, *cariad*, the damage is done. Go."

Outside Rhys's stall, riders went through the motions of preparing for the afternoon's competition, but the normal spirit of eager excitement was missing. Hoel stood in the very center of the barn, his body as rigid as the massive timbers that supported the peaked roof. As she walked toward him, he turned without a word and led her to the far end of the barn, where a small door stood open. Through it, Emma could see the dirt yard they used as a gathering area for riders. Beyond that, hills rose that eventually formed forbidding cliffs. Above it all, Yr Wydda reigned supreme. The great mountain watched impassively as Emma's life twisted.

Tristan was already in the yard. Hoel and Emma joined him. When she saw what was before her on the ground, Emma felt her stomach attempt to come out her mouth. Bronwyn's body had been brought back to the barn. Dust covered the once-lustrous brown coat and black legs. The mare's black wings lay crumpled and dirty beneath her.

"Why is she here?" Emma gasped. Horses' bodies were usually burned without ceremony.

"You need to see what you have done," Hoel said. He nodded to Tristan.

Tristan lit a torch and approached the horse's body. Emma gasped as he lit the straw and sticks placed beneath Bronwyn. The tinder caught quickly, and flames licked at the horse. Emma felt sick.

"You chose to betray your family and ride for a rival," her father said in a wooden tone.

She didn't dare point out she was helping a friend. Da had never approved of her friendship with Morgan's sons.

"Your inexperience in the air caused the death of a valuable asset to our barn."

And she'd almost died as well. He didn't mention that. The flames flared as the black mane and tail caught fire, then the horsehair. Emma refused to think of this hulk as Bronwyn, the pretty mare who used to take apples from her hand.

"The loss of this mare affects our breeding program. That hampers our plans for growth as well as our patron's profits. Lord Farley will not be pleased. He is dining with us this evening, and your mother is busy with a sick colt."

Guilt worsened Emma's sick stomach, as he probably knew it would. The smell of burning hair and flesh didn't help, but she refused to wrinkle her nose.

"Go back to your mother. Nurse the colt and free her to supervise dinner preparations. This isn't Morgan's manor, with a staff that handles such things."

"*Iawn, Tad,*" she answered. Agreeing in Welsh always seemed to please him.

The fire blackened the body until it was unrecognizably charred and hidden by a wall of flame. Without another word, her father turned and headed back into the barn.

Tristan said, "He's a good leader, you know."

Emma held up her hand to stop his words. "No. I won't discuss this with you, Tristan."

She returned to Rhys's stall without encountering her father. Numbly, she took directions from her clearly worried mother. Neste seemed as concerned for Emma as she was for Rhys, but Lord Farley's pending visit prevented discussion. Emma busied herself tempting Rhys with water and cleaning his stall. The poor baby had not even been assigned a groom yet. She ventured out of the stall in search of more tasks to keep her occupied and away from her parents. The rest of the day was spent polishing tack, currying sweaty horses, chasing down riders due to compete, and checking on Rhys.

By dinner time, Emma was dirty and exhausted. The first day of the Aerial Games had concluded, and the riders dispersed to their meals. Emma trudged next door to the small house where she'd lived all her life. Her mother was in the kitchen, buried in fabulous smells and bubbling pots.

"Emma! There you are! How's Rhys?"

"He's no better, Mum, but he did drink a little water." She picked a bit of straw out of her hair.

"All right." Neste was distracted. "Lord Farley is due any time. Emma, I'm sorry, *cariad*, but your father prefers you stay in your room tonight. I'll prepare a tray for you." She wrung her hands, clearly worried what Emma's reaction would be.

It had been a very long day. "Fine, Mum."

She trudged to her room, cast out by her father, by Aer, the god of flight, and by Rhiannon, goddess of horses.

The next morning, after a restless night, Emma had to get away. Running up the hill behind Tremeirchson's barns, she pumped her arms in time with her legs, dodging nimberry bushes. Her cap hung down her back, as usual, and tangled in the flying twists of her hair. The grass leaned as if trying to follow her. The wind whipped Emma's tunic away from her body and wound her skirt around her legs, trying to trip her, but she outran it, outran concern for Rhys, and outran her father's iron hand. Below her, the hill fell away in a tumble of rocks and above her the morning sky was full of horses. The sight clutched at her breath, leaving her gasping from more than just the run up the hill.

A swish of braking wings and the soft thump of landing hooves spun Emma around. It was Clyth, with Evan aboard. The horse trampled through a patch of wildflowers as Emma ran toward them.

"Not a day to be on foot!" Evan called.

"No, it isn't!" Emma agreed, patting the pale brown horse on the nose.

Jealous of his winged horse, she tried not to look up at Evan, so handsome in his green and gold rider's colors, so confident astride his young stallion. But it wasn't jealousy that tickled her insides when Evan smiled.

"Want to join me, Em?"

"Can I? Really?" Her mind was excited, but her stomach clenched, wondering if she would ever enjoy flight again.

In response, Evan held out his hand. Emma took it and leaped while Evan's muscular arm pulled. Although she wasn't wearing her divided riding skirt, Emma had on the thick woolen hose her mother claimed was as good as the men's trousers. Astride behind him, she adjusted her bunched skirts and buckled the safety straps he handed back to her. For the second day in a row, she put on a green and gold helmet.

At his rider's urging, Clyth moved into a canter, then stretched his wings out from his sides and his neck before him. Almost immediately, he was aloft, climbing above the village of Tremeirchson.

Emma tightened her arms around Evan's waist, his wool coat rough under her fingertips. Her legs molded themselves to his, touching along the entire length, and her hair blew straight out behind her. The spicy scent of his skin made her lean closer, then away, embarrassed.

"You all right?" Evan turned his head to shout over his shoulder as they soared above the village.

Emma just nodded with relief. She was more than all right, she was home. Like her father, she was a creature of the air, even though her dreams and his didn't match.

Wynne flew by with Evan's mother in the saddle. Emma waved, glad Elen's back was feeling better today. Streaks of brown zoomed past on their left. Glossy black Bryn approached and Tristan frowned at her, but Emma looked away. She refused to forgive him for yesterday's accident.

The chill of the wind bit into her cheeks, balanced by the warmth of the horse beneath her. Everywhere that her body touched Evan's, she tingled. Self-conscious, Emma tried to remember when her friendship with Evan had changed. They weren't children any more.

They flew above the farms and fields of the village all the way to the foothills, then Evan turned Clyth in a wide, banked turn. Emma matched her body to his as he leaned into the turn, and the ground sped by. The hills nudged the foot of the mountain here, and red-brown cliffs lurched for the sky. Fuzzy gray-green foliage softened the angles of the mountains wherever they could establish a tenacious hold. Emma surrendered herself to the joy of flying, the joy of being with Evan.

Her eyes followed the hills as they softened into the valley floor far below. The road snaked through the undulating landscape, covered with wagons and horses without wings. It would be a busy afternoon with visitors from other villages coming to watch the Aerial Games. Heart singing the song of the wind, she imagined the day when she would have her own wings. She remembered, as a child playing in her father's barn, mares nudging her with velvet noses and colts flapping awkward wings and stallions rearing with exuberance. She loved them all.

But two years ago Adain had been born into Morgan's barn, bred from Deryn and Wynne. She'd gone with Evan and Davyd to see the baby, pride of the barn, first observing that his pale brown coat was lighter than his sire but not as white as his dam. Then Adain looked at her, the chocolate brown pools of his eyes warming her, pulling her into him somehow so that he became part of her and she part of him. Since then she'd spent some of every day visiting the colt, and the rest of the day figuring out how to become his rider. That thought made Emma frown. She only had five weeks to change destiny.

Evan landed Clyth in the road next to her father's barn. Nervous at this bold move, Emma laughed as Clyth primly folded his wings. She dismounted first, with Evan's strong arm helping her down. He swung down close beside her, and her legs began to buckle. He put his arm around her waist to steady her, but she leaned away, afraid she would swoon in his arms.

"Emma! There you are!" Her father's voice threw anger at her as he walked out of the barn.

She muttered to Evan, "You'd better go."

"What's he going to do to me?" Evan asked with a saucy head tilt.

"Thanks for the ride," she said quickly, grimacing and calling to her father, "I'm coming."

"Your mother needs you in the barn." Hoel glared at Evan, who dropped his arm from Emma's waist.

"Thank you for your company, Emma *verch* Hoel," Evan said formally, although his tone twisted the polite phrase into something insolent. She winced, but her father didn't say anything. That wasn't like him.

He did take her arm too firmly as they walked toward the barn, then snapped at her. "What are you doing? Trying to encourage a son of Morgan? Not my daughter. Do you understand?"

"*Iawn*, Da, okay," she muttered, nodding. They took a couple of steps in silence, and Emma felt his anger drain away as the muscles in his arms unclenched. Puzzled, she turned to look at him.

"Your mother's worried about a couple of the horses. She wants your help." Her father's brow furrowed, his eyes far away.

"A couple?"

"Rhys and Pedr have no energy and they're not eating."

"Pedr too? Oh, no."

Riders came in after their flights, and her father

stayed outside to talk to them. Emma went inside to find her mother. The dimness of the barn and its steamy warmth enveloped her in a familiar cocoon. This barn, after all, was home. It just wasn't home to the colt she needed. A pang of guilt lanced her.

"Emma? In here, *cariad*."

Emma entered the stall Rhys shared with his mother. Neste held Rhys by his halter, offering him a handful of sweet hay that he just stared at. Neste brushed a strand of chestnut hair out of her face and patted the mare that stood next to the colt. The mare flicked her tail. Both mums looked tired.

"He's not eating?" Emma asked.

"I'm really worried. Pedr is the same way. I wish I could isolate them until this passes, but there is just no room. I've put some feverfew and willow bark in the water, but I can't get them to drink it."

"I'll go see if I can get Pedr to take some."

Her mother nodded and turned back to Rhys, who half-heartedly nibbled at the hay, dropping most of it on the floor. "Grab a treat from the bag out there."

Emma left the stall and found a bag of the molasses horse snacks her mother made for the barn. Stuffing two in her pockets, she went to see Pedr.

Two stalls down, coal-black Pedr was lost in the shadows of his stall. Emma cooed softly to him and to his mother, a dainty black mare with the softest mane in the barn. She stroked the mare and fed her a treat. Pedr looked on listlessly. She waved the snack under his nose. Pedr tried to turn away, but she broke off a piece of the molasses treat and put it in his mouth. He gummed it a bit, but didn't spit it out. Emma broke off another piece.

No one liked to see a sick baby, especially a cute one. She stroked his velvet nose, looking him over carefully. With those long legs, he might be an aerial dancer. His chest muscles were strong, though. Maybe he would be a racer. His wings were still too short to tell, but he would grow.

Emma mentally compared Adain to the black colt in front of her. Adain was a year older, of course, and was beginning to show signs of being a good distance racer. That didn't matter, though. He whickered when he heard her outside his stall, and by the time she got there his ears were pricked so far forward they looked like arrows pointing at the door. Adain loved her. And she loved him. They belonged together.

"You belong here."

Startled, Emma stiffened at her father's tone. He appeared out of nowhere and echoed her thoughts like he was reading her mind. She offered Pedr another chunk of the treat, looking at the colt instead of her father. "He's not eating. He'll need more than this to stay healthy."

"With you here to help your mother, they'll both be fine. And you will have bonded with Pedr."

"So why am I locked in to Pedr, Da? Every other sixteen year old in Tremeirchson has the opportunity to be chosen as rider for any of the two year olds, but not me. I have to wait another whole year for Pedr."

The colt spit out a mouthful, and she bent to retrieve it from the floor.

"You are my daughter, my only child. You must continue in my barn, and we have no two year olds. You spend too much time over at Morgan's. A barn should be

33

chosen for family loyalty, or strength of the herd's bloodlines, not because the barn leader's sons are good looking."

Emma felt her cheeks turn pink, and she nuzzled the colt to hide it from her father. "Da!"

"Tomorrow you are not to leave this barn. No rides with Evan, no trips to Morgan's barn to see that colt you're mooning over. Stay here and nurse Pedr. He's your future, here in this barn where you belong."

Emma didn't answer. Pedr pushed at her with his nose, and she fed him another bite of molasses treat as her heart withered. Pedr was cute enough. But Adain would be a champion! A sigh escaped.

"Emma."

"All right," she muttered, not looking at her father. "I'll stay and help Mum until the colts are well."

His bootsteps faded as he moved away from Pedr's stall. It sounded like he was going to tell her mother he'd succeeded in tying her down for awhile. Mum would be grateful for the help, at least. And it *was* important to make sure the youngsters didn't get any worse.

She couldn't help sighing as she led Pedr a few steps to the water trough. He wouldn't drink it. Turning the handle, she added fresh water and splashed a bit on the colt's nose. The same odor she'd noticed yesterday in Rhys's water was present here. Was it the herbs her mother used? Pedr licked a few drops before he once again lost interest. Emma talked to him softly, stroking him on the neck and ruffling his forelock. She tried again to feed him some hay, but Pedr wouldn't eat it.

Her thoughts went back to her father's words. No, they had no two year olds for her to ride. Two years ago the barn had been just as full as it was now and her father had traded two fillies for Mael, an unremarkable brown mare with a cantankerous rider, leaving no horses for his daughter to ride when she turned sixteen. He thought she could wait another year. He didn't realize how much she needed to fly now.

Brushing her hands on her skirt, she left the stall and leaned on the closed half-door watching the listless colt. Above her, the cavernous barn disappeared into shadows.

Tristan came to stand next to her, leaning casually on the stall door. His nearness placed his arm along hers. Surprised, Emma moved away a few steps.

"How's he doing?" he asked.

"He's sick," she said.

"I'm sorry about yesterday. Hungry?"

Emma stared at him. Yesterday he had killed a horse and injured a rider. He had almost killed her, too, and today he wanted to share a meal.

Behind Tristan, her mother approached from Rhys's stall. Lined with worry, her face brightened when she saw them. "Why don't you go rest a bit and eat something? I can watch these two for an hour or so." Her mouth smiled, but her eyes were tired.

Emma just barely kept her mouth from falling open in shock. Mum needed her help desperately if she was at Morgan's barn, but apparently not when one of Hoel's riders came by.

"Come on then," Tristan said, taking her elbow.

Still stunned, Emma followed him from the barn, her traitorous stomach growling.

They walked along Aer Road until it ended at

Tremeirchson's massive stone fountain, which presided over the village at its very center. Visitors admired the trio of winged horses carved from colored stone, and they climbed on the basin to watch the competition. Emma pushed away her own fond memories of playing there with Davyd and Evan as children.

Leaving Aer Road, Tristan led her down the second of three main cobblestone streets, named for the stone horse-gods of the fountain, that separated Tremeirchson into pie-shaped sections. Alon Road led into the residential section of the village. Ystrad Road led to the merchant section, and during the Aerial Games it was full of colorful tented market stalls. Tristan walked in a businesslike fashion, facing straight ahead, not slowing, headed for the tavern. Emma wanted to look at some of the merchant's offerings but really didn't want to shop with Tristan. She'd come back later.

They entered the bustling tavern and found a small table in the back. Tristan turned to Emma with a warm smile. "Doesn't it feel good to get away?"

"It does," she admitted.

A familiar girl swayed up to them, her long dark hair covered with a tight-fitting white coif, tied under her chin. She turned cold green eyes on Emma and forced a chilly smile. "*Helo*, Emma."

"*Helo*, Jenett. How have you been?" Emma had known the barmaid since they were children, but they had never really been close friends. They'd grown apart even further once Jenett had learned to walk with a sway to her ample hips that drew men's eyes. Her encouraging smile was always warm for powerful men. Jenett hung around the barn and flirted with the riders, especially

Tristan. Sure enough, when she turned to greet the rider her entire demeanor changed.

"*Bore da*, Tristan. What can I get for you?" Her eyes and voice and posture dripped sweetness and light. Emma wanted to be sick.

"*Helo*, Jenett. How are you this beautiful day?" Tristan asked, then ordered meat, bread and ale.

"I'll bring it right out for you," Jenett promised. "Got to keep you riders strong enough to win races."

She and Tristan laughed, and Emma forced herself to join in.

While they waited for the food, Tristan said very little to her. She was annoyed, but at least she didn't feel like she had to make conversation. He was just one of her father's riders, after all. Jenett arrived with their meal before long, and Emma took a bite of the warm rye bread and a sip of her ale.

Tristan looked at her over the rim of his mug. She needed to say something, but he beat her to it.

"I'm really sorry about yesterday."

She nodded. "Why did you do it? Swerve at me like that?"

"I couldn't believe my eyes. I know you too well, and it wasn't Elen on that horse. You didn't have to react so violently, though, pulling away from me and Bryn."

Bristling, she opened her mouth to argue, but he forestalled her.

"You handled it well, though. It could have been bad."

Bronwyn's death wasn't bad? Emma took a bite and mumbled something she hoped sounded appreciative. She chewed, watching Tristan. He had arrived in

Tremeirchson about eight years ago from Merioneth and too quickly found a place in her father's barn. As Tristan leaned over the table to eat, a blond piece of hair fell across his eyes. Blond, like Evan. But Tristan's eyes were dark and anonymous, not the clear blue of Evan's. She imagined if Evan were to look right at her for awhile, she could see herself reflected in his light eyes. She drifted into dreams of blue, but Tristan's voice snatched her back.

"Why are you so drawn to Morgan's barn?"

What? Her friendship with Davyd went back to early childhood, when Evan, two years older, was their hero. Tristan must know that. It wasn't like there were many people her age around Hoel's barn. Just Tristan, four years older. "I have friends there," she said.

"Sure." His eyes were so intense they made her squirm. She looked away. He finished his ale with a slurp, then said, "But is it more about friends or more about defying your father?"

Emma's mouth was full, so she didn't respond right away. Tristan was the closest thing her father had to a son. Lately, that relationship seemed closer than the legitimate father/daughter one. Tristan was not her friend in this. She should remember that. Before she could form a retort, he continued.

"Look, I don't get the whole thing about having to be part of Morgan's barn, all right? You're like the spoiled rich kid who complains Da bought her a brooch with amethysts instead of garnets. She still has a brooch, right?" He paused. "You don't appreciate what you have in Hoel's barn, Princess. Don't toss it all away before you take a long look."

How dare he say these things to her! In her father's barn she would be shackled to Pedr. She'd have to wait another year to become a rider, another year of being told what to do. In Morgan's barn, she would join a team. All her dreams were tied to Adain, and Davyd and Evan — people and horses in the wrong barn.

Or maybe Tristan was referring to himself. He could solidify his position with her father by courting her. The food suddenly tasted like sawdust. "Tristan, I need to get back to the barn."

"Running away?" he taunted her. "Remember this, Princess. Only a few people get to follow their dreams. Be happy you get to fly. Don't cry over not getting the barn you pine for."

She got up and walked out of the tavern. Tristan was a dolt. Emma walked past the fountain again, and turned on Aer Road, steps slowing as she passed Morgan's barn, looking for Davyd or Evan in spite of herself. They'd be getting ready for the late afternoon races. She'd root for Clyth secretly and dream of Adain.

On a Wing and a Dare

Chapter 3: Under Control

Davyd hurried back to the barn from the officials' tent, a battered ledger under his arm. Up the street a beautiful girl walked away from him. Actually, he couldn't tell if she was beautiful without seeing her face, but she moved with the grace of soaring flight, drawing his eyes and holding them. Her long chestnut hair shone in the sun. She was tall, with long legs, but her figure was round and soft in all the right places. He couldn't take his eyes off the swaying of her skirt.

She turned, darting a furtive look toward the barn, and Davyd nearly choked. *Emma?* She continued up the road without seeing him, and Davyd stared after her in disbelief. She was sixteen like him, but blinded by the Emma-child that was his friend, he hadn't seen the Emma-woman. Davyd inhaled a deep breath and let it out slowly.

"A beautiful woman," Evan said as he joined Davyd, leading a saddled Clyth.

The words echoed Davyd's feelings so closely he winced. They watched Emma until she turned into the lane that led to Hoel's barn and disappeared from sight.

"She grew up overnight, didn't she?" Evan asked.

"Yes, she did." Agitated, Davyd rubbed his finger over the leather binding of the ledger. It didn't feel right discussing Emma with his brother. Talking about girls with Evan was a rather recent development anyway, and it felt odd for the girl to be someone they knew so well.

"I took her for a ride this morning," Evan offered.

Davyd looked up, horrified. "On Clyth? You took her for a ride after yesterday's accident?"

"She *loved* it."

His tone had sensual overtones that made Davyd frown. "You shouldn't talk about a friend like that." His words sounded lame and childish. Davyd wished Evan would go away so he could figure out why his heart beat so oddly at the sight of an old friend walking up the street.

Evan slapped Davyd on the shoulder with the end of Clyth's reins and laughed. "She'll be a good rider, and a good wife for a barn leader."

Davyd swallowed hard, dismayed by Evan's confidence. Opening the ledger to where he had written the day's schedule, he forced a professional tone. "Assignments are up for your group. You're in the third race. Top two in each heat advance to finals."

"*Iawn.*" Evan nodded and peered at the page.

Davyd knew his brother couldn't read the words. It was nice to have a useful skill that put him above Evan, even if it was something Evan considered unimportant and had always avoided learning.

Tristan approached, coming from the same direction Emma had. Davyd wondered if his cocky swagger was natural or intended. Tristan acknowledged the brothers with a nod.

"Racing today?" Davyd asked.

"Not today," Tristan responded.

"Da's grounded riders for less," Evan muttered. The reference to yesterday's incident was clear, and the air shimmered with tension.

"It was an accident. I've apologized. In fact, I just left her."

Davyd frowned again. Emma was already gone. It looked more like Emma had left Tristan.

"Glad to hear it." Evan stuck out his hand, and Tristan shook it firmly. "Have a good Games."

"You too. *Hwyl*, Davyd."

"*Hwyl*." No handshake for Davyd. He didn't know whether to feel slighted or relieved as Tristan walked off toward Hoel's barn. He turned to Evan with a question in his eyes.

Evan stroked Clyth's nose as he stared after Tristan. "Remember when he hung around our barn for awhile? When he first came to the village? Too many sons at our barn, though. He's in a good spot over there as Hoel's second." Evan hesitated a moment, clearly remembering. "He's ambitious. I should keep an eye on him."

Davyd nodded. He didn't really know Tristan, who was two years older than Evan.

"Maybe I can go see Tristan and manage a visit with Emma at the same time." Evan winked at Davyd and led Clyth toward the race start.

Davyd wanted to hit something. Taking a deep breath, he walked toward the barn. Wynne's stall, dim and quiet, embraced him. He paced past the mare a couple of times, then kicked the water trough. At the hollow thunk, Wynne flicked her ears and looked at him.

"She's friends with both of us," he mumbled, laying his cheek along the mare's warm neck. "Why would she flirt with Evan? Or eat dinner with a guy who almost killed her?" Davyd pounded his fist into the plank wall. The ensuing pain drew his attention, allowing him to breathe and calm down. "More importantly, why do I care, Wynne? Evan's had girlfriends before. I don't care about his girlfriends." He threw an arm over the mare. "And that's it, isn't it? I do care. I don't want Emma to be Evan's next girl. And I don't want to be a rider."

There. He'd said it out loud, if only to Wynne. The silence in the stall seemed to recoil in shock, as if the whole barn held its breath, waiting for the world's reaction to Davyd's proclamation. He let his own breath out slowly and sank to a sitting position along the wall. The sounds of the barn began to reach him again. Wynne snorted in her water trough, and next door a horse scraped a hoof against a feed tub. Faraway crowd cheers announced the end of the first race of Evan's group, but everything was muffled by Davyd's awareness of the great wrongs in his life.

And here he was, hiding in Wynne's stall again! He leaped to his feet and ran his hands through his curls in frustration. "What can I do, Wynne?" he groaned. The horse flipped her ears toward him and away.

Her water trough was almost empty, and he turned the spigot to fill it. Frowning as a slight odor teased his nose, he sniffed. Definitely a stronger odor than usual, but the water looked all right. Davyd drained the trough, leaving only a small bit in the bottom, and hoped it wouldn't make Wynne sick. He'd tell her groom to check it out.

So if he didn't want to be a rider, he'd have to find something else to do. He'd grown up around the winged horses and loved them. He could be a groom. His father would be so disappointed. Mum would probably understand, but he didn't even know how he would start that conversation. He'd better figure it out since time was growing short. In a little more than a month, the horses would have riders and it would be too late.

Evan's race was in the air when Davyd emerged from Wynne's stall. He didn't look up. Instead, he returned to the officials' tent and picked up the next stack of race assignments. It would be a busy afternoon chasing down riders and making sure they reported for their competitions.

The next morning, Davyd concentrated on the Aerial Dances. His father, on Deryn, and his mum, on Wynne, were the favorites in this event. Davyd managed the patrons as well as the riders, and that took organization. No barn could survive without the financial support of at least one lord. Each year, potential patrons shopped for barns that would enhance their image. In the lowlands, bragging about backing a barn of flying horses in the mountains seemed to be a requirement of elevated status. His father's barn had the support of one main lord who no longer came up from Merioneth.

As a boy, Davyd remembered the elderly man being treated as a god by the entourage that attended him during his stay. There'd been someone to hold his horse and someone to run messages to the barn and someone to wipe the sweat off his brow. Davyd shook his head at the memory. The man's money had paid for the aqueduct that brought water to the barn, though, and put food on the table so that Davyd and Evan didn't have to learn to run a shop or grow vegetables. That bought the old man some deference. Now he was remarried, and Lady Margery oversaw their investment in Tremeirchson.

Riders milled about, some stabling their horses and others hanging out until the dances started. Morgan and Elen ducked into Wynne's stall to change while the grooms brushed their mounts. In scant minutes, all was ready. Their coordinating brown and white tunics, with his leggings and her divided skirt, blended well with the wings and hides of their horses. They were confident and relaxed.

"Davyd, you got this in hand, *cariad*?" his father asked.

It was a routine question, one that he asked before every performance. Davyd appreciated the acknowledgment, however minor, that his father relinquished management of the barn to his son while he flew. "*Iawn*," he affirmed. "Now get over there before you're detained." Davyd nodded toward the fountain, where stewards for Tremeirchson's patrons were starting to hurry in their direction.

His parents laughed, leading Deryn and Wynne toward the restricted start area. Davyd inserted himself in the path of the well-dressed men. They milled around him like colorful roosters among the seed corn. Davyd felt almost as inept with these stewards as he did with his mother's chickens. He cleared his throat noisily to gain their attention. "Come now, you all know Morgan and Elen need to prepare for their competition. They'll speak to you afterwards," he said in a firm voice.

"Davyd, is there a reason Hoel's barn scratched from the dances?" one of the younger men asked.

Davyd frowned. Hoel's barn wasn't competing? "I'm sorry, but I never comment on someone else's barn."

"But we can't get anyone over there to talk to us. And we trust you, Davyd."

The man was the steward for an officious patron who attended the Aerial Games every year and paid to support two or three of the smaller barns. The lord was full of opinions and eager to share them. Davyd quelled the desire to make a flippant reply that would have the village gossiping for days. He shook his head, but before he could formulate a proper response someone spotted one of the top female racers from another barn. The group hustled to intercept her. The steward who had questioned Davyd followed reluctantly.

Davyd sighed with relief. Dealing with stewards was tricky. If you antagonized one, the lord they represented might refuse to support your barn. Then maybe that lord's companions would follow. No use risking the barn's livelihood over something trivial even though it *was* odd for Hoel to take his barn out of all the dances.

Davyd turned a few pages in the ledger, checking the Games' results for the first two days. Pretty normal. Hoel's barn had won a couple of races, placed in a couple others. Then today, scratched from the dances. Davyd returned to the official's tent and checked the upcoming events listing. No withdrawals from Hoel's barn for the series of races after the dances.

Maybe Emma could tell him if anything was wrong. Davyd scratched his head. Emma hadn't been to the barn since the opening day accident. That was unusual, too. He headed for Adain's stall.

Adain's groom, Owain, was brushing the colt as if he'd raced instead of just taken a short flight without a rider. Davyd hid a grin. At twelve, Owain was younger than most grooms and eager to please. Adain thrived on the attention.

"*Bore da*, Owain. Have you seen Emma around here today?"

"*Bore da, syr*. No, *syr*."

Sir? No one ever called him that. Davyd looked down, hiding another smile.

"Why, sir? Is something wrong? *Syr*?"

"*Na*, it's all right. I just wanted to ask her something and I know she usually stops by every day, doesn't she?"

"Oh, yes, *syr*. She visits Adain every day, *syr*."

"But not today. Thank you."

Davyd left the stall as Owain resumed grooming and talking softly to the colt. Emma's father must be keeping close watch on her. It wasn't going to be easy to convince him to let her have Adain.

Familiar music wafted over from the musicians near the viewing stand, and Davyd looked toward the sky. His parents were up. He grinned with pride at the cheers they received. They struck a pose in the sky and began their dance with a dramatic upsweep of wings.

Davyd didn't watch. He listened to the musicians and saw it in his head as he'd seen them practice it for months. He assembled performers for the next set and arranged a spot where he could control access to his parents. All the patrons would expect individual interviews, which was impossible. His parents were gracious, but it was up to Davyd to make sure it didn't interfere with the schedule of the rest of the barn.

A massive roar punctuated the finish of the dance. They'd done well. Davyd hummed their music as he waited. If the scores were close, they might linger inside the restricted area until the final standings were announced. If, as usual, they blew away the competition, then they'd be here any minute.

Davyd double-checked that the next riders were ready to go, then he saw his parents leading their horses back to the barn. Their arms were around each other's waist, and Elen was looking up at Morgan, laughing. Their obvious happiness warmed Davyd.

"Where will we be, Davyd, *bachgen*?" an imperious voice asked.

He turned to greet the first of the stewards, grinding his teeth at the too-familiar diminutive but smiling anyway. Even his parents no longer called him *little boy*. Morgan and Elen smiled, the grooms led the horses away, and the men formed a tight group outside Deryn's stall as three more pairs completed their dances above and ended the pairs competition. His parents would be needed for the award ceremony soon.

Davyd admired their poise as they stood on the cobblestone road in front of their barn. Behind them, the audience of potential supporters could see a well-run barn, with grooms busy currying sweating horses that had completed their events. A few horses, not dancers, had their heads over the half-doors to their stalls and were monitoring the bustle with watchful eyes and flicking ears. Wings and coats gleamed, and grooms whistled and skipped. The barn itself was sparkling. And the stars of the pairs dances held court, as close to royalty as anything Tremeirchson had to offer.

The pompous stewards asked the same questions they asked every year: How many horses would receive riders this summer? Are any of your top riders considering retirement? Do you still enjoy working together after all these years? His parents were courteous and gracious. No one asked about Evan's win in his race yesterday, although Morgan did mention it with pride.

At that point, Davyd stepped in. "I'm sorry, but we'll have to stop there so you'll have time to get in position for the awards ceremony. Another blue ribbon for Morgan and Elen!" He ushered a few toward the fountain and the others followed. He even managed to avoid the steward with the questions about Hoel's barn.

Later that evening, Davyd's family gathered in the Great Hall for supper. It was rare to be all together for a family meal, especially during the Aerial Games. That and their recent wins gave an air of celebration to the usual bowls of pottage. The cook had added a slice of pork to each plate, so she must be proud of the family's success at the Games today. After reliving every minute of Evan's race and their parents' dance, Davyd remembered the water.

"Mum," he said, "you might want to check out Wynne's water. It smelled odd this morning. Did her groom say anything?"

Elen frowned. "*Na*, this is the first I've heard of it. I'll check it out after supper."

"You did a good job around here today, Davyd," Morgan said.

Davyd beamed. "Thanks. I'm glad everything went smoothly."

"You're the best little clerk around," Evan sniped.

It didn't bother Davyd. Reading and writing had always come easier for him. "Someone's got to tell you when to fly or you'd miss every race flirting with some fan," he told his brother.

"That's enough, you two," Morgan said. "Many skills are needed to run a barn as successful as ours. Someone needs to ride well and lead by example in the air, but someone also needs to organize the ground affairs. And not just during the Aerial Games. There are always air and ground needs. I admit I have trouble keeping my head out of the clouds, but that's why your mother and I make a great pair." He leaned toward Elen and she kissed him on the cheek.

"I love to fly too," she said. "But I guess I'm just more practical."

"What I'm trying to say," Morgan continued, "is that someday the two of you will be just as ideally suited to lead this barn. It will make me very proud to hand over control to the two of you to run as a team."

"*Diolch yn fawr iawn*, Da." Evan thanked his father and nodded. "We anticipate the honor of doing so."

Davyd mumbled something less formal. His father's dreams included both sons in the air. He didn't have to be a rider to run the ground operations. He knew that but wasn't sure his father did.

On a Wing and a Dare

Chapter 4: Secret's Out

The sun rose over Tremeirchson's barns and illuminated a glorious blue sky. Little birds chittered, greeting the day with song. Everything else was still and waiting. Before long, spectators would awaken for the fourth day of the Aerial Games, shattering the silent beauty of the early morning. Emma leaned against the doorjamb, looking out the back of her father's barn. The rising sun silhouetted two smaller barns. Peace washed over her but dissipated instead of lingering. Every muscle in her body, including her heart, ached.

Neste appeared out of the shadows, looking as tired as her daughter. "*Bore da, cariad*. Try to get the colts to take some water. I put three sick adults at the far end. What a shame they are all dancers." And Neste was gone, heading down the barn with a fresh bucket of oats, not taking time to appreciate the outside world.

With a sigh, Emma turned her back on the sun. She entered Rhys's stall and was shocked by how the colt had faded. Stroking the unresponsive colt's nose, she took a firm hold on his halter. His body radiated heat.

"Easy now, Rhys," she whispered to the colt, but he didn't flick an ear at her words. His wings hung listlessly at his sides. Yesterday her mother commented that she'd never seen such a quick, high fever.

Rhys didn't turn to look at her, nor was he interested in water or food. Emma sniffed the water. She frowned. She moved on to the other colt's stall and tried to entice Pedr to drink some water. His water still had the odor, too.

Pedr moaned, hanging his head. Instinctively, Emma tried to hold him up, but the colt sank to his knees and rolled over onto the ground. He lay there, breath shallow and labored, eyes glazed, one wing crumpled under him and one held awkwardly for a moment before it sank to rest across his body.

Emma screamed for her mother while she held the colt's head. "Hang in there, Pedr, come on, boy," she whispered urgently.

In the hallway, running feet headed down the barn.

Neste rushed in and flung herself to the ground beside Pedr. The colt thrashed his head once, emitting a tortured moan. In the next stall, his mother neighed and fidgeted, not used to being separated from her baby. Neste whispered to Pedr, stroking him as she looked him over, tension emanating from every muscle in her back.

Emma held the baby's head in her lap and crooned nonsense. His eyes rolled, exposing the whites, but then his entire demeanor changed. She could feel calm settle over him as his muscles relaxed. His rasping breaths softened, his eyes cleared. For a minute, Emma believed he recognized her. Then the eyes closed. The shallow breaths spaced further apart. Then they stopped.

Shock and anguish made Neste cry, "Oh, Emma, what else could we have done?"

"Mum? He's gone? Truly gone?"

In less than an hour, Rhys also died.

Neste squared her shoulders and stood up slowly. "I need to tell Hoel. He'll want to see them."

Emma turned away, unable to breathe normally. She admired her mother's will to move on, to be so controlled when they'd just watched two of their precious horses die in their arms.

"How many are sick?" Her father stood in the middle of the barn, anguish etched into every gesture.

"Three adults," her mother said, adding softly, "and two deaths."

"Hoel? My Llyth...." A rider's broken voice interrupted. "Llyth won't eat."

"Another," Hoel muttered as Neste rushed to Llyth's stall.

"We are cursed," moaned a rider from the shadows.

Riders gathered around Hoel, waiting in silence for Neste to return with news.

Neste couldn't speak. She held up four fingers, her face bathed with sorrow. Four horses sick, two dead. Emma blinked hard. If her parents could stay in control, so must she.

Hoel pulled himself up straight. "We must keep this between us. We can't risk jeopardizing this year's patronage while we figure out what's going on. No one says a word to anyone outside the barn."

Visions of the colts' deaths haunted Emma. Her father wanted to build his barn, to gain strength and win more races. He would need patrons to do that. He would be unable to increase his herd this year with the colts dead. The mare, Gwen, was pregnant. She'd have to be protected.

"And inside the barn?" Tristan asked, looking at Emma.

Emma glared at him. He was her father's second in command, but that didn't mean she had to like him. He was clearly insinuating she couldn't be trusted.

Other riders' voices tumbled over each other to be heard.

"Rhiannon is displeased with us."

"The wrath of Alon! We've been too tied to Aer and have neglected the others."

"We need to isolate the sick horses," Hoel declared, silencing the others. "Sign up for every race your horse can manage. Keep them out of the barn. We handle this ourselves."

Tristan nodded agreement, gesturing for riders to disperse. Their voices and their bootsteps faded away. Tristan winked at Emma before he followed the other riders, leaving Hoel, Neste, and Emma standing together in the aisle.

"A curse?" Hoel asked Neste, his face grim.

Emma held her breath, but her mother shook her head. "*Na, cariad.* That lot will never believe it, but it will run its course. We'll get through it."

Hoel nodded, and his furrowed brow eased a bit. He turned to Emma. "And no one says anything to anyone outside the barn," he repeated.

"And which of us would do that?" Emma asked with an edge to her voice. Obviously her father was talking about her. Her mother wasn't a rider. She rarely left the barn, especially with sick horses.

"You haven't shown much judgment in your friends. I thought it needed to be said."

Emma's irritation turned to hurt. "I've never betrayed the family."

"What guarantees that? If Evan or Davyd insists it's in the good of everyone, you'd side with them. You have before."

Emma shifted uncomfortably. He was right, but never for something like this. She remembered when her father decided to breed his horses within his own barn when common practice was open breeding between barns. She'd mentioned it to Davyd and Evan in conversation. It hadn't really been like tattling on her father. She was truly concerned. Evan told her that horses bred to the same bloodlines all the time would eventually be weaker. She'd talked to some of the riders about it, and they put pressure on Hoel. Emma supposed she could have gone directly to her father, but she doubted he would have listened to her.

Neste put her arm around her husband. "I'm sure Emma understands her duty to family."

Emma still had a lump in her throat as she headed back to Pedr's stall. She straightened the colt's legs and the wing she could reach and curried him lightly with his brush. Scuffling steps behind her made her tense.

"He would've been a good flier, with that deep chest."

It was Tristan. She nodded acknowledgment

without speaking.

"Pretty convenient for you now that Pedr is gone, Princess. You'll have to become rider to one of Morgan's colts. Probably marry one of Morgan's sons, too," he sneered.

Emma stood up and faced him. Legs apart and hands on hips, she glared at him. "Your nasty comments are ill timed, rider. We have work to do and you are interfering. Leave now and I won't report your behavior to my father."

She hoped Tristan would argue because she would love to release her rage at the colts' death on him. But some self-preservation instinct took hold and Tristan disappeared. Emma took a few deep breaths to calm her shaking nerves before rejoining her parents in the tack room.

Hoel looked worried. Deep lines gouged his face, and he frowned. Neste put her hand on his arm. Mum was the quiet strength in the family, calming her father's explosive temper. She always laughed that being a rider was not an option for her since she cared for Hoel and the riders and all their horses. And Emma, of course. But Mum had been a rider and lost her horse in a flying accident with Morgan. It had happened before Emma was born, but she knew those memories must be coming back now.

"This can be stopped?" Hoel asked.

"I can treat symptoms." Neste shrugged helplessly.

"Is the smell in the water from the medicine? Could that be it?" Emma asked.

"Could be anything at this point, *cariad*. I'll check."

"Help your mother." Hoel turned on a boot heel

and stomped from the room.

"Why is he...."

"Not now," Neste interrupted. "Let's deal with the horse crisis as a family, all right? Unified?"

"*Iawn, Mam.* How can I help you?"

Neste directed the grooms to set smoking pots of thyme around the barn. It would cleanse the air of impurities that might be making the horses sick. She told the riders how to rearrange stall assignments so that the sick horses were as isolated as possible. With Emma, she filled porous sacks with charcoal and attached them to the spigots that filled the horses' troughs from the aqueduct. Hopefully the charcoal would filter out whatever was making the odor. It was the best they could do for water and air.

Emma brought a handful of water to her nose. The odor was still there. "See, Mum? It smells a little like nimberry tea."

Neste smelled the water, thought for a moment then smelled it again. "You know, the nimberry is an interesting plant. The ugly little leaves make quite a tasty tea and the beautiful red berries are extremely poisonous."

"Someone put nimberries in the water?"

"Well, I don't see berries. I'll check the cistern that feeds the lane and see what I can find, and I can send some to the apothecary. He may be able to tell what's in it."

They moved to the next stall and worked companionably for a short while.

"So I hear Evan won his race yesterday." Neste cautiously opened a spigot.

Emma looked up from her task and peered at her mother. "Yeah, and Morgan and Elen won the pairs."

"Of course. They're the best."

Her mother's even tone puzzled Emma. Mum didn't sound ecstatic for Evan's parents, but she didn't sound sarcastic either. "Does everyone hate Morgan's barn? I really thought it was just Da."

The last couple of days had been tough, and today wouldn't be much better. She missed the ease of Morgan's barn. She missed Adain. Her loyalties to family and loyalties to friends threatened to tear her world apart.

Neste took Emma's hands in hers. "*Cariad*, I never got a chance to tell you how glad I am that you are all right after. . .you know."

"Oh, Mum." Emma's chaotic emotions tried to burst forth as tears. "Were you watching? Did you know it was me?"

"It didn't matter at first that it was you. It was a collision. I could only think of my beautiful Llawen and our own accident. Then I was consumed with setting Catrin's leg and trying not to pay attention to Bronwyn's death." She paused for a deep shaky breath. "When I learned you were aboard Wynne. . ." Neste swallowed hard and squeezed Emma's hands. "When I knew it was you, I discovered new depths of anguish. You can't know what it's like to have a child. Your own feelings pale when your child is in danger."

"Da doesn't seem to agree." Emma tried for hard core sarcasm but she was betrayed by the tear that dropped from her eyes onto her mother's hand.

"Your father's first responsibility is to his barn, and

he takes that very seriously. It doesn't mean he loves you any less, *cariad*. In this, I was the parent. He had to be Barn Leader."

"He doesn't even try to understand me."

Neste laughed. "He understands you better than you know. You are very alike, the two of you."

"I would never have been so rude to Morgan. He embarassed me, Mum."

"*Cariad*, don't bother yourself. Morgan is a good man, and a good leader. The accident that caused Llawen's death wasn't his fault, really, but your father had to blame someone and this feud between barns is older than both of them. Your friendship with Davyd and Evan is strong. The three of you will look after each other, I know, for your whole lives. Don't let our adult issues cloud that, ever."

"And this summer? Will he let me be Adain's rider?"

"That will be very hard for your father to watch, but I understand. I will do everything I can to make that happen for you."

Emma fell into her mother's embrace with relief, mumbling, "Thank you, Mum."

Hoel and his riders were airborne early the next day, entered in as many races as the barn could possibly manage. Emma worried that some of the horses might be overtaxed by too many races in one day. Neste busied herself with the four sick horses, but by midmorning she shooed Emma out of the barn, telling her daughter to take a break.

Emma left the barn and walked toward the center of village. She longed to visit Adain, but didn't dare. The fountain spray mingled with the gray sky, dampening the air as well as her spirits. She walked around it, stopping before Aer, the lightest stone horse. Splashing water from the basin, she cleaned some dust off a wing. She understood the concept of the fountain, that air, earth, and water should be in balance. Silently, she offered a prayer. *Aer, protect our winged horses. Help us all.*

She looked to the stone pillar between the horses, and the flame that burned at the top of it. In all weather, the flame burned, except in the heaviest rain. Rhiannon's Fire, with the power to destroy or to create the warmth of a family hearth. Emma's internal flame burned for the air. Her passion was for flight.

With her back to the fountain, she sat on the lip of the basin. Someday she'd have a home, and a husband and children. She wanted them, really she did, but not as much as she wanted to fly. Assuming that burning desire would be tempered a bit once she actually became a rider, then she could think about the more balanced parts of her future.

Surrounding the fountain, Tremeirchson's shops were opening for the day. Visiting merchants opened tent flaps and arranged their wares. The scent of hot buns made her stomach rumble. A farmer unloaded a half-dozen crates of clucking hens, and the ox pulling his cart bellowed. Hoel's barn was aloft, but other riders walked along the wooden walkways in front of the stores, calling greetings to each other. Only Hoel's barn seemed to worry who talked to who, Emma observed. Everyone else seemed to get along fine.

She spotted Evan walking up from his father's barn. His blond hair waved a bit as he walked. She liked it long. He was confident, striding toward her, and she smiled.

"Aer was always your favorite, wasn't he?" he greeted her.

"Yes. Yours, too."

He smiled and sat next to her. His arm touched hers, and its warmth didn't surprise her as much as the tingling sensation it gave her. She wanted to snatch her arm away, but she also wanted to press it harder against him.

"Davyd always liked Ystrad best, I think," she said.

"Ystrad? Really?" Evan looked at the brown stone horse.

Ystrad was the earth horse, representing practicality and nurturing. No air dreams for earth people. Emma thought about her mother's earlier words. Neste was a dreamer who was living in a practical, earth world. Apparently it was true. You could learn to balance all the pieces inside you.

"I saw Hoel take off this morning. Was that the whole barn?"

Evan had noticed the missing horses. He was familiar with every horse in every barn, and he probably knew exactly which four were not with Hoel today. "A couple stayed in the barn. Nothing big."

"Nothing big? Then why can't you look at me when you say that, Em?"

"I promised my father I wouldn't say anything. Don't pry, Evan, please." She longed to tell him, but she knew she shouldn't. The comfort he gave her wouldn't be worth it if her father found out she'd talked.

He looked at her for a long moment. "For you. I won't."

She almost cried with relief. Evan moved the arm that touched hers. She missed it for an instant before it reappeared around her shoulders. Tingles rippled down her back and disrupted the butterflies in her stomach. He leaned close, smelling of horses and sweet hay.

"Races are beginning. Want to watch with me?"

She'd love nothing better. But she couldn't. She shook her head, knowing she had to get back to the barn. "Give my love to Adain, will you?"

Evan didn't move his arm. "You aren't sneaking over to see him? He'll miss you."

"I don't dare. You don't know how bad it's been." She hesitated and felt those traitorous tears welling up again.

"Em, you are going to have to confront your father sooner or later if you plan to ride Adain."

The concern in his tone spread a foolish smile over her face. Yeah, she still had to confront her father. Currently the water portion of her soul was going with the flow. Evan thought he knew what she should do, but he obviously didn't know what his brother was going through. She almost laughed at the irony, but it came out as a choked sob.

"Em?"

They had always stayed together, the three of them. Every childhood trauma, every secret, had been shared. As a result, Davyd and Evan trusted her and she them. She had never had to agonize alone like this. "Pedr was the first to die."

64

Evan let out a low whistle. *"Mae'n ddrwg gen i."* He hugged her, the condolence leaving warm breath on her hair.

"I feel bad. I didn't want to be his rider, but I didn't want him to d…die." She choked on a sob and pressed her face against his chest. The thrill of being so close melded with the comfort of his arms.

"Of course you didn't."

"Rhys died, too. We have four more sick, and this morning others are showing symptoms. We don't know what it is. Some of the riders say it is a curse."

"A curse?" Evan snorted. He clearly didn't believe in curses. Emma felt her clenched heart ease a bit. "Has Hoel asked for help?"

"Da wants to keep this a secret until it passes, or at least until the Games are over and the patrons have left the village." She leaned away from him, not far enough to pull away from his arms, but far enough to face him.

"But the Games have two more days. What if other horses in other barns get sick? We need to talk about it, to share information. Figure out how to help."

"You speak for the other barns now?" she asked, managing a little grin.

"Na," Evan said grimly. "But I should. A Barn Council is long overdue."

Emma smiled at the familiar refrain. Evan had been arguing for a Barn Council since before he became a rider. Most riders seemed tired of the idea, but Evan insisted it would strengthen Tremeirchson's herds, and this illness might be his proving point.

"We need to contain this, but we don't know how yet," she said.

"First step is to stop overflying your horses." Evan indicated the sky with a tossed head.

"He'll not be able to handle accusations that his barn started this, especially if they come from your father."

"We don't know that his barn did. How many other barns might have sick horses that we don't know about?"

"I know, I know, a Barn Council would be the best way to handle a crisis like this." She smiled sadly.

"It would." He removed his arms and turned away reluctantly. "I'd better get back. I have to find a way to convince my father to take the lead. They'll listen to Morgan if they won't listen to his son."

Chapter 5: Barn Council

Davyd surveyed the storage room in dismay. Located at one end of his father's barn, the space collected everything the hurried riders left behind: racing saddles, colored blankets, clothing, half-eaten meals. He picked up a plate with a chunk of moldy bread. Today was the last day of competition, and tomorrow was the Farewell. Then life would go back to normal. Davyd moved the plate to join an empty ale mug on a shelf and sat down on an old stool. Normal.

Once the Games ended, he was virtually off duty for a month until the new riders joined the barn and a new round of training began. This year, his chosen course would be known to the world by then. He would not be a rider. He would be. . . something else. His parents' disappointment, villagers' speculation, and his brother's derision would die down, hopefully, and he would be able to move on.

Running feet drew his attention to the wooden walkway outside. Evan appeared in the doorway.

"Where's Da?" he gasped, trying to catch his breath.

"In Deryn's stall, I think. What's going on?"

Evan didn't answer. Davyd followed as his brother ran to Deryn's stall.

Morgan met them at the door. "Why are you running?"

"Hoel's had two horses die already and more are sick," Evan blurted out.

Morgan's face sobered. "Come inside."

He closed the stall door behind the three of them. Deryn munched hay calmly as Evan spoke in an urgent whisper, explaining what he and Emma had talked about.

Davyd listened with half his attention. The other half was stabbing his heart with the image of Emma sneaking out of her father's barn to meet Evan. He shook his head, clearing it of troubling images. "Some of our water smells odd, too," he offered.

"It's time for a Barn Council," Evan said. "We need to be very clear about where this illness strikes and how to combat it. If not, we could lose every horse in Tremeirchson."

"Now, son," Morgan cautioned. "No need to panic. They have two dead. That's a tragedy, but there are nine barns in Tremeirchson, and well over a hundred horses. A Barn Council would take time to implement properly, even if everyone agreed."

"I don't think we have time," Evan insisted. "It can't really be a curse, can it?"

"People are always quick to cry curse, but what have we done to bring down a curse?" Morgan asked. "Now what do we know about this?"

"What are the symptoms of the sickness?" Davyd asked.

Evan looked at them, puzzled. "I didn't ask. First we need to get everyone together to discuss it."

"First, we need to make sure our horses are safe," Davyd pointed out. "Do all the barns use the same water source?"

Evan began pacing the stall, clearly frustrated. "I have no idea."

Morgan shook his head slowly, brow furrowed. "The barns share water. The aqueduct was put in by a group of patrons years ago. It draws water from a common cistern outside of town near the fields. I don't know if it is separate from the village's well or not." He paused for a moment, lost in thought. "Why hasn't Hoel come forward?"

"Emma told me they had two dead and four sick," Evan repeated.

Davyd pictured Evan and Emma, very close together, commiserating over the deaths. Her smile was not one she ever showed Davyd. Evan's blond hair coordinated nicely with her brown, and Evan's lanky build complimented her graceful movements. There was no room in that picture for Davyd's solid bulk. He forced the image out of his head and focused on his father's words.

"She must have overstated the threat, Evan. We can't panic about a sickness in another barn. Leaders do what they think is best for those they lead. If Hoel wants our help, I trust he'll ask for it."

"How many horses have to die before we make him accept help?"

"We don't make him. It's his barn."

"Da, that's not right." Evan's voice rose, betraying his frustration.

"*Iawn*, it is. We take care of our own." Morgan's voice was controlled.

"A Barn Council wouldn't ignore dying horses."

"And that's why so many older riders are opposed to the idea. They don't want other barns meddling in their affairs."

"Meddling?" Evan's voice rose.

Morgan had made his point and turned away from his son, examining Deryn's eyes and listening to his chest. Evan stalked out of the barn.

"I'll make sure all our horses are healthy," Davyd said quietly.

Morgan nodded and waved him out of the stall.

Davyd started with Wynne. She looked up when he entered the stall and twitched her ears at him as he talked to her. "Eyes bright, sniffing for a treat. You look fine, Wynne, *del*."

He emptied her water trough. The mare would need water, but he didn't want to take any chances. He paused to calculate. He'd need a barrel a day for three horses, although Deryn drank more than that. It would be hard to find enough traders to bring that much water by wagon from Merioneth. There must be a closer source, a lake or something. Davyd shook his head. The local waterways filled the cistern that fed the aqueduct. Until they knew the source of the illness, the cistern water could not be used.

Moving from stall to stall, Davyd checked the horses. He asked grooms about behavior and eating habits. Frustrated, he wished he knew what he was looking for. He did sniff water in every stall. Wynne's water smelled strongest, and Hefin's, but the odor was present in all stalls. Davyd instructed the grooms to scrub the water troughs with vinegar and not refill them. He set buckets of smoking thyme along the walkway, dampening the thyme to increase smoke. That would show those crying curse that something was being done to pacify the god Aer.

He left the barn then and walked up Aer Road past the fountain to the tavern on Ystrad. Davyd forced a cheerful smile on his face as he walked past spectators. Hoel was probably right to keep this quiet until the Aerial Games were over and the visitors gone. It would be much harder to deal with an emergency if they had to stop and explain themselves every half hour to every visitor who fancied they had influence with a lord.

The fountain splashed in the sun, the water sparkling as if on fire. Davyd stopped for a moment, watching people walk past it or stop to visit the tents of festival vendors. All that water. Davyd turned away from the fountain, unable to maintain his smile.

The tavern was a popular spot for locals. The interior seemed dim after the bright sun outside. Davyd stood just inside the door until his eyes adjusted. The walls were covered with memorabilia from past Aerial Games. A large painting of his parents in their pairs dancing costumes of maybe five years ago hung over the fireplace. Tacked to the frame were more recent drawings of the pair and their horses. The owner spotted Davyd and waved.

"Robert," he asked quietly, "I'm going to need to

order quite a few barrels of water. I'll need access to the traders that supply you here. Can you handle that for me?"

The storekeeper furrowed his brow. "Water? What's going on?"

"I'm not sure yet. I just need to put the horses on a protected water source for awhile."

Robert whistled. "Expensive. I can arrange delivery directly to the barn, though."

"Great," Davyd said.

They worked out quantities and pricing quickly, stopping twice to allow Robert to wait on other customers. Davyd was pleased that Robert's current supply of water could be delivered immediately, but disappointed to learn that today's traders were gone and no more were due until tomorrow. At least the Aerial Games ensured daily visits. Once the Games were over, the traders' visits were much more irregular.

When the order was complete, Davyd shook Robert's hand. Before he turned to go, though, he asked one last question. "Robert, do you know anything about the village's drinking water?"

"Drinking water? Lucky for me, most of the villagers drink ale."

Davyd laughed with the tavern keeper and took his leave. He stood just outside the tavern for a minute, watching the crowds of people and the horses in the air. Up the street, the fountain innocently splashed as he approached. Pretending to wet his face, he smelled the water. No odor.

The festive sounds of the last market day swirled around him. A vendor selling pies did a brisk business nearby, and the scent of hot sweet berries made Davyd's stomach rumble. Beyond that, a man called to passersby that he had the most beautiful jewelry in the region. Going by the amount of interest, Davyd suspected his very beautiful wife or daughter modeled for him.

By the time he was once more outside his father's barn, the late afternoon sun stretched pale arms across an empty sky. This year's Aerial Games were over. Tomorrow, Tremeirchson would belong to itself again.

Davyd was pleased to see Robert's water delivery had been made and a barrel of water distributed to each groom. The top door to Adain's stall was open, and he heard Owain talking to the colt.

"I know, Adain, *del*, I know. You're still thirsty, aren't you? You're a growing boy, you are. Let me give you just a bit more. Just a bit won't hurt you."

The spigot creaked as Owain opened it, and water gurgled into Adain's trough. Davyd leaped for the door and crashed into the stall.

"*Na!*" he shouted, startling both boy and colt. "Turn off that water!" He grabbed Adain's halter and jerked the colt's head away from the trough as Owain hurried to obey.

"Can't you follow orders?" Davyd roared as Owain cringed. Adain's eyes rolled and his ears lay back against his head. Davyd fought to calm himself.

"I'm sor...sorry, *syr*." Owain's eyes were as big as the colt's.

"It's all right." Davyd took one more big breath. "The water may be poisoned. Do not give any of the horses any water from the pipes. Do you understand?"

He didn't think it was possible for Owain's eyes to

get any wider, but they did. "Yes *syr*."

Still shaking, Davyd left Adain's stall and checked each horse to make sure the grooms understood. By the time he got to Deryn's stall, he was calm.

Two days later, Davyd stood in Hefin's stall, leaning on the sill of the open half door. In the cobblestone courtyard before him, grooms and riders moved hurriedly about their business but their heads were down, their conversations muted. Across the courtyard, the manor house stood watch over yard and barn, its dark windows projecting concern. Davyd looked past the manor and stared into the sky.

Thin herds revealed how many horses were sick or had died. Quick visual counts were the most telling sign, since barn leaders were keeping to themselves the extent of sickness in their barns. It was painfully obvious that the illness was pervasive, but everyone seemed to be afraid the disease's spread would be blamed on them. Davyd had brought in wagonloads of water barrels from Merioneth for two days, but his efforts had not been good enough. He turned back to the colt.

Hefin's labored breathing and listless eyes told the story. He hadn't eaten anything since yesterday morning, and getting water in him was much harder. To make matters worse, the last shipment of water barrels had smelled odd. But the horses had to have water. Davyd reached out to stroke the colt's fevered head.

"How is he, *cariad*?" Elen poked her head into the stall.

Davyd just shook his head, for once not minding

the dancing of his dratted curls. His mother looked worried and distracted.

"Any others showing signs, Mum?"

His mother looked away, wiping hastily at her eyes. "Wynne didn't eat her breakfast."

Davyd sucked in a breath of air. "Wynne? Oh, maybe it's a coincidence, Mum. Wynne's strong. She'll be fine." His voice trailed off, betraying his concern.

"We'll know by tonight," Elen said grimly. The eyes she turned on him were as hollow and forlorn as the windows of the manor house.

They helplessly watched Hefin breathe for a moment.

"You know the worst thing, Mum?" Davyd said slowly. "Here you have this gorgeous animal, blessed by Rhiannon with the ability to fly, and he won't have the chance. He's just a baby, and he won't have the chance."

His mother turned to look at him. "And you'll be free?"

Horrified, Davyd spluttered, "*Na*, that's not what I meant! Of course, I know Hefin was intended for me, but I'm not thinking about riding him. Or, I am, but. . ." He subsided, a torrent of emotions flooding him. He didn't want Hefin to die, but it did solve his problem. He couldn't become a rider if there were no colts. The disloyal cruelty of that thought brought him up short. He didn't want Hefin to die like this. Then a new thought struck him. "How did you know?"

His mother shook her head. "I'm your mother. I've suspected for years, waiting for you to say something. But this is not your fault, *cariad*, and no one will say it is. Oh, they will commiserate with you and say how awful it is that you can't become a rider as soon as you want to, but it's out of your hands."

Stunned, Davyd couldn't believe his mother knew about his fear and wasn't troubled by the knowledge. "And what about Emma? Will she be able to keep Adain?" he asked.

"Assuming Adain is well through this, I don't see how we can keep Emma off him. That colt is as besotted with her as she is with him. Did she tell you he almost kicked in his stall last week when he heard her and couldn't see her? Owain could barely calm him."

They smiled and Davyd felt the fist that clenched his heart ease. His mother seemed to think it would be all right. As a child, his mother had made everything rosy. Now that he was older, he still turned to her to fix situations that were unfixable. He couldn't rationalize it. He felt better because his mum reassured him, just like every son in the province.

It was a momentary easing, though. Hefin died within the hour and Wynne didn't eat her dinner. Two other horses were sick, and the entire barn was worried. Morgan decided it was time to go have a word with Hoel. Davyd thought bleakly that it was about time Morgan took action. Mums were for reassurance, but fathers were for acting to protect what belonged to the family.

As he prepared to leave the barn, Morgan turned to Davyd. "I'm really sorry, *cariad*, about the colt."

Davyd acknowledged the gruff words with a nod.

"Will you come with me to Hoel's barn? I hope you and Emma can help us old adversaries come to agreement on this."

"Glad to help," Davyd said, and he was. If he could be useful, maybe he could keep his mind off his guilt over the relief he felt at Hefin's death. He knew the animosity between his father and Emma's ran deep, but both men had lost good animals, and the riders in their barns were grieving. These men were leaders, responsible for the continued well-being of their barns. They would know that this was a crisis that crossed barn boundaries.

They walked to Hoel's barn without speaking. Hoel's riders were milling about, looking reluctant to put their horses in the barn. Hoel met them at the door. From the corner of his eye, Davyd saw Emma rush up. She looked tired but beautiful. He'd missed her over the last couple of days. She certainly hadn't been to see Adain. Maybe she'd been sneaking out to see Evan.

"We have one dead and more sick," Morgan reported bluntly. "We need to know what you know about this illness, where it came from and how to treat it."

Hoel snorted derisively. "You and I aren't the only barns with illness, or even death, and we have no time to hold your hand. Most of my riders are calling it Rhiannon's Curse. You'll have to deal with it on your own."

He turned to walk away, but Emma stepped forward. Hoel hesitated.

"Treat the fever and diarrea as usual," she told Morgan. "Force clean, fresh water down them. It's almost more important than food for the first day. Keep them as comfortable as you can. The illness works fast." She subsided, tormented by the sickness she'd seen. "We have two that might recover."

Morgan thanked her. *"Diolch."* Turning to Davyd, he asked, "You got that?"

"Yes, I think we've got what we need for now," Davyd answered. "We may even have compresses to spare for fever. I'll bring a few over." Emma nodded, the tension in her shoulders lessening a bit. "And Emma? It was Hefin, not Adain." Relief washed across her face, but she immediately tried to hide it.

"You dare to mention Adain here?" Hoel roared.

Morgan stepped forward. "Who knows how many horses will be left come summer? Maybe no one will be riding. Forget about the colt."

Muttering, Hoel stalked into the barn.

"Diolch, thank you for coming," Emma said graciously, "and for the compresses."

"When the time comes," Morgan said, "you will do your Barn Leader proud, Emma *verch* Hoel."

Davyd smiled to see the flash of pride in Emma's eyes, and he winked at her. She blushed and hurried into the barn. Whistling to himself as he returned to his father's barn, Davyd thought about how beautiful Emma looked when she was official barn representative, and when she was proud of herself, and when she was embarrassed. She tossed her head with confidence, her chin lifted, and her chestnut hair swung over her shoulder. Emma never wore a cap on her hair like other women, and he liked that. He was fascinated by the way her dark eyes sparkled with delight and dimmed with sorrow. Dark eyes that seemed to see only Evan. His whistling ceased as a guttural growl erupted from his throat.

Chapter 6: Hard Times

When Davyd returned with the promised fever compresses, Emma was waiting for him. Her heart had fluttered alarmingly when she watched him with Morgan. She'd never seen Davyd in any kind of leadership role and guilt lanced her as she realized the depth of her dismissal. Davyd always deferred to Evan and was always in his shadow.

As children, their games often mimicked what they saw the adults doing in the sky with the horses. They'd pretended to be horses themselves and galloped across Tremeirchson's hills. Emma's hair streamed behind her like a horse's mane, and she'd tossed her head and whinnied as they created complicated patterns in the grass or run races. Her long legs allowed her to keep pace with Evan pretty well, but with his shorter, stockier legs Davyd fell behind. Emma would turn back or circle around as if herding Davyd onward, but Evan never waited. And Davyd never gave up, never went his own way. The two of them always followed Evan.

Yes, Davyd deferred to Evan. Yet earlier today he

On a Wing and a Dare

had stood beside his father, representing their barn, and spoken confidently and knowledgeably about the current crisis, his brown eyes focused on Hoel and an errant brown curl bobbing as he moved his head to emphasize his words. So she waited for his return like a little girl mooning over a mysterious knight, wondering which Davyd would return.

He walked across the road toward the barn with assurance, waving to a rider. Emma admired the sun on Davyd's brown hair, and the way his shirtsleeves were rolled up past his elbows, exposing his tanned muscled arms. His stubby childhood legs had lengthened, giving him the smooth stride of a confident man although he would never be as tall as Evan. Her heart fluttered again. She accepted the compresses from him and tucked them on a shelf inside the barn. Then she turned to her friend with a deep breath and a smile.

"Want to go for a walk? Mum wants me to stop at the apothecary's to see what he was able to discover about the water." She tried for a casual tone as she snuck a look back at the barn.

"I'll come along. Good idea." He grinned back at her.

Suddenly shy, she started walking. Davyd fell into step beside her. Above them, horses flew in scattered groups.

"Lot of spaces up there," Davyd observed.

"Too many, I know."

"Riders still crying curse?"

Emma rolled her eyes. "They say Rhiannon's Curse will ruin our lives." She laughed grimly. "More likely, our lives will be ruined by moaning riders and villagers

80

who do nothing but complain."

Villagers' superstitions seemed silly compared to the glory of winged flight. Anyone who had flown above the earth, freed from the constraints of the earthbound, understood the limitless power of the air. No curse could topple that. But villagers, grooms, and even some riders still believed Rhiannon was angry, and Aer was helpless in the face of the goddess's wrath.

The cobblestones around the fountain were littered with debris from the vendors who'd left as soon as the Games concluded. Davyd kicked aside a short length of rope, too frayed for the merchant to save. Emma bent over to retrieve a bit of green and gold ribbon. She smiled as she tied it into a bow and slipped it into her skirt pocket. It might be the only piece of Morgan's barn she'd be allowed to have. Her smile slipped. "I'm really sorry about Hefin," she told Davyd quietly.

He nodded. "*Diolch*," he said softly.

They walked a few steps in companionable silence. The village around them seemed quiet, but maybe it was just the absence of the clamor surrounding the Games. A young boy drove a small herd of pigs down a lane between shops, and a couple of elderly women chatted on a stone bench near the fountain.

"Does Evan spend much time at your father's barn?" Davyd asked.

"Evan?" She was puzzled. "My father doesn't like him any better than he likes you." She laughed apologetically.

"Just wondering."

Davyd seemed ill at ease when she peered at him.

"Nice day," he observed. He glanced up at the hazy

sky, then quickly down, eyes darting side to side as if looking for something to fasten on to.

The sky must have reminded him of sick horses, as it did her. Her father's barn was being decimated by this disease, which most people were now calling a plague. Her heart wrenched every time a horse died that she had loved growing up. She thought she was numb, but another horse had died that morning and ripped a new hole in her heart. Emma blinked quickly and swallowed. She mustn't cry now. She wanted to enjoy this walk with Davyd and took a deep breath.

"Pretty nice," she agreed, managing a small smile. Davyd had always been her friend, and she'd never had trouble talking to him before now.

Circling the fountain, stone-walled shops opened onto the street and hid living quarters in the rear. Some of the shops were dark and closed. It wasn't unusual for merchants to take a few days off after a successful Games and head down the mountain to visit friends or family. Even so, a lot of places were dark. Up ahead, Emma could see Ranald, the tailor, loading a wagon.

"*Dydd da*," Davyd greeted him. Emma echoed him.

Ranald turned to them with a grimace. "Good day? In whose world? Yours, where horses continue to die or mine, where trade dries up overnight?"

Emma looked down, uncomfortable with the man's forthright challenge.

"Tremeirchson has seen hard times before," Davyd said quietly.

The tailor shook his head. "Maybe so, but the winged horses always brought us back. With them came the patrons, the visitors, the money. Without them..."

His voice trailed off.

Emma noticed four small children curled amongst blanket-wrapped bundles in the wagon. "Ranald? Are you leaving?"

"We cannot stay, miss. It will get worse, and my family has to eat. It's already started. No one here is thinking of new tunics or festival clothes. With the water scarce, people are hoarding everything. We are heading down to Merioneth. More people, more trade. I hope." His tone was defeated, his shoulders slumped.

His wife called from the doorway, and Ranald hastened to help her with a heavy piece of furniture.

A small boy emerged from under a blanket in the wagon and crawled to the side. On his knees, gripping the wagon side, he stared at Emma and Davyd. Emma waved at him.

"They're not the only ones," Davyd said, indicating other wagons and a few shops that were already shuttered.

"And all we can do is let this run its course? What if it *is* the water and it can't be salvaged?"

"Ranald's right. If the horses die, Tremeirchson dies with them."

"Then we must save the horses," Emma said. "We can't disappoint that boy."

Davyd laughed. "That's the only reason to save them?"

She scowled at him, pretending to be angry, then laughed. Her heart felt so much lighter, just being out of the barn and away from the constant pressure to do more than what was possible. She could pretend everything at the barn was fine if she could just stay out walking with

Davyd.

Davyd took her arm and they continued walking around the fountain, looking down Alon Road. Here the residences were mostly wattle and daub, the gray of the mud walls matching the gray of the ground. The thatched huts were separated by garden plots that supplemented what food was grown in the fields. Chickens scratched in a few of the yards. At the far end of the street was the mayor's stone manor. It was similar in size and grandeur to Morgan's manor; they were the best houses in the village. In lowlander towns, the best houses belonged to the landowners, who came up the mountain to buy a share of a barn and increase prestige in their world by becoming patrons. In Tremeirchson, though, the real power was in the air. Morgan's barn was the largest; so, therefore, was his house. The mayor's authority was a pale imitation. Today his courtyard was full of people, mostly men. Quite possibly the women were home packing to leave the area. The obvious tension in the air sobered Emma.

"They want answers he doesn't have," Davyd commented. They watched for a moment as the villagers milled and emotion mounted. He had kept hold of Emma's arm, and he pulled her on around the fountain, back toward the barns, away from the growing crowd.

"I had no idea," she breathed. Davyd's grip was reassuring, comforting.

The apothecary's shop was in an alley behind the main road. The dirty window was covered with shelves of colored bottles, giving it a stained-glass look. A cat hissed as Davyd pushed open the door, its eyes glowing from a dark space under the counter. Kenn, the proprietor, pushed aside the black curtains hiding his back room and glided to the counter.

"Ah, Emma *verch* Hoel," he said. "You've come for your mother's report?"

His black-cowled robe with its belled sleeves smelled as if he hadn't taken it off since before she was born. But she'd known the old man her whole life, and his eyes sparkled like a kindly grandfather.

"Yes, I have. What did you find?"

"And this is Davyd *ap* Morgan, correct?" Kenn was not about to be hurried.

Davyd nodded. "Yes. And may we know what you have found?"

Kenn picked up a small vial as if looking at the clear liquid inside would reveal all its secrets. "You were partially correct, milady," he said to Emma. "This was contaminated by the nimberry. Did you know that the poison in those lovely berries is not the fault of the berry at all? Let me demonstrate."

He shuffled through the crowded shop to a small tub on the floor near the window. Emma recognized a nimberry bush, laden with red berries. Her mouth dropped open as Kenn picked a handful of berries and popped them into his mouth.

"You see? Tart, they are. Juicy. Not poisonous."

"I don't understand," Davyd said.

Emma shook her head. She, too, was confused.

"This is a special bush. Please don't try that on a wild nimberry you find on the hill." Kenn shook an admonishing finger at them before rustling through a box of small jars. "Ah, here it is. Do you recognize these?"

On a Wing and a Dare

Davyd and Emma peered into the jar. Four or five tiny red segmented worms wriggled over each other. Emma turned away, but Davyd was intrigued. "What are they?"

Kenn twisted the jar, holding it up to a lantern over his counter. "These, my young friends, are *Lumbricus Rubellus*, a special type of red worm that lays their eggs in the nimberry, right in the berry. They secrete a toxin into the berry that protects the larvae. These little fellows are the cause of the nimberry's poison."

Davyd gestured toward the nimberry plant in the tub. "So if you have a nimberry without worms, you have nimberry without poison."

"Very true, my young *syr*." Kenn beamed at Davyd.

"But what does that mean for our horses?" Emma asked, impatient with the details.

Kenn's face fell. "I'm not quite sure. I know nimberry toxin appears in the water sample. I know how it gets into the berry. But how it gets from the berry to the water source? I have not yet discovered that."

He pushed his way behind the counter and indicated a bookshelf filled with leather bound books so old the pages were yellowed and crumbling. "The answer may be here. These are ledgers from apothecary studies in three countries. All I need is time to search."

"And time we don't have," Emma said wistfully.

"Can I help?" Davyd asked. "With the Aerial Games complete, my days are mostly free. I can help search these books."

Kenn's face lit up. "That would be wonderful, young man, truly wonderful! A service to your town and to my profession as well."

Davyd nodded. "I will be here tomorrow morning."

He took Emma's arm and led her from the shop. Odd as it was, Emma was relieved to know a bit more about the poison. Even if they didn't know how the worms actually poisoned the horses' water, it felt like progress.

They turned down Aer Road and left the cobblestone street for a hard-packed dirt lane that led to the lesser barns. For the first time, Emma saw her father's barn as a visitor might. It was smaller than Morgan's, but not by much. The tightly thatched roof and sturdy clay walls weren't pretty, but they were functional. Adjacent to the barn, the house sat amidst a straggly flower garden. Her mother rarely had time to garden even in the best years, which this wasn't.

Davyd stopped before walking her right up to the door. Leaning over, he picked a purply blue flower and handed it to her. She took it, confused. She really didn't know much about flowers.

"Milkwort," he said. He smiled, let go of her arm with a last reassuring squeeze, and waved as he turned back up the lane.

Emma watched him go for longer than necessary. It was like the wrapping had been removed from a gift. The gift looked nice, but when it was unwrapped its true value was revealed. She twined the milkwort flower into her hair.

"So it's like that, is it?" her mother said, amused, from the doorway of the house.

"Like what?" Emma knew she sounded defensive.

"I always figured it would be one of Morgan's boys," her mother teased. "I was never sure which one it would be."

"Neither am I."

Emma took deep breaths to calm herself and turned away, entering the barn. She looked in on horses that she had grown up with and loved like family members, family members that were now in need of relief she could not give them. She stopped in front of Lleu's stall and stroked the brown nose. Her father's stallion pricked his ears, monitoring all sounds within his barn.

Her mother's soft footsteps approached. When Emma told her what the apothecary had discovered, she said, "The hills are full of nimberry bushes. Why hasn't it been a problem before?"

Emma shook her head. She didn't know.

"A barn can't exist without a village," Neste observed. "And a village can't exist without clean water. . ."

"So we move the village?" Emma joked.

Her mother was silent.

"Mum?"

"Better than watching the entire village die. And not as impossible as it seems. Really, Emma, what's keeping us here?" She raised her arms to indicate the barn. "Sure we have history, but the future is not assured. We have to protect what we have and I'm no longer sure we can do it in Tremeirchson."

Mum turned and walked away. Emma stared after her, mind staggered by the idea of moving the village. It would be a huge undertaking. There was no way one barn could organize it. They would have to work together, and they hadn't ever done that well.

Restless, Emma left the barn again and headed for

her favorite thinking spot. Seated on the fountain's rim under Aer's feet, she felt protected. The stone fountain had absorbed the heat of the sun all morning, and it radiated warmth now. It wasn't enough, however, to unchill her heart. Burying her face in her hands, she wept for the dead horses, for the exhausted riders, and for the demise of her father's barn. He was so proud of his horses' bloodlines and of the family of riders. So far, her father's stallion, Lleu, was fine. Pregnant Gwen would be the future, but first they had to figure out where they could guarantee her safety.

She gulped a couple of deep ragged breaths, then wiped the tears out of her eyes. There was no time to indulge herself like this. She was about to force herself to rise, to return to the barn, when Evan's voice stopped her.

"Are you all right, Em?"

The concern in his voice caused the tears to well up again. "Never better," she said, trying for a cheerful tone but ending up with a growl.

Evan reached out to take her hand, sending electric impulses up to her heart. "I'm sorry your father's barn has been hit so hard."

She tried to smile, but his nearness made even her lips quiver. "*Diolch*," she whispered.

"You know," Evan said, "Adain is thriving. Shows no sign of illness."

"I miss him so much."

"There's something you should know, though."

She looked at him, waiting.

"Tristan has been around the barn." He looked at her with a grim expression.

"Tristan?" she repeated, confused.

"He's talking to the riders, but not to Da yet, anyway. He's pushing for Adain to be given to Davyd."

Shock slammed the breath out of her body. Tristan didn't want her going to Morgan's barn, but there was no colt for her in Hoel's barn. He must not know that Davyd did not want Adain.

"I thought you should know."

Emma took a deep breath. "Thank you for telling me." He was so confident and handsome. She wanted to touch the blond lock of hair that fell across his face, push it back, then stroke his cheek. Embarrassed, she fumbled a few more words and looked away.

Her friends in the village often talked about the male riders. Emma was considered an expert, since she was the only one actually connected to a barn, and they sought her out for information on their favorites. On Emma's recommendation, the girls had decided Evan was the most eligible rider. Jenett had argued against Evan. She clearly had a crush on Tristan. She could have him, Emma decided, wondering what the attraction was. Of course, at the moment she was staring into Evan's blue eyes.

"Too many horses are dying," she said, looking away and trying to change the subject.

Evan nodded. "I know. What does your mum think we should do?"

"Move the village." She blurted out the words without thinking, then blushed. He would think the stress of the last few days was driving her mother mad.

"Move the village?" Evan looked at her incredulously. "Is she serious?"

"In the way a dreamer is serious about anything. I mean, really. Where would we go?" Emma brushed off the suggestion, but Evan stared at the mountains thoughtfully.

"Sounds like someone should do some exploring," he said softly.

"You expect to find a nice little village in the mountains?" Emma asked.

"*Na*, but there are probably nice valleys up there that the horses would like. A source of fresh water, at least. A summer camp, maybe? A place to ride out the illness until Tremeirchson is safe?"

He was serious. Coming from him, the idea didn't sound so farfetched. Hope ignited a tiny warm spot inside her. Emma realized he still held her hand. She stepped toward him as he encircled her with his free arm, and lifted her face to his. His lips touched hers, and pleasure suffused her. She felt safe, and loved, and some feeling she had never experienced before but wanted more of. The tiny warm spot grew. Feeling her cheeks turn red, she looked up at the most eligible rider in Tremeirchson and caught her breath. His arm tightened to steel around her.

She panicked and put both hands firmly against his chest, pushing. Her mind was screaming at her to get away, but her body longed to melt into his arms. Confused, she turned away as soon as he released her, too embarrassed to look back. She wanted him near her with a ferocity that scared her and made her push him away. What sane person could explain that? "I need to go," she mumbled.

Evan laughed, making it worse. Emma's cheeks

burned as she relived her childish reaction.

"*Diolch*, Evan," she said quickly, "for cheering me up."

"My pleasure, milady." He swept into an exaggerated bow, bending almost to the ground.

Her face flushed again. He was making fun of her. She gathered her skirts in one hand and fled across the cobblestones as if pursued by demons.

"I'll let you know what I find in the mountains, Em," Evan called. "Maybe we can go together to check out possible sites."

Not trusting her voice, she waved and nodded, hurrying to the familiar safety of her father's barn.

Chapter 7: Nimberry

True to his word, Davyd went to see Kenn the following morning. Walking through the usual predawn mist, it was easy to believe conspiracies existed all around. He shook off his trepidation. After all, he'd been born in Tremeirchson and was accustomed to the year-round gray of early morning. Nonetheless, he appreciated the warm mustiness of the apothecary's back room. Every bit of horizontal space that wasn't covered with jars held a stack of books. The walls were hidden by floor-to-ceiling bookcases full of leather-bound volumes gathering dust. Davyd had never seen so many books in one place.

"We have our work cut out for us," he said to Kenn.

The apothecary had a book under his arm, tucked in comfortably as if it belonged. "We need to find incidences of bad water crossed with nimberry poisonings," he told Davyd.

Davyd eyed the immense piles of books. "Where do we start?"

Kenn cleared the corner of a table and pulled up a rickety stool. Indicating it with a sweep of his hand and a dramatic bow, he said, "Anywhere you wish, milord."

Davyd laughed. It was probably best to be systematic. He perused the stacks of books until he discovered what passed as a shelving system for the apothecary. Assuming Kenn would be familiar with all the chemistry tomes, Davyd selected a shelf of books that looked like journals. Leafing through the first one, he saw that it was the personal reflections of an apothecary who had lived in Tremeirchson before his grandfather was born. None of the volumes were indexed. It was a chronological record of cases. He would have to read every one. Running a hand through his hair, he took the first three journals to the table and perched on the stool.

By the end of the first hour of reading, Davyd had learned to skim an entry for the word 'nimberry.' He found nothing in the first journal. Kenn hummed to himself as he assembled jars of salves and other concoctions for customers. In between, the two men read, with only the sound of brittle pages turning, sometimes a shift of body weight on a hard stool, or the hollow thunk of another book settling onto the discard stack.

"Are the riders still calling this Rhiannon's Curse?" Kenn asked once.

Davyd nodded.

"Well, the wrath of the horse goddess is more dramatic than a tiny red worm. You have to admit."

"Maybe so." Davyd smiled and turned bleary eyes back to the journals.

It was another hour before Davyd found a string of cases involving nimberry poison. He was tired of reading by then and unable to make sense of the words. "Kenn, do you mind if I take this one journal home? I'll look at it later and see if I see a pattern in these cases."

Kenn waved him out the door, deeply engrossed in a thick dusty tome of his own.

Davyd carried the precious book carefully. The sun had burned off the morning fog while he'd been toiling over the journals, and it was a perfect spring day. Perfect, except for the nearly empty sky. The barn had awakened while he pored over the journals. Grooms curried horses, and riders chatted in small subdued groups. Inside, his father and brother sat at the table in the Great Hall, tension snapping between them.

"I know what you are saying, Evan, but I'm not in a position to change the minds of other leaders," Morgan said, rubbing his eyes. The dark circles under them did not go away.

They were all tired. Davyd set Kenn's book on the table, poured himself a mug of ale from the pitcher, and stared into the hearth fire. He hoped Evan wouldn't do or say anything stupid.

Evan leaned forward in his own chair and tried again. "Da, we must protect the horses that are healthy. We have to get them away from Tremeirchson."

"I agree isolation is advisable, but do we take them into the mountains to maybe a different threat? And what about the grooms? And rider and groom spouses? Children?" He shook his head and rubbed his eyes. "*Na, cariad*, it's not a weekend outing, even for one barn."

"First step is to find an acceptable place, right? Can I at least do that?"

The older man looked up at his son and nodded.

"*Iawn*. That much is necessary. Try to find something not too far away."

"It's a beautiful day. I'm on my way," Evan said as he rushed out the door.

"If it's there, he'll find it," Davyd said.

"I know," Morgan agreed. "But hopefully it won't be soon. It's a big decision to move the whole barn to a strange place."

Morgan poured a second mug of ale. "I'm taking this down to the barn. Your mother was there all night watching the horses. I think she sees plague in the smallest snort at this point. Riders are tired, too, and a few might be sick."

"*Na*," Davyd said, hefting his mug of ale. "Who's foolish enough to drink water when there's good ale to be had?"

Morgan grunted and left the room.

Davyd finished his ale and followed, tucking the book under his arm. The late May sun was warmer than it had been only days ago during the Aerial Games. The paddock beyond the barn was full of horses, wings astir. The paddock effectively kept them grounded, since they didn't have room enough to gallop into a takeoff, but they were milling around flapping dust everywhere with their wings.

Heading for the storage room and a place to read in solitude, Davyd felt annoyed when Owain came out of Adain's stall and walked purposely toward him. Davyd entered the storage room and left the door open. He sat on a stool in the corner and waited. Owain came in almost right away. The boy was growing fast, Davyd observed. The frayed cuffs of his shirt ended well above his wrists, and his pant leg swung free above his boot top. Owain ran his left hand through his mop of red hair. Davyd smiled, recognizing his own gesture.

"Morning, *syr*, I mean *bore da*," Owain said, raising his right hand to his hair.

"Welsh is not necessary, Owain. Have a seat."

The groom perched on the edge of a box. Both hands lifted toward his hair, but he made an obvious effort to redirect them, twining them nervously in front of him.

"What can I help you with, Owain?"

"Well, *syr*, I don't know if it's important, sir. It may not be."

Davyd waited, trying to put a patient smile on his face.

"*Syr*, I know Lady Margery was here during the Games, but Lord Andreas wasn't."

"Andrew," corrected Davyd automatically. He didn't care how the lord styled himself, but Owain should.

Owain stammered, flustered. "Ah, *syr*, yes…I'm sorry, *syr*, I forgot Lord Andreas prefers the Saxon version of his name. Lord Andrew, I mean. Sorry, *syr*."

Davyd waited until the boy calmed himself.

"Anyway, *syr*, I saw *Tew* in Deryn's stall the other day. When I called to him, he waddled off." Owain flushed, embarrassed by his choice of words.

"*Tew*?" Davyd racked his brain for a face to go with the name.

"Yes, *syr*. Siorus, Lord Andrew's steward. We call him *Tew* because he eats so much." Now Owain's face matched his unruly hair.

97

On a Wing and a Dare

Davyd tried not to laugh. Lord Andrew's steward was an unpleasant boy, about Owain's age. Siorus loved food, that was true, and yes, he did waddle. "So what was he doing in Tremeirchson, Owain? Much less in Deryn's stall?"

"I don't know, *syr*. I thought you would know, *syr*."

"Thank you for telling me." It was very unusual for the steward to be in town without the lord, and unheard of to be here secretly.

"*Syr*? What is that, *syr*?" Owain pointed at the book.

Davyd was tempted to point out it was a book, but Owain was already nervous and probably regretting asking. Instead, he held the book out to the boy and opened it to the entry he'd been reading earlier. "It's the journal of an apothecary who lived a long time ago."

"Oh?" Owain leaned closer and peered at the script.

"Can you read?"

"A bit, *syr*."

"Give it a try."

Owain took a deep breath and placed his first finger on the page under the first word. His fingernail was bitten ragged, and dirt was ground under it, but the boy seemed eager. "The horse. . .um. . .um. . .of fever and. . .um. Sorry, *syr*." Owain sat back, defeated.

"*The horse exhibited symptoms of fever and diarrhea.* Tough sentence. Good try, though." Davyd smiled at the boy.

"Fever, *syr*? And diarrhea? Isn't that what the horses have now, *syr*?"

"Very good, Owain. Yes. I'm trying to see if there have ever been any cases like this. Kenn seems to think the nimberries have poisoned the water."

They sat in silence for a moment, each busy with their own thoughts.

Davyd spoke first. "Owain, are you free for an hour or so? Want to come with me to the cistern? I want to see if anything's amiss there."

"Oh, *syr*, I'd love to come, *syr*!"

"One condition."

"*Syr*?"

"You stop calling me *syr*. I'm Davyd."

"Oh, yes, *syr*, I mean, Davyd." The boy grinned.

"That's better. Come on, then." Davyd put a hand on Owain's shoulder, feeling thirty years older rather than just four years older than the boy.

Davyd secured the precious journal in the storeroom before they left, walking along the barn away from the center of town. Once they left the last barns behind, it was easy to see the plateau that housed the town. On one side, cliffs disappeared into the last remnants of mist, lingering high in the sky. On the other, the ground dropped away in undulating waves. In between was a flat piece of perfection. Tremeirchson was nestled at one end, and cultivated fields stretched along the cliffs. Davyd and Owain walked toward the river-fed cistern in the middle of the plateau.

Originally stones had been stacked in the river to divert the water for the town's use. More recently, patrons had cooperated to make the stone basin bigger and line it with hardened clay. Clay-lined trenches led back to the barns and the town. Nimberry bushes thrived in this area, their berries so red they appeared to be glowing.

Davyd stared at the berries, then at the cistern. "So

how did those berries get into that cistern?"

Owain squinted at the bushes. "They would have had to fly upward and then what, twenty feet? Not possible without help, Davyd." He tried to hide his grin, probably still self-conscious about using the name.

Davyd knelt to examine one of the bushes more closely. He turned over a fuzzy gray-green leaf. Two tiny red worms clung to the underside of the leaf. He almost recoiled, but remembered Kenn saying the poison was in the berry. With his belt knife, Davyd cut a small clump of berries free. Carrying them by the branch, he found a low rock and splayed them out. Owain leaned forward, curious. Davyd cut open a berry, almost butting heads with Owain as he bent to examine it. No worms, just dark seeds and juice. He did find larvae in the next berry, so small that they looked like white seeds.

"This?" he said in disbelief. "These tiny white specks poisoned the horses? It must have taken a lot of them."

"Couldn't have been an accident," Owain observed.

"No, it couldn't have been an accident."

Davyd and Owain walked the entire length of the water trenches, looking for places where nimberry bushes grew too close to the water, possibly in a position to drop berries in, but found nothing but grass and horse droppings. Nonetheless, Davyd believed that the nimberries were the culprit. Nothing in the apothecary's journals would solve their problem. It was a people problem now. They had to figure out who would want to poison the horses, and how they had managed to do so.

When they were once more outside the storeroom, Davyd asked Owain to watch the barn carefully. "I need to know if anyone unusual comes by and where they go."

"Like *Tew*?"

"Yes, like Siorus."

Owain returned to Adain's stall, and Davyd considered Siorus. The steward belonged in Merioneth with Lord Andrew. It was plausible that he might travel to Tremeirchson with Lady Margery, but neither patron had been in town when Owain had seen Siorus. What possible reason could bring the steward to town without the patron?

On a Wing and a Dare

Chapter 8: Lord Farley

No fanfare sounded, but it was no less a ceremony. Four pairs of wingless horses, decked in blue and silver livery, trotted through Tremeirchson, stopping for no one. Their riders, anonymous in helmets, carried shields and looked straight ahead. Behind them came a matched team of six big roans pulling a showy carriage that caused the villagers to stop and stare. Following the carriage were four more pairs of horses, all in blue and silver livery. They clattered through town as if it was an inconvenience.

Emma had been sitting on the edge of the fountain, thinking about her mother's idea of moving the village. When she saw the livery, her face paled. While those around her were pointing and staring, Emma raced home, clutching her skirts above her ankles to run faster. Heedless of her hair whipping around her or her heart beating faster in panic, she burst into the barn. Without slowing, she headed for her mother's surgery.

"Mum! Lord Farley's carriage!" Gasping for breath,

she barely had time to take in her mother's stricken face, suddenly devoid of color, before Neste rushed from the room.

Emma took a moment to catch her breath and attempt to smooth her hair and skirt with shaking hands. Stepping back into the barn was like jumping on a moving wagon. Grooms and riders scrambled to curry horses and pick up scattered ropes, brushes, and blankets. Emma shook her head. It was far too late for that. Her parents hurried toward the barn door, and Emma joined them. Lord Farley had left town when the Games ended three days ago. His return was as unprecedented as the illness.

The entourage entered the lane and milled about in the scant space near Hoel's barn.

"Where in Rhiannon's name are we going to put twenty-two horses?" Hoel muttered.

"Not to mention that outlandish carriage, and people to feed," Neste said.

With great ceremony, the driver dismounted and held open the carriage door. Lord Farley's steward got out first. Padrig cowered as he stepped down. Emma resisted the urge to make a face at him, knowing the timid boy would cry. Padrig carried a heavy ledger that made it difficult for him to help the lord out of the carriage. The driver stepped up to assist.

Lord Farley's polished black shoes with shiny brass buckles appeared first, followed by legs encased in fitted dark trousers. A richly embroidered tunic, covered by an elegant tabard, topped the outfit. Lord Farley wore a fur-trimmed cloak pinned to his shoulder. It was almost laughable, given the warmth of the spring day, but it did clearly establish the patron's wealth.

"Welcome to Tremeirchson, milord," Hoel said, bowing.

Emma thought her father looked old and pale next to the lord. Neste curtsied, muttering her own greeting, and pulled Emma into a curtsy. The patron swept past them into the barn, leaving all his entourage in the lane. It irked Emma that he acted as if he owned the place. Technically, she supposed he did, but he was only here a handful of times each year. Lord Farley did not belong here, and an unscheduled visit was rare.

Her father hurried after the patron. "To what do we owe the pleasure of your visit, milord?"

The patron ignored him. Stopping outside Lleu's stall, he remarked, "Fine animal. Strong wings. Still healthy?"

"Yes, milord."

They continued down the barn.

Neste slipped away, hurrying toward the house to make preparations for a hasty meal. Emma lurked in the shadows, wanting to observe but not be put on the spot. Lord Farley had scared her since she was a toddler. Tristan joined her, having dutifully thanked Lord Farley as he praised Bryn.

"Any idea what he wants?" Tristan asked.

"None."

Emma turned to look at him. "I hear you're hanging around Morgan's barn now."

Tristan returned her gaze. "And I hear your mother wants to move the village."

"She has a point. Do you?"

He smiled, a tight little smile with no mirth. "You're

105

so lost in dreams, Princess. You skip merrily through life just knowing everything will turn out fine for Hoel's blessed daughter."

"That's not how it is." She was not going to let him turn the topic of conversation to her. "Why are you trying to give Adain to Davyd?"

Tristan whistled. "Wow, you do have good information. Why not?"

She waited, not about to tell him why not.

"I wasn't born in Tremeirchson, Princess. No built-in barn affiliation for me. I've worked hard to be your father's right hand man. My loyalty is stronger than yours at this point, but I can't tell your father that."

"How does spending time at Morgan's barn show your loyalty to my father?" Emma asked, but almost before she finished asking she was figuring it out. "It's not about you. It's about me, isn't it?"

"If you don't ride for Morgan, you have to stay here."

"But someday Da will give me the barn, not you."

Tristan winked at her. "Hoel would support his top rider wedding his daughter. I'll do it if I have to, although there may be another way."

Emma's emotions ran from shock to anger to embarrassment to horror. She didn't know what to say, but it didn't matter. Tristan was already walking away. She watched him give Lord Farley a quick upper-body bow, saying something that made the lord smile. Emma escaped from the barn, rushing to see if her mother needed help.

By the time a glowering Lord Farley appeared with her harried father, Emma had sent trays of ale and bread and meat out to the lord's entourage. She'd pressed a half-dozen grooms into service, instructing them to keep the food and drink coming until all the men were full. It was a long trip to stand around and wait. They might as well eat.

The hall was not as large as Morgan's and would never accommodate Lord Farley's entire group. Neste had found time to spread a clean linen cloth across the table, and the cook had assembled a hasty platter of sliced pork, vegetables, and leftover pie. A large pitcher of ale completed the offering.

The men sat at the table. Padrig stepped up and put the ledger down near his lord, then slunk off to the shadows. To Emma's dismay, her father pulled one of the grooms aside and asked him to fetch Tristan. When Tristan arrived, he ignored Emma and joined the men at the table. Neste and Emma hovered, ready to replenish food platters or refill mugs and ready to listen.

"So, to business," Lord Farley began, laying a hand on the ledger but not opening it. "You have no two year olds ready for riders this year. You've lost your pair of yearlings, so no new riders next year. You have one pregnant mare. You've lost four aerial dancers, and three racers are ill."

"Two have recovered," Hoel put in. His voice sounded weak and tired.

"The cause of this tragedy is not known, nor is its cure." Lord Farley continued as if Hoel had not interrupted.

"We are following Neste's instructions for treatment," Tristan said. "Isolating the sick horses as much as we can, treating symptoms. We hope to have control of this soon."

Lord Farley acknowledged Tristan with a nod, which made Emma frown.

The lord continued, "My problem is this. With no new riders, the barn is not growing. With the deaths, it is in fact diminishing. As is my revenue. If the future were assured, I could invest with an easy mind. As it stands, the next new addition to the barn won't be ready to compete for three years." He shook his head. "This barn is fast becoming a losing proposition."

Hoel's shoulders had slumped while the lord was talking, and his eyes were fastened on the table in front of him. Emma wondered why he didn't try to defend his barn. It sounded like they were about to lose their only patron.

"Other barns are dying, too," Hoel muttered.

Emma winced. Next to her, Neste groaned softly.

"Lord Farley," Tristan said in a strong, calm voice. "Hoel is correct. Deaths have hit every barn in Tremeirchson. We are not the only one suffering. First we must stop the illness. Then we rebuild."

"It takes strength to stop an illness of this magnitude, son. It's only fair to let you know that I am looking for barns to merge with this one. It's possible we can survive by joining two weakened barns into one."

Emma gasped.

Neste murmured, "Oh, no."

Hoel didn't give any indication he'd heard.

"I think we would like to avoid that if we could, milord," Tristan said.

"My pocketbook is running out of time, son. Fix this. Show me progress. I will be making a decision soon." He stood suddenly, and Padrig scurried forward to retrieve the ledger. Tristan and Hoel followed them from the room.

Neste sank into a chair.

"Oh, Mum, what will we do if he stops supporting us?"

"There is always some lord or another who wants the prestige of owning a barn of winged horses and fancies getting rich off stud fees and revenue from the Aerial Games. Merger is worse, *cariad*. Your father will never be able share the barn his father's father's fathers built. It will break him."

Heart still racing after Lord Farley's visit and Tristan's declaration of his malicious intent to take over the barn by marrying her if he had to, Emma escaped as soon as it was feasible. Slipping silently down the lane, she followed the tugging on her heart to Morgan's barn. To Adain. Maybe because her heart was so sore from the losses she had seen, maybe because of the high emotions at her own barn, Morgan's barn seemed bathed in loving warmth. Being in Morgan's barn was like being with Morgan.

Adain recognized her footsteps hurrying along the walk, and he poked his head out of his stall. She stroked his nose, her hand reaching to scratch his ear and finger-comb his mane. Laying her palm flat against his neck, Emma leaned her forehead against his. Horse breath warmed her chest. Her head and the colt's melded their warmth. With every fiber of her being, Emma could feel life in the horse, contentment that they were together.

She let herself into the stall and picked up a curry comb, talking softly to the colt as she brushed him.

"Ah, my precious, my *cariad*, my sweetling, I have missed you. You are balm to my soul."

The horse's ears twisted and turned, following every sound she made. He turned his head and pushed at her with his nose. She laughed and hugged him.

"*Helo*, Emma, he really missed you." Owain appeared, leaning on the half-door of the stall.

"Owain! You've been taking very good care of him, I know," she said, smiling at the boy.

Owain blushed, muttering, "He's worth it."

Emma's laugh rang out and Adain tossed his head. "See? He's laughing, too," she said.

"He's happy you are here," Owain said.

"A lot of noise around here," observed Morgan, coming into Emma's view beside Owain. "*Helo*, Emma. Nice you could come by today. The colt's missed you."

Emma beamed at him. "And I him."

Morgan entered the stall as Owain left, muttering something about having work to do. Emma remained as close to Adain as she could get, needing to be leaning on him or touching him.

"You look tired," Morgan observed.

"It's been rough," she said, trying to smile.

"I'm sure you and your mother are doing everything you can. I'm very proud of the way you've stepped up to help in this crisis. Most young women would be cowering in their mother's homes crying curse." He laughed. "Most are, as a matter of fact."

Self-conscious, Emma hid her face in Adain's neck. She didn't know what to say.

"Hey, now," Morgan said gently. "I don't mean to embarrass you. You're a strong person, Emma. You do what's needed, and that's important."

"Thank you," she said, "but I don't think I always do the right thing."

"Who does? Real strength is in making choices and living with the results. Those who hide from decisions never enjoy life. Sure, they are safe and secure, but only in taking risks can you truly live life to its fullest. The setbacks make the successes even sweeter."

Adain's ears flicked to catch their words, and he pushed at Emma with his nose. She smiled and scratched his ear. "So life must be setting up for a real sweet spell, then," she told Morgan.

He reached into his pocket and found a bit of treat for Adain. He stroked the colt's soft nose then took Emma's hand in his own. "Emma, if you need someone to talk to, need a different viewpoint, I am here. I've seen a lot of young grooms and riders over the years, and you have great potential. Don't agonize. It will work out. You have plenty of support where you need it."

His blond hair, unevenly cropped, was very much like Evan's, but his brown eyes were Davyd's. Emma smiled. "Thank you, Morgan."

As she walked back to her father's barn, the troubles of the world hadn't gone away but they were significantly less worrisome.

111

On a Wing and a Dare

Chapter 9: More Deaths

The faint glow of dawn strengthened into day, but the normal waking sounds of the barn failed to distract Davyd. Deep into the words of the journal, he catalogued information as he came across it, trying to answer his most pressing questions. First, how many nimberries, diluted in water, would it take to kill a horse? Second, how and where would it have been introduced to the aqueduct? Third, who would have done such a thing?

A truncated shout and hurrying feet broke his concentration. When nothing followed, he got up to check. At the far end of the barn, the horses in the paddock were still restless. A knot of people were gathered outside Wynne's stall, their body language screaming tension. Davyd broke into a run, reaching the crowd and pushing through. The stall door was closed. Hysterical female sobbing emanated from inside. Davyd opened the door, closing it gently behind him. Smoky clouds of thyme assailed him. Wynne lay on her side, her white body pale against the dark floor. Her wings rested at an odd angle. Davyd didn't have time to ponder that because his mind was caught by the sight of his mother draped over Wynne, dark against the white horse, sobbing.

A horrible rasp came from the horse as her entire body convulsed, trying to draw breath. Morgan stood helplessly, the mug of ale still in his hand. All barn sounds faded to insignificance as they all willed Wynne to breathe. The bone-chilling rasp came again. Davyd cringed, but exhaled with momentary relief. He held his breath again, waiting for another of the mare's breaths. One, then two more shallow breaths. Then nothing.

Davyd stared, slowly realizing what he was seeing. Wynne was dead. A noise drew his attention away from his mother and Wynne.

His father took a few halting steps toward his mother, laying a hand on her head as she sobbed over the mare, now lying still on the stall floor. Davyd moved toward them, numb.

"*Cariad,*" his father murmured, stretching out an arm to his son.

"Will she be all right?" he whispered, hugging his father.

Morgan's eyes were sunken more than they had been during their earlier conversation. "I don't know."

"What should we do?" Davyd asked quietly.

"Nothing yet. Let her cry until she's exhausted. That's what I'd want to do."

Davyd stared at his mother, the pillar of strength in his life. "Da, why don't you stay here with Mum? I'll make her some breakfast."

"Good idea," Morgan said, his haunted eyes on

Elen.

Davyd hesitated, one hand on the stall door, and looked back. Morgan leaned over Elen and held her tightly.

"I'm so sorry, *cariad. Dw i'n dy garu di*," he whispered.

"I love you too," she choked. Her sobs lessened but her grip on him seemed desperate.

It pained Davyd to see the naked emotion, and he left them alone.

Mum would need a lot of support. Evan would need to be reined in before he pushed them into a hasty decision. Da would need help with both of them.

"First, we need food," Davyd said out loud.

He returned to the kitchen of the manor and rummaged through the cupboards, assembling a tray of bread and sliced meat while ignoring the glare of the cook. Maybe no one would eat, but it gave him something to do. Grief hit him then, and tears burst from his eyes. Oh, Wynne.

Emma would understand the loss of a horse, at least. Davyd suddenly felt an urge to tell her about Wynne, to share the grief. He wanted to spend more time with her and enjoyed being near her, but girls were harder than horses. You were never sure what girls were thinking, never sure they meant what they said.

He set the tray on the Great Hall table. The big doors opened, causing the candles in the sconces to flutter. Elen stumbled a bit, leaning heavily on Morgan as they entered. Both of them looked as though they had aged ten years in a day. Davyd indicated the food with his hand.

"*Diolch*," Elen said automatically, her voice barely audible, her eyes not even looking at the food she was thanking him for.

Morgan helped her to the table where she tore her bread into bits before pushing it away. The men looked at her, then each other, then the table.

"I think I'll go lie down. I'm exhausted." She stood up slowly and made her way upstairs, waving away Morgan when he started to join her.

"She'll be all right when she's had a chance to rest," Davyd said optimistically.

By midday, news of Wynne's death permeated the barns. Morgan and Elen were well respected, and the mare's loss keenly felt. Davyd was glad for the support but exhausted from dealing with it all.

Evan appeared as the sun began to drift toward the horizon. Davyd waited under the barn overhang for his brother to dismount and lead Clyth into his stall.

"I found the perfect place!"

Davyd just stared. He had to tell his brother about Wynne. "Evan," he began.

"I know, I know, wait until Da is here. But it's secluded and big enough, and it can even be gated to prevent anyone from bothering our practice runs."

"Wynne died today."

The vitality that drove Evan escaped from him in an audible whoosh. He slumped against Clyth. "*Na, na.*"

Without speaking further, the brothers walked across the courtyard. Their father sat alone in the darkened hall, staring into the flickering flames of the fireplace. The sconces were trimmed low, and the rafter shadows loomed over the room like vultures.

"Da? I need to tell you what I found today," Evan said.

Morgan looked up, waiting.

"Pretty meadow, high in the mountains. Big enough, access all right, I think. Hard to tell from the air."

"Good news, *cariad*," Morgan said softly. "Maybe no one else's horse will have to die."

"Wynne was special," Evan said quietly. "There aren't many horses that turn pure white, and she was a good one."

"No argument here," Davyd said.

"Clyth is pretty light, and there's a white mare in a barn down the road."

Davyd nodded. "I know the one you mean. But the color isn't what's important. It's Mum's spirit in Wynne, and hers in Mum. And that's broken."

"We can honor them both by honoring white horses."

Davyd looked quizzically at his brother.

That evening Morgan called his riders to a meeting, which didn't happen often. Davyd lingered in the kitchen doorway and watched as somber men and women gathered in the Great Hall. The two riders whose horses had also died that day entered hesitantly, as if unsure of their status. Elen acknowledged them with particular empathy. Davyd frowned as he remembered the conversation with his brother about attending this meeting.

"It's for riders," Davyd had said. "I'm not a rider

and Hefin's gone."

"You can attend as my right hand man," Evan had offered. "I'll need help convincing them all to move the barn into the mountains, and you will do that."

Davyd had been irritated. "Why would you assume I would do that?"

"Hey, I'm only trying to help. I'm offering you a chance to be a part of the barn activities, to help me. Eventually I'll take over the barn, you know, when Da retires. You'll have real power then, even more so if Tristan convinces Da to let you have Adain."

What? He would never be a rider whether they tried to give him Adain or not. But he didn't say anything. Evan would never understand how he could walk away from the power of being a rider in Morgan's barn.

Morgan began speaking in a low voice. "I didn't call you here to discuss our losses. We must ensure that the remaining horses stay well."

Morgan sat with his shoulders hunched like an old man. His clothes were rumpled like he'd slept in them, and his eyes were dark with fatigue.

His mother, too, looked barely functional, a shell of her normal self, leaning against the kitchen doorway as if she couldn't manage to stand upright on her own.

He returned his gaze to his father as Morgan continued. "We must move our herd out of the village." He paused, waiting for reaction. It was mixed.

"But we have families here, roots in Tremeirchson!"

"The sooner the better! I thought I heard Branwen cough this morning."

"You are running away from the problem!"

"The curse will follow us. You can't outrun an angry god."

Davyd raised his voice above the others. "It's the responsible thing to do to ensure the safety of the horses in our care."

Silence fell hard and lay uncomfortably in the room. Riders' eyes flicked to Morgan, then back to Davyd. Some turned their backs on Davyd and faced their leader, Morgan. Davyd felt the chill of their emotions envelop him even as his cheeks heated with an embarrassing flush. He took a few steps into the kitchen, intending to flee, but his mother's firm grip on his arm stopped him.

Davyd forced himself to relax, feeling his mother's hand ease its grip as soon as his arm muscles released their tension. She left her hand there, now resting casually on her son's arm. Davyd raised his eyes to meet his father's. He raised his chin a bit and swallowed hard.

Morgan's nod was barely perceptible as he turned to address the room. "Although riders can survive on ale," his words brought a few chuckles, "we cannot bring in enough water to meet the needs of the horses for an extended time. We have no idea if the cistern water will ever clear up. The horses we have left. . ." His voice caught, then continued. "The horses are currently all healthy. We remove them now, before any more get sick, and we keep our herd intact."

Davyd started to speak, but his mother's grip tightened again.

"While we scout a place, I need you all to protect your horses so no more fall ill. Prepare yourselves to move. Initially, we move just the horses and grooms.

Riders if they want to. If this continues, we all go."

No one met Morgan's eyes. No one muttered or complained. Reality had finally sunk in. Riders filed out, sober expressions on their faces. Surprised that Evan hadn't said anything, Davyd sought his brother. Across the room, Evan leaned against the wall and watched the departing riders. A satisfied smile played across his face.

On the morning after Morgan's meeting, Davyd was sitting in the solar when Elen awoke. He poured her some ale as she sank into a chair in front of a cheery fire.

"Mmm, *diolch, cariad*." She sipped gratefully. "So what did you think of the meeting last night?"

"Evan suggested I go and support him." He attempted a wry smile, but the resulting grimace was unconvincing.

"That's interesting. Evan's gathering supporters."

"Did he tell you about the valley he found? He's quite sure he will be the savior of the village. You just have to ask him."

"Morgan mentioned it, that's all. He needs to go see it before any other horses fall ill." She drank deeply and, after a moment's silence, continued. "I just can't fathom the idea of moving."

"You want to stay?" Davyd tried to conceal his surprise.

"*Na*, not necessarily. It's just that it's going to be so much work. So much work. Maybe it will be good for me. . ." Her voice trailed off.

"I'll help, Mum. You know I will."

"I'd better get some rest." Elen rose and turned

toward the curtained-off bedroom.

Davyd frowned. She'd just gotten up. He'd cover the daily barn support duties until she was herself again. Tired riders needed to rest. And they needed to store food for horses and people in preparation for the move.

Davyd shook his head to free it of worry, and doubt crept back in. He'd been unable to save Wynne. He picked up his mother's mug as well as his and went downstairs, shutting the door softly behind him so as not to disturb his mother. He deposited the mugs in the kitchen and left through the kitchen door.

Davyd crossed the courtyard absorbed in thoughts of provisioning the barn for the immediate weeks as well as planning for a move. Preoccupied, he went directly where he always went, every morning. Wynne's stall. Both halves of the door were closed, but he was inside before he really noticed. The emptiness of it horrified him, clawing at his heart and chest until he couldn't breathe. He whispered the mare's name in a choked voice.

Brushing the tears away furiously, he left the stall without a backward glance. He had to be strong to marshal the barn to keep on. He had to believe in his function in order to survive, in order for the barn to survive.

Morgan was in Deryn's stall. He leaned against the stallion, head pressed into the horse's neck, shoulders slumped. Davyd hesitated, then unlatched the stall with a loud clank that announced his presence. Morgan straightened and turned.

"Mum's resting. I'll see to the barn."

Morgan just nodded.

Avoiding the stalls he knew would be empty, Davyd walked the length of the barn to the storeroom. He spent the morning rearranging and cleaning it, tossing out old horse paraphernalia that thrifty riders over the years couldn't bear to part with. Broken bridles, frayed harness parts, blankets with holes or tears all went into the trash. Davyd cleaned what he decided to keep and arranged it on shelves, appraising the empty spaces thoughtfully.

"Here you are!"

The familiar voice warmed him. He turned to greet Emma, standing in the doorway smiling like the sun. She pushed away all worry, all concern, with that smile, and he grinned back at her in spite of the ache in his heart. "*Helo*, sunshine. Good to see you here."

"On my way to visit Adain. What are you doing?"

He couldn't answer. Feeling joy melt from his features, he told her about Wynne. When her face crumpled, he felt guilty about stealing her pleasure in visiting Adain. He hurried to explain that he was trying to keep busy, gave her a tour of the storeroom, explained the purpose of his morning's efforts.

"It looks like Morgan will move his herd out of Tremeirchson," he told her when he finished. "I need to fill these shelves with provisions we will need to start anew."

"Start anew? Where?" Emma's voice was full of unshed tears.

Davyd waved toward the mountains. "Up there. In some fabulous meadow Evan has found. I just hope he knows what he is doing."

"Evan? Or Morgan?"

"My father will consider everything carefully and act in the best interests of the barn. My brother is impulsive. He's still trying to impress the other riders, I think."

Strong, confident bootsteps echoed down the walkway. Davyd and Emma watched expectantly as Evan approached.

"What are you doing hanging around dirty storerooms?" He might have been teasing, but his tone didn't quite pull it off.

Davyd bristled, but Emma answered first. "It's not dirty. Davyd's been cleaning. Looks good."

Her words were supportive, but she tilted her head and looked up at Evan sideways, smiling. She had come to find Davyd but was flirting with his brother right in front of him. He picked up a broom and continued sweeping the floor, maybe a little more vigorously than before Emma arrived.

"So nice to see you productive," his brother said in an oily tone.

Davyd's knuckles whitened on the broom handle.

"Saw Emma here," Evan continued, "and thought she might like to visit the valley I found."

Emma's squeal of delight pierced Davyd's heart. He kept his attention focused on his task, not wanting to see the look she was probably giving Evan. He swept furiously as she and Evan headed for Clyth's stall.

When they were gone, he leaned on the broom and let the dust settle. He would have to keep his mind off the girl, off family tragedy, and on the job else he would be driven crazy. He leaned the broom against the wall and left the storeroom.

Heading away from the barn, Davyd spared no glance for the area where Evan was, no doubt, helping Emma aboard Clyth. Provisions. He must begin to gather provisions. That meant a visit to Robert at the tavern.

Robert had come to Tremeirchson from Merioneth when he was a young man, and he was full of concern about the horses. He told Davyd that since he had no ties to any of the barns, he felt tied to them all. They discussed water problems for awhile, then Davyd changed the conversation to other supplies.

"I need to set aside food that can be easily stored."

Robert frowned. Davyd held his breath, waiting for the tavern keeper to ask questions. After a long thoughtful pause, though, Robert began suggesting items. "Jerky, rye flour, ale. . ." After a minute, he whistled. "Sounds like you're preparing for a siege."

"Maybe I am."

Chapter 10: Love in the Air

With stars in her eyes, Emma followed Evan to Clyth's stall. Thrilled with both the opportunity to ride the winged stallion again, and with Evan's offer to visit the site he had found, she could hardly keep herself from skipping along the barn walkway. Impulsively, she grabbed Evan's hand and smiled more brightly when he squeezed it and held on.

Evan led Clyth out of the stall, and then put on his helmet and handed an extra one to Emma. He also gave her a spare riding cloak he had stashed in Clyth's stall. She inhaled the leftover scent of male sweat in the cloak. It was too big, of course, and she wrapped it tightly around her. Evan looked her over critically.

"I don't have any spare gloves here. Keep your hands inside the cloak. It can be cold up there." His head tilt indicated the mountains, not the sky.

"I'll be all right," she promised him, thinking with a blush of how his touch warmed her.

Evan helped her aboard Clyth then swung up himself. After strapping them both in, he moved Clyth into a trot. As they reached the end of the road, Clyth increased speed to a gallop and effortlessly leaped into the sky. Powerful beats of his wings brought them to flying altitude. They circled Tremeirchson, and anguish tugged at Emma. It seemed impossible that everyone would leave this village. The sun shone on the stone fountain, and it seemed as though Aer waved at her with his hoofs. The flame on top of the stone pillar burned as bright as the hopes of the people. Emma blinked away tears as Evan turned Clyth toward the mountains.

The wind snatched away conversation, but now and again Evan would shout to her, point out a rock formation or tiny valley. Once Clyth raced a bird and Emma laughed so hard she almost lost her grip on Evan.

She sat close behind him as she had before and locked her arms around his waist. She certainly didn't have to do that, since the riding straps held her safely, but she wanted to and he didn't seem to mind. He let go of Clyth's reins on occasion to pat her arm. Each time, shivers of delight ran through her.

Below them a silver river played peekaboo among the trees and cliffs. Evan circled Clyth in to land on the lip of a drop where the river spilled over into a rushing waterfall. Emma caught her breath at the sight of all that lovely fresh water. They didn't dismount, and in just a few minutes Clyth dove off the edge and soared through the mist that rose from the crashing deluge. Emma lifted her face to be covered in spray and laughed as she licked the clean drops off her face.

By the time Clyth landed them on a plateau overlooking a beautiful high meadow, Emma was happier than she had been in days. Thoughts of death and illness had been pushed deep into her subconscious by thoughts of love and desire. Evan was a handsome man, a rider, destined to be a powerful leader. And he cared for her. She would not push him away again.

They stood at the edge of a plateau that sloped down to the most perfect meadow she'd ever seen. Soft green spring grass waved in the breeze. In contrast, hard rock cliffs towered over them, protective.

"I could sit here and stare at this view all day," she told Evan.

"Picture it with horses flying above that meadow."

"It's beautiful, perfect."

Evan turned his back on the view. "This is where the village will be. The road can come in over there, and we'll have to build something here with a courtyard for viewing the meadow."

"Perfect!" She pantomimed sitting in a chair and watching horses in the meadow, grinning at him with stars in her eyes. "I'll start every morning right here."

"Oh no, you won't. Come on."

Evan grabbed her hand and led her away from the flat area, up a little bit onto the hillside overlooking the plateau and meadow. It wasn't far, but it was steep, and she was breathing hard from exertion and his nearness by the time he stopped.

From this spot, the village would be downhill a bit on their left. The mountain dropped away below them, down beyond the village site, and stretched away into the meadow.

"This is where the first barn will be."

"First?"

"Sure. We'll need to house the horses immediately,

but we won't be able to build a village full of barns right away. This is where you'll spend your mornings, Em, here with Adain." He turned and took both her hands in his. "And me and Clyth."

"Oh, so lovely."

The view lost interest as the intensity of his expression captivated her. Instinctively she leaned toward him and closed her eyes. His lips met hers and she melted. She clung to him and kissed him back, wondering why she had ever pulled away.

After the kiss, she could see the stars she knew were in her own dark eyes reflected in his blue ones. He pulled her to the ground, and they sat. She leaned into him and put her head on his chest. His arms encircled her like the mountains encircled the meadow, and he kissed the top of her head. She placed a hand on his chest, feeling his heart racing to match hers.

Striving to breathe normally, she asked, "So what do you plan to call the village?"

"Has to be *Dolydd Uchel*. High Meadow."

"High Meadow, home of Clyth and his rider, Evan *ap* Morgan." She turned her face up to him.

"And Adain and his rider, Emma *verch* Hoel." He kissed her again.

As they kissed, his hands wandered over her body, igniting flames. Her hands explored the solid muscles of his back and slid to his waist. Evan awakened every nerve ending in her body from her toes to her cheeks. His kisses became less gentle, more demanding, and she felt a moment of fear before reminding herself that this was Evan, the man she loved.

A sudden rush of wind and clattering of loose rock

startled her. They broke apart and jerked their heads toward the noise. Clyth walked up from where he'd landed, nuzzling Evan.

"Oh Rhiannon, Clyth! You about gave me a heart attack!"

"Me, too!"

They laughed too loudly, too hard. Emma stood up on shaky legs and busied herself brushing dust off her skirt. She finished and looked up to find Evan watching her intently.

"You are beautiful."

She felt blood rush to her cheeks. "As are you."

Sparks flew between them, but reason had returned. She dared not step closer to him because she knew she wouldn't be able to stop him, wouldn't want to stop him.

He turned away, gathering up Clyth's reins. "I hope Davyd will be here with us. I know Morgan is looking for a colt for him."

"Davyd?" Emma almost stumbled in surprise. Davyd would never live at Evan's barn. "He still plans to be a rider?"

Evan turned to face her again, his eyes boring holes. "As far as I know."

Emma fidgeted and looked at the ground. Davyd had never mentioned a change in plans, but she'd assumed Evan knew. She wrung her hands in her skirt. Evan should have known.

"Em?"

"Shouldn't we just leave him alone?" she whispered. When he frowned, she added, "It's just that he's so afraid."

"Afraid? Davyd's afraid to fly?"

"Please don't say anything," she begged, panicking at the surprise in Evan's tone. "We have to help him."

"Sure," Evan said thoughtfully. "I won't say anything."

They walked hand in hand back down to the plateau where they'd left the helmets. Emma wanted to sing. She was in love. But she also wanted to cry. She'd told Davyd's secret. But Evan should have known. The three of them never kept secrets from each other.

Once again aboard Clyth, they circled the plateau before heading over the barn site. It was a short flight from there to Tremeirchson. Emma clung to Evan, knowing that once they returned to the village she would be parted from him.

Dismounting near Morgan's barn, she looked up at Evan, kissing him with her eyes. A shout from the barn drew her attention. A groom was running for the manor house, calling for Morgan.

They hurried toward the barn. Emma hung back, watching Evan demand answers from flustered grooms. Another horse was down, breathing hard, fevered. She could feel the panic escalate as the riders and grooms gathered.

"Help me!" The hoarse cry was unrecognizable.

All eyes turned toward a boy staggering down the walkway. His shiny black boots were brand new, and his leggings never patched. Over his shirt, he wore a fine silk tunic.

"It's *Tew*!" exclaimed Owain.

"Who?" murmured Emma.

Siorus rubbed his chest, moaning. Grooms and riders fell back until Evan stood alone. The sick boy collapsed to his knees in front of him. Ramrod straight, Evan barked, "What's wrong? What is it?"

"I can't breathe," Siorus rasped. He crumpled the rest of the way to the ground.

Emma felt her heart beat faster.

Owain ran to assist him. "*Syr*, how can I...."

"*Cer o'ma!* Get away!" Evan snapped. "Do you want to die, too?"

Emma gasped. Owain paled and melted back into the crowd. Evan peered at the man on the ground. Running bootsteps drew attention toward the storeroom and Davyd, approaching fast.

Emma shrunk back, trying to preserve memories of the mountain meadow, the feel of the sun and the cool water, Evan's kiss. The crowd began to mutter again as Davyd knelt to help the patron on the ground. He looked up at his brother, and even Emma could see the accusation.

"What?" Evan snarled.

"He's dead."

"What could I have done?"

Davyd ran a shaking hand through his curls. "I don't know, but this is our lord's steward. You don't just let him die at your feet!"

Troubled, Emma turned toward her father's barn before Evan responded. Human deaths. Morgan would *have* to act now. His decision would affect the whole village. His barn was the largest; others would follow. For generations, the only winged horses in the world had been here in Tremeirchson. Shops sprang up and livelihoods thrived around the barns. Tremeirchson itself would die if it didn't go where the horses did.

Emma knew in her very bones that Adain was her destiny. Where he went, she went. She would have to leave her parents, her father's barn, for Adain. Although she'd known this for over a year, she hadn't planned to physically go further than down the street. If she moved up into the mountains, though, the rift with her father would never heal.

Yet the world wasn't that bleak. Evan had kissed her. Her heart sang with the memory as she floated toward her father's barn. Evan loved her, and he'd help make everything all right with her parents.

"Emma!"

The hiss startled her out of daydreams. Standing behind the huge oak tree near Hoel's barn, a shadowy female figure beckoned. Emma stepped closer. Jenett had a crush on Tristan, Emma remembered with a smile.

"Jenett?" she asked as she joined the girl in the shadows.

"I'm so glad I caught you." Jenett spoke in a loud whisper. "Is Tristan in the barn? Can you tell him I'm here?"

Emma could barely believe it. If Jenett could distract Tristan, maybe he would stop trying to court Emma and stop trying to convince Morgan to give Adain to Davyd. "Of course, come on."

Jenett stepped out of the shadows with Emma and brushed her skirt with her hands. Emma thought a comb through her frizzy dark hair would probably help more, but didn't say anything. They rounded the corner to see Tristan leaning against the barn, long legs encased in black leggings as usual, one black boot on the ground and one up against the wall. His black shirt stretched across a broad chest. Emma heard Jenett sigh.

Tristan turned to face them, flicking his eyes over Jenett before addressing Emma. "Another horse died, but three seem to be recovering."

Emma's heart thudded back to reality. "A patron of Morgan's died just now." Remembering Jenett, she said, "Jenett's here to see you."

Jenett came alive. "*Helo,* Tristan. I wanted to compliment you on how well you are handling this crisis."

Emma bit her lip. Tristan grinned.

"*Diolch,* miss." He actually nodded his head to Jenett, like a bow! And Jenett fluttered her eyelashes!

"I'll leave you with Tristan," Emma said quickly. "I must go find my mother and see what's going on."

Neither Tristan nor Jenett responded.

Neste looked up from the brown mare as Emma entered the stall. "*Cariad.*"

"*Helo, Mam.* More horses ill?"

She turned away from the mare and tucked a stray lock of hair under her cap. "Same thing. Fever, diarrhea, not eating. Some horses are recovering, but weak. None of them have had dirty water. The hillsides have been plucked free of thyme. Every barn in the village is burning it to cleanse the air. The charcoal is worthless. How is Morgan's barn faring?"

She looked so defeated Emma didn't have the heart to protest that she hadn't been to Morgan's barn. "A person died, Mum, just now. Their lord's steward. And another horse is sick."

"A person?" Neste blanched.

She left the stall and Emma followed her. They walked the length of the barn, their footsteps echoing.

Only two weeks ago the barn had been full to bursting with healthy horses snorting, eating, moving about their stalls, rustling their wings. Now the emptiness echoed and they were even more unsure about saving those that were left.

"Three of our riders are sick, too," Neste said.

"Three?" Emma's voice squeaked in panic.

Neste nodded. "I checked the barrels. All the water is fine. Normal warming season phlegm can be fought off by a healthy body, but the horses are sick and weak; riders are tired and weak. There's no strength to maintain a healthy balance."

Emma remembered Davyd's nimberry research. "Are they drinking right from the aqueduct?"

"I don't know. We can't keep this secret, though, especially since one has died. Have you seen how many herds are flying light?" She gave Emma an intense stare. "And keeping it a secret didn't work the first time."

Emma nodded. She understood. Her mother wanted her to tell Morgan that his patron's steward wasn't the only sick person, hopefully before her father declared his riders' illness a barn secret. And her mother needed to know what was going on, too, with the illness in Morgan's barn. "Mum, Evan's found a beautiful meadow in the mountains. They're looking to move the barn, maybe the village."

Neste faced the direction of the mountains with a faraway look that saw through the barn walls. "Good for him. It's an idea that must be pursued."

"What's a good idea?" Hoel said.

"Oh, Da!" Emma said. Why did he always sneak up on them like that?

"Moving the village," Neste replied smoothly. "We

134

have a mare and three riders sick. We can do nothing but wait until it runs its course. With a fouled water supply and a new illness, we could all die, horses and people."

Hoel stared at her, and Emma used the opportunity to slide backwards out of view.

She was just slipping out of the barn when she heard her father roar, "Abandoning Tremeirchson is foolish! I will never agree to such a thing!"

She ran back to Morgan's barn.

Clyth's groom had put the stallion in his stall. No one was outside the barn, and Siorus's body had been removed. The door to the storeroom was open, and the light on. Inside, Davyd was sitting on a box, slumped over, head in his hands. Guilt washed over her at the sight of him. He didn't look up as she joined him, but he moved over and made room on the box. Emma sat. Davyd's arm was warm against hers. Something made her want to snuggle against him where she would be safe. *Na!* She was his brother's girlfriend! Suddenly uncomfortable, she inched away from him, half falling off the box.

"Owain found this on Soirus." Davyd opened the sack and held up a jar full of nimberries.

"Oh, no."

"There's another jar here of a thick red liquid. I'm going to take it to Kenn. A couple of people in the village have died, too," Davyd said in a flat tone. "We have a horse sick. You?"

"A horse and three riders."

Davyd stood up and retrieved a ledger from a nearby shelf. "We have to get started on this move. It's our only hope."

"For Morgan's barn or for Tremeirchson?"

135

Davyd's brown eyes delved into hers. "For anyone who wants to be safe."

Something about Davyd's sleeves rolled up to his elbows, or the efficient way he began checking things off on his list, reassured Emma. He was strong, and he was secure. Davyd would not let this thing conquer Morgan's barn. He would fight.

Hoel would hide. At one time her father must have been young and strong, a respected leader. Riders still followed him, but his ideas were old. It was no longer shameful to ask another barn for help, or to share resources and ideas. The younger riders embraced Evan's Barn Council idea, but the older ones, the leaders, still clung to their old ways. It chafed. Especially if horses and people continued to die.

"What can I do to help?" she asked.

"The best thing you can do is convince your father to stay out of our way."

His words stung, but Emma knew he was right.

Chapter 11: High Meadow

The sun came up with a blood-red dawn on the eleventh day of the plague. Davyd watched the brilliance fade to streaks of pink, then be consumed by cloudless blue sky as he summoned some strength of will to ignore the groaning muscles in his back and shoulders so he could face the day. Ten days, and he estimated that Tremeirchson had lost fifty horses. The number was so staggering, he couldn't say it aloud without a gasp. He couldn't think it without a pain in his midsection doubling him over.

Even worse for morale and the future of Tremeirchson, both riders and villagers were ill. Eight people had died. Barrels of fresh water continued to be dumped into the cistern, an attempt to dilute the poison even though it didn't seem to be helping. This malady couldn't be seen so it couldn't be killed. Tired and heartsore, people went about their chores with little hope, some muttering about Rhiannon's Curse and some about plague. Davyd shook his head, refusing to believe it was a curse.

Kenn had confirmed that the jar found in Sorius's satchel was a concentrated nimberry poison, stronger than he'd ever seen. His voice had shaken as he'd told Davyd it was absolutely strong enough to kill, even when diluted in water. So now they knew how it had gotten into the water supply. Evan believed Soirus had poisoned Hoel's barn, but that didn't make sense to Davyd. Horses in all barns, including their own, had died. People and horses were still dying. It was possible Soirus had intended to eliminate Morgan's biggest competitor and it had gotten out of control. If so, had he acted alone or on Lord Andrew's orders? And clearly he hadn't poisoned himself. Davyd had to discover answers. And he had to find out how the poison was spreading.

Few villagers accepted the reality of moving out of Tremeirchson. Davyd understood the physical difficulty of moving households and businesses. Unlike Evan he also understood the emotional pull of historic Tremeirchson. Traditionalists would never leave. Evan's growing frustration with them, and his enthusiasm for High Meadow, divided the village even further. The water supply may be tainted, but some insisted this winter's melting snow would bring fresh water to renew it. And then there was the issue everyone tried to overlook. How had the water become tainted in the first place?

Davyd's storeroom was almost full now. The laden shelves meant hope for his father's barn. Morgan continued to delay a firm decision, and his barn continued to lose horses. Davyd wondered what his father was thinking. The road to High Meadow was almost ready, although it was little more than a roughly cleared track, and the first barn's temporary walls and roof would take only a few days to rig. Evan, however, insisted they could move immediately.

Tired of waiting for the older riders to come around, Evan had begun meeting with younger riders from each barn. It might not be an official Barn Council, but it was a beginning. With summer approaching, these riders argued the horses did not need a barn, and the people could pitch a tent. Other riders agreed privately with them although no one had yet committed publicly.

Davyd left the storeroom and walked down the barn, past empty stalls, to Adain. The colt pricked his ears with interest at first, but looked away when he saw Davyd.

"Looking for Emma, *del*?" he said. "She misses you, too. Soon she'll be your rider."

Adain wasn't interested in his empty words. He pricked his ears again, though, as another person approached. He turned away when it wasn't Emma.

"I want to talk to you about that," Morgan said.

"About Emma?"

They leaned on the open half-door of Adain's stall.

"Without Hefin..." Morgan's voice trailed off.

Davyd's stomach clenched. He wasn't going to...

"I was thinking about Adain, and how much Hoel needs Emma. I'd like to put you on Adain, *cariad*." Morgan turned to his son.

For a moment, it seemed to Davyd as if he rose out of his body and hovered above, looking down on some husky young man with his father, leaning companionably on the stall door. The lines around his father's eyes were new, Davyd observed dispassionately.

More gray streaked his hair, and his eyes were shadowed. He was doing what he thought was best. And Davyd would have to have this conversation after all. A rushing sound roared in his ears like the wind of a hundred wings, and he took a deep breath.

"Adain is Emma's," he ventured.

Morgan shook his head. "*Na*, Adain is mine. My sons take precedence over a rider from another barn."

Davyd forced himself to take deep, relaxed breaths before jumping off the cliff. "I don't want to be a rider, Da."

The words hung between them. He couldn't call them back. He wouldn't. For a moment he could almost see the words grow larger, blocking out his father's face entirely. The world spun in his head.

"You don't want to be a rider." It wasn't a question.

Davyd waited.

"What do you want to do, son?"

Now he sounded confused. Davyd knew his answer wouldn't help. "I don't really know. I like organizing." Organizing? That was pretty pathetic.

"You do. Well, you're good at it." Morgan rubbed his neck as if a great pain had settled there. "Let's think about it awhile, all right?"

Morgan laid a heavy hand on Davyd's shoulder for a long moment before walking away slowly, stooped like an old man. Tears tickled Davyd's eyes. Should he have insisted his father understand? He'd planted a seed, that was all. This discussion was not over.

Davyd took a calming breath and continued down the barn. Vigorous noises reached him from Wynne's stall. His mother. Elen didn't lie in bed all day any more but spent her days obsessively cleaning Wynne's stall. His brow furrowed as he heard voices. Someone was with his mother.

He peeked into the open stall. Mum was wiping out the water trough. A girl with long dark hair was sweeping the stall. She turned. Jenett?

"*Helo*, Davyd," she said with a smile and a little wave.

"Oh, you two know each other?" Elen smiled. "Davyd, Jenett is a dear. She's coming by to help me, all on her own."

Davyd's eyes narrowed a bit. The stall was empty. It didn't need two people to clean it. "How nice," he said in a flat tone. He had never known Jenett to be particularly interested in barns, just riders. His mother was vulnerable right now. He didn't want Jenett taking advantage of her.

"It's wonderful to be part of the barn," Jenett gushed.

"And you're a big help, *del*," Elen told her.

"*Diolch*, Elen. It is truly an honor. Tomorrow then?" At Elen's nod, Jenett waved to Davyd and headed back into town.

"Now there's a pretty girl. About your age, too, *cariad*."

"Mum. . ."

"*Na, cariad,* I know." His mother smiled at him for the first time in days.

"Some of the horses are getting better," Davyd offered, trying to change the subject.

"That's true, thank Rhiannon," his mother responded. "I think the water must be clearing of the poison, but I wouldn't want to risk it yet."

"Good idea, Mum." He walked toward his storeroom.

"There's the future rider now!" Evan's call was harsh, taunting.

Davyd closed his eyes. Being his brother's target was new, and he didn't like it. Evan approached, one arm loosely around Emma's waist, leading his saddled horse.

"*Helo*, Davyd," Emma said, not meeting his eyes. She, at least, had the grace to look abashed.

They were always together now. Evan treated her as if he owned her, and it made Davyd sick to watch his brother with the girl they both loved. Not that it did any good to love a girl Evan had chosen. She'd never have eyes for him after riding behind his brother on Clyth. Evan was exciting where Davyd was quiet. Boring, even.

"What are you up to?" he asked his brother diffidently.

"Off to check progress on the road to High Meadow. Richard says he should have it through to the plateau today. Want to come along on Clyth?"

Davyd narrowed his eyes. "Wouldn't that be Emma's place?"

"I have to get back to the barn." Her eyes darted between Evan and Davyd.

Evan ignored her. "Oh, that's right. You don't fly. And Da so eager to push you off on another colt."

"You know, I think I'd like to see High Meadow," Davyd said through clenched teeth. Emma must have revealed his secret to his brother.

"Excellent!"

"Are you sure, Davyd?" Emma looked guilty, darn

her. He didn't answer.

Evan tossed him the helmet Emma usually used and swung up on Clyth, leaving Davyd to scramble up behind him as best he could. Once in place, Evan strapped them in and urged Clyth into a gallop.

Davyd had only a moment to regret his hasty decision before Clyth's easy gallop turned into a leap and a glide. They were airborne. Davyd shut his eyes and clenched his hands on his thighs. He would *not* grab his brother. The wind whistled past his face, slashing like knives, all trace of possible spring warmth gone.

Breathe, he told himself. Breathe and don't open your eyes.

Emma had once told him that not looking made it worse. She claimed that his imagination made heights higher and the drops farther. He couldn't discredit her claims since he'd never actually looked down from a drop. Today he didn't need to look. He only needed to survive the trip. Breathe.

"Wahooooo!" Evan turned Clyth in lazy eights, leaning right then left.

Davyd grasped his legs tighter with his hands, and his legs gripped the somewhat solid warmth of the horse beneath him. At one point Davyd heard a loud roaring that did not seem to be the blood rushing through his head. He cracked his eyes open in time to see a rushing waterfall. Evan guided Clyth close enough for the spray to wet their faces. Davyd shut his eyes again. Finally, Clyth plummeted from the sky, seeming to leave Davyd's stomach aloft. The landing was gentle, but Davyd was spent.

Evan leaped off Clyth's back and took off his

On a Wing and a Dare

helmet, grinning up at Davyd. "How was that, brother? Did you see the waterfall? All that fresh water!"

Davyd tried to still the trembling in his legs. He just needed to get off this cursed winged animal without sprawling in the dirt. Forcing casualness, he tossed a leg over Clyth's neck and slid down the horse's side. His feet touched the ground, and the horse held him up until he could stand on his own. "Great."

Evan was already away, heading along a rough dirt road toward a small knot of men near a large wagon with four horses hitched to it. "Richard! Are we in time?"

"Sure are, rider! Want to ride into High Meadow the way us villagers will do it?"

Davyd walked over to them, greeting Richard and his crew by name and shaking their hands. Evan and Davyd clambered into the back of the wagon, which creaked as it started up the last part of the hill.

The track was steep here, but Davyd could see where it would someday be a nice sweeping turn onto the plateau.

"Over there is a good spot for the gate," Evan said, pointing to rocks looming alongside the road. "Natural defenses on three sides make this location even better."

Davyd dutifully admired the approach as Richard drove the wagon team across the plateau and stopped near the meadow edge. Evan jumped down, enthusing about the road. Now they could start bringing lumber up for the barn. Davyd knew they'd rigged carry straps between two winged horses for smaller supplies, but lumber was beyond them. It also wasn't easy to get riders to carry loads to High Meadow. Most either resisted Evan's idea or worried about overtiring their animals and

144

making them susceptible to illness.

"Come on, I'll show you where the first barn will be."

"Go on, Evan. I'll be along in a minute."

Evan scampered up the hillside. Davyd looked out over the meadow. It was a beautiful spot. He could easily imagine winged horses soaring in the valley. Forcing himself to look down, he realized the plateau was not that high off the valley floor. Maybe the way it rolled into the meadow gave the illusion of shortness, but the look down did not frighten him. He relaxed. This was his spot. He'd take a minute to enjoy it before listening to Evan rave about the barn site.

Behind Davyd, Richard shouted at his crew. Something about marking the perimeter of the village. Davyd turned and walked over to the foreman, who was unrolling a large piece of parchment. "Richard, is that the village plan? Who drew it up?"

Richard looked uncomfortable but handed the roll to Davyd. "Well, I sort of did. Evan said he wanted a village and a barn." He shrugged. "Gotta know where the streets go, at least, in order to cobble 'em, right?"

Davyd struggled to hold the thick paper open. He looked for the spot overlooking the meadow. A street was pencilled in. Richard had called it Main Street. Not very original, but serviceable. There was room on the side of the street with the view for buildings. Davyd peered at the tiny script. *Tavern? Market? Town hall?* Richard's ideas were plain. Davyd handed the plan back to him and returned to his spot.

He thought about what type of shop would go well here. No, people would want to sit and look at the view, a casual meeting place for High Meadow's villagers. He thought of the tavern in Tremeirchson. It was a place that cared for the heart of the village — its people. That appealed to him. A tavern would be perfect, but he'd need help. Maybe Robert would relocate. Grinning with his own excitement, Davyd went to find Evan.

His brother was pacing out the dimensions of the barn, giving specific instructions to one of Richard's men, whose face scowled as he concentrated. After sending the worker off to show Richard what was required, Evan turned to Davyd. "Well?"

"It's perfect. Got a spot picked out down there for my own."

Evan frowned. "Spot down there? For what?"

"I thought a nice tavern, with tables overlooking the meadow. People will come and relax, watch the herd fly."

"I thought I was supposed to be the dreamer. Where do you get this stuff? This is where the barn will be, the first of many barns in High Meadow, and this is where you will live. With your winged horse."

Davyd felt his grin slip. "My winged horse."

"Come on, you know Da is negotiating for another colt for you. You talked him into keeping Adain for Emma, but he's looking for a barn that has a colt that's not claimed. He'll get one. You'd better be ready."

Davyd walked a few steps along the bluff, staring unseeing at the view. "I'll never be ready, Evan. I can't be a rider."

"*Na*, I know. You're afraid of heights." Davyd cringed at Evan's sarcastic tone. "Better get over it. The Rider Ceremony is coming up in a month. You know, the

146

ceremony where you will get your winged horse. So you can *fly*."

Evan's words stabbed Davyd's heart, but his tone froze Davyd's very soul. Evan was enjoying this. "Da is considering merging our barn with John's. John has lost over half his horses, but he has three foals that are still healthy."

"Merging? John would agree to that? And give up one of his foals, too?" Davyd was surprised.

"If he agreed to a merger, he'd be giving up total control of all his horses. Riders, too. It's really more of a takeover. All so you can have a winged horse."

Davyd's stomach squirmed. John was a nice guy. Not a particularly gifted leader, but a nice guy. He'd been rocked by the losses his barn had suffered and was probably being pushed into something he'd regret. Obviously Morgan hadn't believed Davyd earlier. Or maybe he felt his son could be talked into becoming a rider, especially since he didn't seem to have any other plans.

Even though Deryn remained healthy, Morgan spent the bulk of his time consoling Elen. Riders apparently thought Evan would lead the barn out of this crisis. The very notion chilled Davyd. There was something malicious about his brother, something that enjoyed Davyd's anguish. It might be seen as confidence amongst the riders, but it was simply arrogance to Davyd. And arrogance was not a good trait in a leader.

He followed Evan back down to the plateau. Evan caught up the reins as Clyth gave up the patch of grass he was nibbling and came over to them. Richard and his crew were preparing to depart, and Davyd headed in their direction.

"Going somewhere?" Evan asked in a singsongy, taunting tone.

Davyd paused. "I'll catch a ride back with Richard. I want to see the ground approach."

"Oh, we can swoop low over the approach if you want." Evan could barely keep the laughter out of his voice.

Davyd's lips tightened. Whatever did Emma see in Evan? She was too good a person to fall for his swagger. He turned back toward Richard, who had caught the conversation and waited by his wagon. The ride back to Tremeirchson was filled with conversation about the road and about the layout of High Meadow. Richard seemed impressed with some of Davyd's ideas about the village and promised to build a tavern in the location Davyd had selected.

Driving was naturally slower than flying direct, so when they pulled into Tremeirchson there was no sign of Evan. Davyd thanked Richard for the lift and climbed out of the wagon. Waiting to greet him was Emma, her face striped with tears.

Chapter 12: Suitors

Recognizing Clyth circling in from High Meadow, Emma raced to Morgan's barn with a smile on her face and energy in her legs. It seemed like an eternity since she had felt joy, and she counted on Evan to make her life joyful. Her smile slipped as her thoughts drifted to another horse, dead just that morning. She must go on. Her mother needed her to be strong, but Emma needed some relief.

The cobblestone road between Morgan's manor and the barn was bathed in spring sun. At the far end, she could see a group of riders leaning on the paddock fence, deep in conversation. A couple of horses stuck their heads out of their stalls, but too many stalls were shut. Deryn's groom had the stallion out in the sun, grooming him. In front of the long wooden barn, Evan dismounted and handed the reins to Clyth's groom. Emma stretched out her hand to him, but he ducked and laughed.

"Help! I'm being attacked by a wild woman!"

Stung, Emma stopped short of taking his hand. The groom chuckled a bit as she led Clyth to his stall. Emma's cheeks flamed and her smile vanished.

"Oh, what's the matter? Can't take a joke? Come here."

Evan threw his arm around her roughly. It wasn't the warm embrace she had been hoping for, and it made her uncomfortable. She hunched next to him, staring at the ground and brushing at her skirt with her hands.

"Just got back from High Meadow," Evan offered. "Davyd rode with me on Clyth. Maybe he's putting his fear aside so he can accept his responsibility to his family and his barn."

Emma's head shot up. That didn't sound right. Her stomach churned as she thought about how scared Davyd must have been. She looked around. Davyd had definitely not come back with Evan. She frowned.

"Nice of you to stop by and say hello," Evan continued, without waiting for her reply, "but I have to go work out some details for High Meadow."

With a quick squeeze of her shoulders he walked away, leaving her standing in the middle of the road in shocked disappointment. This was not what she expected in a suitor. She'd begun thinking of Evan in those terms and assumed that's how he thought of her. If he did, his ideas about suitors were different from hers.

Emma slipped into the shadows of Morgan's barn. The slight cooling of the dim light comforted her. Sick at heart over the continued deaths of horses she cared about, and disappointed in Evan, a few tears spilled. She couldn't let go and cry, however, since she suspected she'd never get control again. Holding back the flood, she stood with her back against the solid wall of the barn and stared into the cruel world. She couldn't even visit Adain and risk upsetting him. The rough sawn planks of the barn wall offered physical support, not emotional. Tears trickled down her face.

She became aware of Davyd about the same time he saw her. He was getting out of the wagon, turning back to say something to Richard before he flicked the reins and drove off, the leather harness creaking and the horses' hooves clopping on the cobblestones. Then her friend was walking toward her. He stopped short when he saw the tears. Hastily, she wiped her cheeks.

"Emma? What's wrong?"

The concern in Davyd's voice threatened to liberate her tears. Not trusting herself to speak, she just shook her head.

"Come on, let's get away."

They walked up to the tavern, busy with villagers and riders getting their midday dinner. Normally she liked the bustle of the tavern, but she didn't have the energy today. Robert must have sensed a crisis since he filled two mugs with ale and didn't offer conversation. Davyd carried the mugs to a table near the window. The fountain across the street was dry and eerie. Even the flames atop the pillar had been doused. It heightened Emma's sense of wrongness. She sipped from the mug Davyd handed her, rolling the liquid across her tongue before swallowing.

Davyd sat down and put a plate of warm rolls on the table. "Are you hungry?" he asked. When she shook her head, he continued. "I found a spot in High Meadow that would be great for a tavern. Nice place to set out tables and watch horses fly over the meadow. It's beautiful up there."

"*Iawn*, it is. I think I know the spot you mean. Very

peaceful."

He bit into a buttered roll and laughed. "Well, it's peaceful now, and I hope it is again someday. In between there will be a great deal of building to mess it up."

"It'll be very nice." Emma selected a roll and tore it in half. The warm smell assaulted her nose and her stomach growled. Maybe she was hungry after all. She really didn't want to talk about High Meadow with Davyd. And he'd asked what was bothering her. Emma lay her hand on his arm. He covered it with his own, warm and heavy. "Gareth died this morning," she blurted out, tears threatening again. She didn't even know if Davyd knew Gareth or his rider, but she knew he would care.

"*Mae'n ddrwg gen i.* I'm sorry. This is so hard."

"The illness? Yes." He really sounded sorry, and she felt a weight lift.

"Was that why you were crying? Gareth?"

"And Evan," she said quietly.

"Evan?" Davyd's tone hardened. "What's he done to you?"

"Oh, nothing really."

Davyd just waited, steel in his eyes.

Emma sighed. "I just wanted a hug. He was mean. Am I being a baby to want a hug from him on a tough day?"

"Absolutely not. Still need a hug?"

Emma looked closely at this kind young man, this childhood friend who had always been the quiet one, the one to go along with others. His was not an air spirit, maybe water the way he followed his brother. Rampant brown curls swayed when he moved, and one hung in front of his face. Soon he would reach up and push it away, but now his brown eyes were fixed on her. She watched the hardness melt like butter. No, he was earth, she decided, nurturing like soil to the crops, solid like the mountains. Davyd never initiated anything. But a hug sounded good. She nodded.

He set down his mug, took hers and set it aside also, then turned in his chair and took her in his arms. Emma was surprised at the warmth that emanated from him. It felt right to be there, in Davyd's arms, but it wasn't right. She was Evan's girl. Right now she didn't care about that. Not at all. He was secure, and he smelled faintly of horses and hay. She resisted the urge to snuggle into his chest.

"Better?" he asked.

"Mmm, *diolch*." She broke away from his arms, her hands the last to break contact with his body. They lingered, reluctant to part with him.

"Glad I could help." He handed her mug back to her and picked up his, taking a long sip.

Emma took a relaxed breath and realized she did feel much better. "I'm so sorry I told Evan about your fear." It was so hard to keep silent. She too often blurted out words that too often should not be spoken.

"I know. It's done. No problem." He didn't look at her.

"Really?" She tried to catch his eye and failed. It was no problem? She didn't quite believe that. "So what do we do?"

He frowned for a moment. "About Evan? Or High Meadow?"

Evan, she answered silently. Out loud she said,

"High Meadow."

"A barn is laid out, a village planned."

"And Evan assumes the whole village will follow him? I thought just Morgan's barn was involved. Why does he need a whole village for just one barn?" She leaned toward him, intent on his answer.

"I think his dreams are bigger than just one barn, but he doesn't talk to me about them."

"Me either."

"Really?" He looked at her quizzically, then munched another roll.

Emma sipped her ale and finished her roll. She wished Evan would confide in her. It was something that was important in a relationship, but here she was, his girlfriend, but not his confidante. She began to wonder what else might be missing. She was no expert on relationships. How could she possibly be expected to choose the right man?

"Emma? You know Jenett?"

Startled, she didn't answer at first. Why would Davyd ask about Jenett? "Of course. Why?"

"She was in the barn earlier with my mum, supposedly helping her." He sounded skeptical.

"Helping?" Emma frowned. That didn't sound right to her either. "I thought she was obsessed with Tristan. What would she be doing over in your father's barn?"

"Tristan? So it's like that?" Davyd thought for a minute and sipped his ale. "Would Tristan send her to our barn for some reason?"

"He's certainly capable of it. I wonder if he still thinks he can make your father give you Adain. I'll have to watch him."

"And I'll keep an eye on Jenett. Things are going smoothly with my father right now. We don't need any trouble from them."

They smiled at each other and warmth spread through Emma. She drained her mug.

"*Diolch yn fawr iawn*, Davyd. Thanks a lot," she said, getting up. "I need to get back to the barn."

"Anytime." He rose to follow her.

She smiled, knowing he meant it. She continued smiling as he said goodbye to Robert, as he greeted a few people he knew, and even as they passed the dry fountain. Passing the garden of a small cottage, Davyd stooped to pick a scant handful of flowers. "Buttercups," he told her.

"Are those milkwort?" she asked, pointing to the purply blue ones.

"Yes." He grinned at her. "You're getting good at this ground stuff."

For the rest of the day, Emma listened for snippets of conversation about High Meadow. At first, she only heard references to "Evan's crazy idea" or "that mad plan of Morgan's son." More and more, though, she heard the phrase "our new village." It was becoming increasingly obvious that firm plans would have to be made about moving to a new village soon.

Emma didn't see Jenett around her father's barn although her father seemed to want Tristan close. Remembering her promise to Davyd, she clenched her teeth and endured Tristan's presence.

"*Helo*, Princess," he greeted her, as if her thoughts

155

conjured him.

He'd called her Princess since their dinner during the Aerial Games, a mistake she never repeated. She wanted to answer something like, *Helo, Swine*, but didn't dare.

"*Bore da*, Tristan." She tried to make her tone flat and disapproving as she leaned against the barn door and looked out across the hills. It was her favorite place, and he was messing it up. She focused on the clear light spreading across the hills, gradually turning everything from green and gold, the colors of Morgan's barn, to shades of purple as the afternoon faded.

"I'm thinking of training Bryn for the aerial dance."

Emma turned, annoyed. All of the dancers from their barn had died, so she couldn't resist asking, "Who are you going to dance with up there?"

"Hopefully you."

She stared at him. His blond hair hung around his face like he hadn't combed it upon waking. His dark eyes were always so intense she couldn't look at them for long. He was short, she realized suddenly. Evan was taller, but Tristan more thickly muscled. He was still trying to curry favor with her father by attaching himself to her. It wouldn't work. "I'll be aboard Adain, in another barn."

He shook his head, smiling. "I don't think so. Hoel's hopes are riding on Gwen's foal. It's yours. If it's female, it'll be a dancer."

"But the foal won't be born for months, and won't be ready for a rider until two years after that. I can't wait three more years!"

"Not even if it means saving the barn? Continuing

the legacy? How selfish of you." Scorn dripped like venom from his words.

Emma lashed out, her morning calm fleeing in a rush of hot anger. "Is that why you've sent Jenett to spy on Elen? Are you taking advantage of her grief?"

"Jenett knows it's important to keep Tremeirchson's barns healthy. And to honor tradition."

"Jenett doesn't care about the barns. She does whatever you tell her."

Tristan grinned. "She loves me."

"So what is she working on now?" Emma paused, thinking. "She's talking to Elen about giving Adain to Davyd, isn't she?"

"Beautiful *and* smart, just like Jenett."

Something about his jaunty attitude made her pause. He wasn't at all upset that she'd figured out his plan. That meant she hadn't gotten it all. There was more. "Tristan, stay out of Morgan's barn. Nothing over there is any of your concern. Recall your trained pet and keep her away from Elen. My mother can tell you about losing a horse. It's not something you get over easily. Jenett might not understand, but I would think you might."

Emma's skin crawled as she walked back into the barn. The benefit of Tristan spending time with Jenett was that he stopped courting *her*. But what could a barmaid bring him that the barn leader's daughter could not? Tristan looked out for himself. There was definitely something in it for him, but she couldn't see it.

She joined Neste, who was laboring over Gwen. It hardly seemed worth the effort since the mare had already stopped eating and her fever raged. Emma grimly offered the horse water again. How ironic that Tristan had been taunting her with Gwen's foal. Mare and unborn foal would be gone by nightfall.

Neste moved the bucket of smoking thyme, causing the smoke to drift through the stall. "She needs water," she said. "Gwen's lost a lot of fluid through the diarrhea. I hope this herb will provide fire, since it's smoking, and air, since it's a purifier, but she needs water for balance."

Her voice was directed inward. It was more like she was reviewing treatment in her head than talking to her daughter. Emma moved the water bucket away and sat behind the horse. She could see the mare's abdomen, just starting to swell with the colt that would never be born, rising and falling in time with the tortured breathing.

Behind the mare were the results of her last bout of diarrhea, her crusted tail twitching through it. Emma retrieved a shovel to clean it up when a flicker of movement caught her eye. Peering at the droppings, she saw tiny red worms.

"Mum?" she said, swallowing hard to control her nausea and pointing.

Neste examined the droppings. "Oh, Rhiannon! Are these nimberry worms? I wonder." She reached into her apron and pulled out an empty vial, scraping dropping and worms inside. "Take this to Kenn as soon as you can."

Emma took the vial and nodded, slipping it into her pocket. She finished cleaning up the mess.

A familiar voice in the barn aisle made her heart flip and her brain boil. Her mother looked at her quizzically and Emma nodded, confirming the voice's identity, and wondered why Evan was here. He greeted a couple of riders and walked right past the stall where the women were working. She heard her father's voice then, and all other voices stilled.

"What are you doing here?"

"*Bore da*, Hoel," Evan began smoothly. "I am here to discuss the move to High Meadow. Is there someplace we can talk?"

Emma cringed, not knowing whether to hide in the stall or run to Evan's rescue before her father tore him apart. The mare's breathing rasped, shallow but regular.

"Talk here." Hoel's voice was low and cold, furious.

Emma shivered, and her mother put a hand on her arm, a clear signal that she should stay put. Emma twisted her hands in Gwen's mane and focused on the words of the men in the aisle.

"Tremeirchson has lost many fine winged horses to this illness. I propose to take the healthy horses and relocate to High Meadow."

"And then what?" Her father was not warming to the idea.

"When the illness recedes and we are sure these barns are safe, they can return, of course."

Emma wondered why she had never noticed how oily Evan's voice sounded. The mare took a deep labored breath and exhaled.

"Morgan's barn supplies riders and grooms?"

"If necessary. I understand the importance of keeping grieving riders together, maintaining the supportive community they are used to. I would never advocate taking them to a new barn, a new village."

Emma was incredulous. Evan said he would never take grieving riders to a new village. That meant he would take her father's horses without their riders. Surely Morgan hadn't approved that. Gwen missed a breath then took a shallow, soft one. Emma put both her hands flat against the mare's neck.

Hoel did not respond to Evan right away. Neither man nor beast moved in the barn. Neste squeezed her daughter's arm and gave a pained smile.

"Let me get this straight, Evan *ap* Morgan." Hoel spit out the words. "You take my daughter, now you think you are taking my horses. I've led this barn since before you were born. Did you really think you could walk in here and take everything with a few smooth words? You are nothing. Your ideas are nothing."

Emma could hear her father moving away down the barn. He hadn't even bothered to order Evan out. She shook off her mother's hand and rushed from the stall. Grooms had melted away so that Evan now stood alone in the center of the barn.

"Evan," she whispered, afraid her father was near.

He turned toward her. "Ah, *cariad*, why is your father so stubborn?"

"Shhh, you *are* in his barn."

"Come on." He half pulled her outside.

In the shade of the tree where they had half hidden before, Evan took her in his arms and kissed her. Surprised, Emma almost forgot to kiss him back. She was disappointed that she didn't feel the warm pleasure that Evan's past kisses had given her. Evan didn't seem to notice. He patted her aimlessly as he broke the hug and walked off toward Morgan's barn as the setting sun dappled the yard with purple shadow.

Emma watched him go, and thought of Davyd.

Chapter 13: A New Kiss

Morgan sat in his usual chair outside Deryn's stall. It was early in the year for him to be sitting there, but Davyd had to admit it was a nice day for late May. The scratched and rickety chair was usually inside the stall, only pulled out when the sun was warm. His father sat, leaned back against the barn wall, boot heels tucked into the chair rungs. Here he watched people pass by, talked to riders and grooms, and pretty much kept tabs on all Tremeirchson doings. Tremeirchson came to him, Davyd realized. The Barn Leader's was a quiet sort of power, but it was effective.

Davyd stepped up onto the walkway and nodded to his father, who was talking to a rider from a small barn. He leaned against the building next to where Morgan sat and bent his knee, resting the sole of his boot against the planks of the barn wall.

"She'd be safer in your barn, Morgan." The rider was pleading with voice and body language.

"How long since your last infection?"

"It's been two days since the last death. Adwen is our last horse. She is healthy."

Davyd's ears perked. Adwen was the white mare. Maybe his mother would bond with another white mare. Nonetheless, Evan believed the rare white horses should be protected. He would want this one.

"We will consider your request," Morgan said, shaking the other barn leader's hand as he professed his gratitude and took his leave.

"Adwen is a beautiful mare, Da. She'd be a good addition to our barn," Davyd said.

"*Na drueni*, a real shame. Good men's dreams and life's work in shambles, with us picking up the pieces." Morgan's eyes turned toward the sky, where only a few horses soared. "A week ago you couldn't tell the sky was blue for all the horses in the air."

Davyd nodded, but didn't comment.

"Adwen's not the first, you know."

"The first?" Davyd looked at his father, brow wrinkled.

"Other barn leaders have come and asked me to take their healthy horses."

"How many horses?"

"Twenty."

Davyd whistled. "That sounds like most of what's left. Not Hoel, of course."

"Hoel is the least likely of anyone to agree to collaboration to fight this thing. Yet Evan continues to needle him. That isn't good leadership."

Davyd would not argue with his father about Hoel. Nor would he take Evan's side. "How many in our barn are untouched?"

"Six."

"So we could move twenty-six healthy animals to

High Meadow now. The roads are in and materials in place. A temporary barn and part of the village will be ready soon. High Meadow needs to be more than a barn, more than a refuge from disaster. It can be a thriving village. It's time to leave Tremeirchson and move on."

"It's easy to say that when you're young. Some of us have history here."

"I have history here, too. It's where I was born. It's also where Wynne died." Davyd snuck a glance at his father and saw his eyes cloud, thoughts far away. He waited.

"I'm too old to drive this." Morgan sounded defeated. "I have enough to do keeping panicking patrons away and soothing superstitious riders."

Davyd tried to keep his tone casual. "Maybe it's time for your sons to take a more active role. Evan is already linked with High Meadow in most people's minds, I think. I can coordinate the people and their needs. Evan will take care of the barns and horses. Your job, Da, will be to take care of Mum."

His father thought for a moment before responding. "This is not how I envisioned the barn carrying on without me." When Davyd began to speak, Morgan held up a hand. "But what you say makes sense, *cariad*. The riders are beginning to respect Evan anyway. This will solidify his position. I'd hoped to get you aboard your own horse before I stepped down." His eyes narrowed. "You really don't want to ride, do you? Well, you're good on the ground. And your mother needs me."

Davyd tried to conceal his shock. After months of agony he couldn't believe it was so simple. His father accepted that he didn't want to ride. Maybe it was his mother who dominated his father's concern now. She'd always been strong until she lost Wynne. He'd never heard stories of his parents' youth. Had they been like Evan and Emma, eager to fly, bonded with creatures whose relationship supplanted their own? He shook his head. No use speculating.

They fell silent, eyes on a darkly hooded figure hurrying up the road. Davyd recognized Kenn, the apothecary, and raised a hand in greeting.

"Ah, Morgan, Davyd, well met, yes. I have just come from Hoel's barn. I believe Neste and I have finally discovered the path this insidious poison is taking through our village."

"Wonderful!" Davyd exclaimed.

"Pray tell," Morgan said at the same time.

"Well," Kenn began, "we know the nimberry extract was placed into the aqueduct above Hoel's barn. His horses drank it and fell ill." Davyd and Morgan nodded. They knew this. "Apparently when the poison was created, the red worm larvae were not destroyed. They hatched in the belly of the horse and were expelled in its droppings. Then the new red worms lay new larvae and secrete new poison. As the droppings dry up, the worms move to wetter places." He paused.

Morgan nodded. "So now we have poison worm larvae on the ground. What next?"

Kenn continued, "Horses drink from the aqueduct, so they stand nearby, right? They leave droppings there, too. The worms moved into the water supply. They are laying eggs in the water supply itself now, and secreting a stronger poison to overcome the dilution. I have tested the aqueducts coming from the cistern to each of the barns. All are contaminated."

Davyd whistled. "So it doesn't matter how much clean water is put in the cistern, it's all contaminated along the way?"

Kenn nodded. He seemed disconcerted that worms were poisoning the water, but pleased he'd figured it out.

"So," Morgan said. "Looks like we'll be relocating twenty-six horses to High Meadow." He turned to the apothecary. "Thank you for this, Kenn. It helped me make a difficult decision."

Nodding and smiling, Kenn took his leave.

Davyd looked at the laden shelves behind him, mentally calculating. "We still don't know who started this," he pointed out.

"I sent a letter to Lady Margery informing her of the circumstances of Sorius's death. I asked her to investigate why he was in Tremeirchson."

"Do you think she is involved?"

"I don't know. I hope not, I rather like her." He grinned. "Our priority now is to move the barn. We need to encourage the villagers, too."

Davyd's brow wrinkled. "We'll need a mix of people. Not all will want to come."

"Build the village and they'll come. Then we stay there. We don't come back." Morgan's voice was flat, his words wooden.

"But build the whole village before we go? That will take too long." Evan had walked up in time to catch his father's last comment.

"We have to offer the people something," his father insisted.

"Da, let me talk to Richard. He will tell us what we

need to do." Evan sounded thrilled that his father was finally fully behind his idea. "He's in High Meadow today. I'll take Clyth and go now."

"And I'll rethink my provisions." Davyd disappeared into the storeroom.

"And I'll go tell your mother." Morgan didn't look excited at the prospect.

Evan had already taken a few steps toward Clyth's stall. He looked back and grinned. "I don't envy you that one, Da!"

Inside the storeroom, Davyd perused the laden shelves. The room was full. He had food and seed. He had household supplies and barn supplies. He had tools. He did not have enough for twenty-six horses, nor did he have enough for an entire village. He grabbed a well-thumbed ledger and began calculating how much would be needed just to get everyone started in High Meadow.

A female voice, whispering from the door, roused him from his calculations. "Davyd?"

He'd never seen Emma looking so vulnerable. Dark circles under her eyes were the result of long hours nursing dying horses. Frustration and fatigue had slumped her shoulders. Today, though, there was something else.

"Come on in."

He brushed off a stack of boxes and gently pushed her to sit on them. He perched on a nearby stack. "What happened?"

"Evan came to see my da. It didn't go well. Oh, Davyd, I don't want to oppose my father in this!"

"You know you have to decide on your own what is best for you. With your father on one side and Adain on

Linda Ulleseit

the other, it's an impossible choice. I completely understand."

"You would have done your duty. You would have found some way to conquer your fear and become Hefin's rider, whether you ever enjoyed it or not. You always do what is expected of you."

"I don't know, Emma. It's true I've followed tradition so far, but I'll never be a rider. It just took me awhile to admit it to myself."

She went on as if he hadn't spoken. "Evan is different." He swallowed hard and forced his smile to stay on his face as her eyes lit up with his brother's name. "Evan dreams of a better place, one where all barns work together for the good of all. He is so close to achieving his dream, and I am so happy for him." The light died in her eyes then, and the troubled look returned.

"Then what's wrong?" Hope flickered that there might be trouble between her and Evan, that he might be able to show her how much he cared.

"It's all right. I guess. Evan is really busy right now."

Davyd took a moment to study her downcast head. He might never get the opportunity to make a future with Emma, but he had to let her know how he felt. Now, before the triumph of High Meadow raised Evan's star to unreachable heights.

He took her hands in both of his. They felt cold, and he curled his warm ones around them. "Emma, *cariad*."

Something in his tone must have alerted her. She looked up at him. He tried to read her eyes but didn't dare hope that he saw encouragement. Before he chickened out, he leaned in to kiss her. Just before he closed his eyes, he thought he saw her lean in to meet him. Sweet, sweet fire coursed through him. Her lips were soft and responsive. He had dreamed of this kiss many times over the last few weeks, but never had it been this fierce.

He let go of her hands and slid his to her waist, around to her back, and pulled her close for another kiss. She didn't resist, and responded to him again, this time moaning softly and putting her arms around him.

He drew a ragged breath and pulled back, reality chasing Emma's fire from him. She looked dazed. What was he thinking? He had just kissed his brother's girlfriend, his childhood friend. *No, he would not apologize.* He lifted one of her hands and kissed it.

"Davyd?" Her whisper was husky.

He couldn't profess his undying love. He wouldn't apologize. Actually, he was quite afraid to hear what she thought. Much better to imagine her response later. He placed his forefinger against her lips to silence her. "Shhh."

She kissed his finger, then turned and left the storeroom, almost running in her haste to retreat.

Davyd sank back on the stack of boxes, trembling suddenly. What an idiot! She'd be too nervous to ever be near him again. What had he hoped to accomplish with that kiss? *Na.* He straightened his shoulders and took a deep steady breath. She knew how he felt now. That was important.

He picked up the ledger with its figures but was too distracted to concentrate. Davyd decided to give it up for now. He latched the storeroom door and headed home.

***

The fire in the hearth cast a flickering orange light over his mother's face, motionless as she stared into the fire. Davyd noticed the hem of her skirt was dirty. She'd been cleaning Wynne's stall again, probably with Jenett. He didn't know whether to thank Jenett or curse her.

"*Helo, Mam,*" he said, crossing the room to kiss her on the cheek.

She gazed up at him with a smile that actually reached her eyes. "*Helo, cariad.* How did today go in the barn?"

She really was recovering, showing interest again in barn affairs. He hesitated though.

"Davyd, I won't break. I'm fine. Losing Wynne...well, losing Wynne was like losing you or Evan. Or your father. But I'm strong. I'll be fine. Jenett has been a big help." She sighed, then smiled. "What did you today?"

A weight lifted. He'd been worried about her, a constant concern that underlaid everything he did. He could tell her about the storeroom and about his father's decision. He'd talk to her about the barn and the horses they were getting from the other barns and maybe Adwen, the white mare Evan so admired.

"I'm in love with Emma," he blurted out. Immediately he began chastising himself mentally. That was *not* what he had intended to say.

His mother's face crumpled in sympathy. "How does she feel?"

He paced the living room. "I'm not sure, Mum. Sometimes I'm sure she loves me and other times I'm sure she loves Evan."

"What are you going to do?"

"What can I do?" Davyd perched on the edge of the couch next to his mother. "I will work as hard as I can to make the transition to High Meadow smooth. I want to open a tavern there that will be a gathering place for villagers. I can keep track of what's happening on the ground while Evan controls the barn."

"A tavern? Sounds lovely. Have you talked about this with Emma?"

"*Na*. Why would I? She will become Adain's rider and join Evan in the sky. They will be together every day up there, while I watch from the tavern's courtyard."

"Don't underestimate yourself. And most importantly, give Emma the choice. If she knows how you truly feel, she can make a choice. Trust me. What do you have to lose?"

Davyd looked searchingly at his mother. "What do I have to lose? Maybe everything important to me."

"But what do you have to gain? *Cariad*, Rhiannon gave us a beautiful world and taught us to balance ourselves within it. Evan and Emma are both air people. If she is smart, she will match herself with earth. He needs that kind of grounding, too."

"Earth." Davyd mulled that over. Family was important to him. He was certainly organized. Suddenly he saw the flaw in her logic. "But you and Da are both air."

She laughed. "All riders are not air people, Davyd. Only the good ones. Your father, yes, and Evan. I loved Wynne like a child and cared for her like one of my own. I enjoyed flying her because it brought us closer, not because I had lofty aspirations of my own. My dreams have always been about having family close."

"You and I must both be earth then," Davyd said, and it resonated within him as truth. "So we agree Emma and I should be together. How do we convince Emma?"

"Show her how you feel and give her the choice. After all, you are both my sons."

Davyd looked at her dubiously, but smiled. "I'll do that, Mum. And thanks, *Diolch yn fawr iawn*."

The door opened then and Morgan appeared. The serving girl came in from the kitchen with a big bowl of pottage, and Davyd's stomach growled. Evan followed his father in, and the family sat down to dinner.

"I've had Robert increase his orders to traders coming from Merioneth," Davyd said.

"Walls are up on the barn, and roofing scheduled for tomorrow. We're ready to move," Evan added, eyes on his father.

Morgan hesitated, then set down his knife and looked at his sons. "We still have horses and riders all over town falling ill. Townspeople are blaming this whole thing on the barns. Riders are still saying it is a curse. I don't see how this is going to end well."

"Maybe it won't," Elen said softly, eyes moving from one son to the other.

On a Wing and a Dare

Chapter 14: Family

"Nine," Emma said out of the blue. She looked back at the tiny building with its peeling paint, nestled under a huge oak that made it look like a dollhouse. "Nine barns in Tremeirchson, and I've seen horses die in each and every one."

Her mother's eyes were sympathetic, and she gave Emma a grimace that was probably supposed to be a smile. The pair trudged back to Hoel's barn, having just lost a beautiful palomino mare with mane and wings the color of clotted cream. Thankfully, each day more horses were recovering. It was a slim hope, but it was the best they'd had in the last twelve days.

Emma was tired emotionally, physically, and spiritually. At least the goddess Rhiannon should be pleased with that kind of balance. A heavily laden wagon rolled by, and she averted her eyes. She couldn't bear it if that palomino lay atop the bodies being taken out of the village to be burned. It offended her that the bodies of the dead horses were burned in mass piles, even though

Tremeirchson's horses were routinely cremated upon their demise. This was different. So many of them were dying that there was no ceremony of loss, no special grieving for a loved one. Just constant despair by the entire village and carrion crows that grew bolder each day.

"Take a deep breath, *cariad*," Neste advised. "Tense your shoulders, then relax them."

Emma obliged, but her mother's strategies never worked. As soon as they entered the barn, Da would pounce on them with accusations and threats they knew he wouldn't carry out. He hated that they were helping all the barns, but somewhere deep under all that antagonism he loved them.

Few people were on the streets, as was becoming the norm. The ones they saw didn't acknowledge Emma or her mother. They walked in a daze, as if Rhiannon's Curse had stolen their will to live. Emma made an abrupt noise of denial. It was hard not to believe in the curse after days of devastating loss.

"Your Rider Ceremony is coming up. Are you excited?" Her mother's voice had a false cheery note.

"Part of me wants to hop aboard Adain and fly away from here for good."

"Isn't that what you plan to do anyway?"

"Mum, High Meadow isn't that far. I'll come visit, but I won't risk Adain."

"I know, *cariad*. I'm sorry. It's totally normal for you to grow up and move on with your life. I hate that it has to be surrounded by all this." Her hands encompassed the village, with its dead and dying horses, exhausted and sick riders, and angry father. "Your father loves you."

"I know, but I don't feel it much lately."

"He thinks he is doing the best for his family and his barn."

"Mum, I know."

Emma was tired enough to snap at her mother, and she was sick of hearing how wonderful her father was. He hated everything she loved. Adain was in the wrong barn and Evan was of the wrong clan. And now, she and her mother had made the wrong choice when they set out to try and save Tremeirchson's horses.

It had been her mother's decision. Neste couldn't sit by and watch. Starting slowly, she had approached the barn nearest Hoel's and begun nursing their horses. It really didn't do much for the horses, since recoveries were so rare. But it did bring relief to the people of the barn. They felt better knowing that someone cared, that someone was trying. Whatever hope still existed caused people to believe that this horse would be different, this one would survive.

"How many, Mum?" Emma knew that her mother kept a running count in her head of how many horses had died. For some reason, she had to know even though the knowledge pained her.

"That palomino was number seventy. Seventy horses gone in twelve days."

Rhys and Pedr had been the first. It was May, a time of renewal, but the deaths kept coming. The horses fell sick with an ease that thwarted all their efforts. Charcoal filtered the water and thyme cleansed the air, but it wasn't enough. Offerings left at the feet of the stone horse-gods of the fountain hadn't helped, either. And now they knew about the red worms. Emma shuddered to think of worms laying eggs inside a horse, not to mention secreting poison. She had no idea how to fight a battle with an enemy she couldn't see. Her mother was better at that. Her mother knew, too, that the riders and grooms needed to cling to the ritual of offerings to the gods and thyme in the air. They would resist the notion that tiny red worms had robbed Tremeirchson, and the world, of three-fourths of its winged horses.

Meanwhile, Morgan wanted every horse to have a rider before the move to High Meadow, and talked about moving up the Rider Ceremony which would pair her with Adain for the rest of her life and his. Emma felt guilty that Adain was still destined for her. Many riders didn't want to replace their mounts, but many did. There were only four foals left in all of Tremeirchson, and Morgan had suggested that none of them be given to riders who had lost their horses. That would eliminate having to choose who got them. Barn leaders had seen the wisdom of this and gone along with Morgan as they seemed to do on everything these days.

"Chin up," Neste said as they approached their barn.

"Maybe he'll be too busy to notice us."

Their footsteps echoed in the barn that had been so crowded only two weeks ago. Only three healthy horses remained. Luckily, Lleu was one of them. Tristan's black Bryn was another. The other horse was Mael, a brown mare that Hoel planned to use to repopulate his barn. Mael was skinny and cantankerous like her rider, who believed Mael's continued health was a result of her devoted care.

"About time you returned." Her father's voice sliced through the silence.

"We're tired, Hoel," Neste began.

"Maybe if you took care of your own barn instead of tramping all over the village trying to bring the illness back here you'd be less tired." He didn't sneer. Not at her mother. Emma kept silent.

"We've had this conversation, *cariad*. I'm not up to it again."

Neste stepped past him. Emma followed, her head down. Unfortunately, he came with them.

"Neste." His voice had turned pleading. "Lleu isn't eating."

Emma's head whipped up. *Lleu?* Neste was already heading down the barn. Emma raced after her.

Big brown Lleu looked at them with soft eyes, his ears twisting normally to catch the softest whispers of affection. Emma went straight for his head, rubbing his nose along its white blaze.

Neste listened to the big stallion's breathing. He shifted his weight a bit, and ruffled his wings. Emma whispered soothingly to him.

"He's fine," Neste proclaimed.

"But he didn't eat breakfast," Hoel insisted. "He's listless."

He had no idea what listless was. Emma compared Lleu to the horses she and her mother had seen over the last few days. Lleu practically capered around the stall. "He's fine, Da. No fever, no diarrea."

"He's probably just reacting to everyone's stress. Keep him calm and he won't get sick," Neste promised.

Emma hoped that was true. Her parents left the stall

together. She fed Lleu a couple handfuls of grain. He liked to be hand fed, the spoiled beast. She wiped her hand, now wet with horse slobber, on his neck as she hugged his head. "Oh, Lleu, *del*, please don't get sick."

She couldn't face her father and had been with her mother all morning. Emma left the barn again and went to the fountain, which had been turned off by order of the mayor. Without water it was dead like so much in Tremeirchson, but habit brought her there, searching for peace and comfort.

"Hey, beautiful."

Emma smiled at Evan, but her hands twisted nervously as she pictured his brother's brown curls overlaying Evan's blond hair and warm brown eyes instead of cold blue ones. It wasn't Evan's fault, though. Blue eyes reminded people of air and water and ice. They weren't as naturally warm as earthen brown. And he'd been so busy with High Meadow that they hadn't had much time to spend together. "Hey yourself, handsome."

He gave her a casual kiss then sat next to her on the fountain's edge. "High Meadow's barn is enclosed. It's not fancy yet, but it will have living spaces for grooms, too. Riders can live there until they can build their own homes. It'll be cozy."

"Sounds great, Evan." Emma loved watching the light in his eyes as he talked of High Meadow. "It will be a great place to raise a family."

"Family?"

"Don't you want kids?"

"Oh. Yeah, I guess so. Someday." He sounded unconvinced.

"My dreams are all about a happy family," she told

him firmly.

"Happy like yours?" he snorted.

"That's not fair," she said quietly. Her family had been very happy until recently. If anything, it was her fault. She'd felt guilty for months that she'd fallen in love with Adain. She'd tried to stay away from the colt, to spend time with Pedr, as was her family duty. It hadn't worked. Evan had reassured her that she made the right choice, and now he taunted her about it.

"You're my girl. I want to make a future with you, but that future is in a village that doesn't exist yet. There will be years of building and moving and consolidating power before I can think of a family."

Emma was stung. They hadn't discussed this before. Obviously, Evan wanted her in his future. But as a member of his aerial team more than as a wife, apparently. She was young. She could wait for him. But something inside her didn't feel right about their conversation.

"Eventually you do want children, don't you?" she persisted.

"Sure." He was dismissive.

She was unconvinced, but afraid of what further discussion might reveal. She changed the subject. "Tell me about High Meadow."

His eyes brightened again. "The barn looks great nestled there against the hill, Em. The base is all stone. It looks like it's been there forever. The walls will be wood, but temporarily they've put in leather tent walls. Inside it will have large stalls. They'll hold two horses apiece until we can build a second barn, and the foals will probably have to be squeezed in there."

"They'll be two year olds by then."

"They'll be fine. It won't be any more crowded than your father's barn used to be."

"Used to be. Not any more."

"I know. I'm sorry." He kissed her, but his mind seemed to be on other things. Emma was disappointed. She clung to him, kissed him again, and waited for magic that didn't come.

"We should've been gone already. Some days I want to climb aboard Clyth and take off." His eyes shone with dreams. "I could make a camp until the buildings are done." Cold killed the light in his eyes. "But I have to make sure High Meadow is mine. If I move up there too soon, I'll lose it all. I have to play this right."

"Play what? What are you talking about?"

"Gotta go, Em."

He pulled back and walked away without telling her where he was off to. Probably High Meadow. She sighed heavily. It was not a good time for dreams of settling down.

That evening, Emma left the barn openly. She didn't flaunt that she had a date with Evan, but she didn't sneak out either. He must have realized he'd upset her that afternoon by the fountain because not long after she returned to her father's barn, Owain had appeared. At first she panicked, thinking something was wrong with Adain, but the boy simply asked her to meet Evan at the tavern later and fled. Evan must be going to apologize.

She pushed open the heavy oak doors and entered the tavern with a smile. She spotted Evan at a table and watched him for a minute. He seemed to be deep in thought, sipping ale and looking out the open window next to the table. A trio of young girls walked past him, giggling and staring. Two older women, seated across the aisle from Evan, also kept glancing over at him. He was handsome, with his longish blond hair and intense gaze. Emma smiled and walked to the table, taking a chair next to him.

Evan greeted her with a quick kiss. "*Helo*, I hope you don't mind. I asked some people to join us."

Emma frowned. "Of course I don't mind." She wondered who they could be.

It was only a few minutes before someone she recognized came through the door and she turned to Evan with shocked consternation. He laughed and waved Tristan and Jenett to join them. Jenett pulled up a chair next to Emma, and Tristan sat next to Evan. In the flurry of greetings and meal ordering, Emma managed to smile and hide her confusion. Why would Evan invite these two here? Small talk about training exercises didn't enlighten her. When the meal arrived, Evan ignored it and leaned forward.

"I hear some of the barn leaders have approached you about consolidation," he said to Tristan.

Emma stifled a gasp, shocked that Evan knew something about her father's barn that she didn't, and shocked that leaders would approach Tristan. Tristan didn't have a barn.

But Tristan nodded. "True. Hoel has agreed to bring them into his barn." His eyes flicked to Emma then returned to Evan. "The riders don't want to ride for him, though."

Evan clearly wasn't surprised. "You intend to stay in Tremeirchson?"

"I intend to lead my barn."

Emma couldn't hide her strangled breath. Jenett clamped a hand on Emma's arm, nails digging into the skin. Jenett was part of a conspiracy against her father. The idea sickened Emma.

"High Meadow is safer than Tremeirchson," Evan said. "There's only one barn there for now, but that will change. The main thing is to move as many healthy horses as possible up there. It's not completely about tainted water. What has made the Aerial Games so commercially successful in the past is that they happen only in Tremeirchson. For High Meadow to work, the Games must happen only in High Meadow. I've had a chance to talk to Jenett at our barn, and I believe you and I might work well together."

Emma watched Jenett. The other girl smiled and widened her eyes, then fluttered them at the two riders, looking very pleased with herself. Emma hoped she'd be able to keep down her meal.

"Let's not play games, Evan. You want me to convince Hoel to move. Is that it?" Tristan's voice was quiet.

Emma's eyes strayed to the window. "Oh, Rhiannon!" she exclaimed. "Look, it's Padrig!"

Outside near the fountain a crowd was gathering. Her father's steward, his clothing mussed and torn, fell to his knees, his grayish brown hair tousled across his eyes, his hands tied behind his back. The mayor climbed onto the fountain. His loud, ringing voice summoned the people of Tremeirchson and could be clearly heard inside the tavern. People left their meals and hurried outside. The four young people stayed inside, watching from the open window.

"The man responsible for poisoning the village's water has been identified and arrested!" A flamboyant sweep of his arm punctuated the mayor's announcement.

Emma looked at the other three. They all shook their heads. No one knew anything about this.

"Working with other stewards, this man conspired to kill off his master's herd and poison another steward, too!" The mayor's voice rang with conviction, and there were nodding heads amongst the crowd.

"I don't believe it," Emma said. "He's so timid that shadows scare him."

Sure enough, Padrig's face was covered with tears.

"Is it the wrong guy, or do they just not have the full story?" Evan asked. "Stewards never act without patrons' orders. Soirus and now Padrig. So was this ordered by your patron? Or ours?" He and Tristan exchanged a look.

"I don't know, and it doesn't matter right now," Tristan said. "Listen."

"What poison can be filtered out of the water has been done. The apothecary from Merioneth estimates that the water will be unsafe to drink until the end of the year when the winter rains come." The mayor's voice rang across the square.

"End of the year," Emma breathed softly.

"All the horses and half the village will be dead by then," Evan said. "We have to move to High Meadow now."

"And if I help you, what's in it for me?" Tristan

asked.

The two riders leaned forward, attention focused on each other. Heads close, they lowered their voices to murmurs that excluded the girls. Emma considered telling Evan about kissing his brother. It would get his attention, but she didn't think she could pull off such a declaration without blushing like a ten year old.

Irritated, she turned to Jenett. The other girl's face was pale, her eyes wide. Emma frowned. "What did you hope to accomplish by getting the two of them together?" Emma asked.

"They are the two most powerful riders in the village. They are either going to save Tremeirchson's herd or destroy it completely," Jenett answered.

"And if Tristan helps save it, he shares High Meadow, is that it?"

Jenett shrugged, her mouth turning up into a smug smile. "Seems right, doesn't it?"

Tristan stood suddenly. "Come on, Jenett, *del*," he said. "We're done here."

Emma peered at him. His meal was untouched. Jenett followed him out of the restaurant and Emma turned to Evan. "What happened?"

"Tristan and I came to an arrangement." Evan sounded pleased.

"What kind of an arrangement?"

Evan turned to face her. "Tristan and I are going to make sure every winged horse moves to High Meadow. Davyd will handle the villagers. High Meadow will be a viable village by the time Tremeirchson's water supply cleans itself."

Together they would take every last horse from

Tremeirchson. Emma wondered what the cost would be as she mouthed tasteless food. She tried to be happy for Evan that his plans were falling into place so nicely, but she didn't trust Tristan. Jenett was clearly thinking only about what was best for Tristan, not caring about Evan or High Meadow. And no one cared about her father's continued refusal to be part of the move.

On a Wing and a Dare

Chapter 15: The Village

High Meadow started to take shape over the next few days. Davyd took charge of the village layout and prioritized construction. Villagers from Tremeirchson staked out plots and raised tents in what would be the residential area. They followed Richard's orders, but Richard followed Davyd. Others noted that and treated Davyd with growing respect. Evan, too, was gaining respect among the barn people, thrilled he didn't have to worry about the villagers since he didn't know what to do with them. For Evan, it was enough to prepare for the horses.

By the end of the week, the barn loomed on the hillside like a protective spirit. Davyd gazed upward, admiring the living quarters taking shape under the leather tent flaps. Evan would live up there, and Emma would join him. But he couldn't think of that.

Main Street was smoothed but not yet hardpacked. That hadn't slowed Davyd. On the cliff side of the street a large building was rising, stone by stone. It would be an inn. Evan didn't think High Meadow would need an inn, but Davyd planned to have villagers live there until they had time to build their own homes. Next to the inn was the tavern, where he headed now.

The building was timbered, and workmen daubed clay on the walls and hung oiled cloth over the window openings that someday would be filled with leaded glass panes from Merioneth. The courtyard area was his pride and joy. Although it was still littered with construction debris, Davyd had set up a plank table with a large pitcher of ale. Davyd was open for business, even though these days the ale was all free.

"*Helo*, Evan, join me for a mug?" he called to his brother, approaching through the doorway.

"Sure. You do have the best view in the village."

"As you have the best view among the barns."

They laughed at what had already become a familiar joke as they watched Clyth gallop down the valley and leap into the air, soaring into a turn that increased in height until he was above their heads and flying back the way he had come.

"Imagine what that will look like with hundreds of horses," Evan commented. "You could have a colt, you know. Da controls all four remaining foals."

"Evan," Davyd warned.

"Think about it. You wouldn't have to fly much. You would be in a position of authority. Together we could rule High Meadow!" Evan's voice thundered with his enthusiasm. Clyth neighed from the near end of the meadow. "You only have to live through that first flight. Come on, let me help you."

Evan jumped up and whistled for Clyth. The horse sailed in and gingerly landed on the courtyard area, picking his way between lumber and tools. His ears twitched toward Evan, who grabbed the harness and bridle. He talked to Davyd, who still sat with his mug of ale.

"A rider's first flight is closely supervised by an experienced rider. I will be there for you. Let's get you to practice hopping aboard without looking like you're being murdered."

"Just get aboard? He won't take off?" Davyd shook his head. Why was he even considering this? But he remembered riding behind Evan three days ago. He didn't like being embarrassed in front of his brother.

"He won't take off," Evan promised.

Davyd stood up. Clyth twitched both ears and sniffed the air. Evan held Clyth's reins looped over his arm as he gave his brother a leg up onto the horse's back. The young horse obediently held his near wing out of the way, pulled back along his body to allow the man to settle into place. Evan fastened the straps. Leading Clyth at a walk, he traversed the courtyard area behind the unfinished tavern.

"Looking like a pro," he encouraged Davyd.

"Not too bad. Clyth isn't much higher than Richard's wagon."

The horse ruffled his wings, fluttering a bit as he stood at the end of the straight stretch along the cliff. Leaning into the horse's ear, Evan whispered, "Go, Clyth!" He flicked the reins against the horse's side.

Trained to obey his rider's signals, Clyth broke into a gallop. Evan tossed the reins to Davyd. "Hold on with your knees, brother!"

The horse reached the cliff edge and stretched his

wings, soaring straight ahead into the air, ground falling away beneath him. Evan laughed at the grimace on Davyd's face and let out a whoop. "Good job, Davyd!"

Murderous rage saved Davyd from being consumed by terror as the world plummeted away, taking his stomach with it. Clyth glided in a tight circle, one wing pointing straight toward the distant ground. Davyd ground his teeth and focused on the stallion's ears.

Evan whistled, and Clyth landed smoothly. He nuzzled Evan, who stroked the horse's nose and looked up at Davyd. "Enjoy your ride?"

"Don't ever lie to me again." Davyd's tone was not that of the weaker younger brother.

"Let me help you down." Evan unfastened the straps and stood firm as Davyd slid toward him on shaky legs. They moved over to the chairs they had been sitting in before the flight.

"Have I flown enough for you?" He spat the words at his brother.

Evan cringed. "Not the best idea," he admitted.

"I will never be a rider." Davyd drew his stocky form up straight and glared at Evan. "Is that clear enough for you now? My place is here, in the village, where I am willing to support you in the barns if you choose to work with me."

Evan was silent a moment. "Sounds good."

"Limiting breeding so the skies aren't overcrowded is your department," Davyd continued. "Mine is the village, but we should limit villagers, too. If we allow everyone to move in and fill this plateau, people will want to build more village up into the hills. That will ruin the view and the charm of the location." Davyd took a breath and watched Clyth fly down the valley. Evan didn't care about the village, but surely he could see the benefit to the horses if the hills remained as they were.

After a long moment, Evan responded. "So let's make a pact. You take charge of the village. Limit the people, do whatever you need to. Tristan and I will control the air."

Davyd nodded. "I'll have to have an elected mayor and probably a village council. I should be able to arrange the composition of that, especially at the beginning."

Obviously losing interest already in village politics, Evan said, "I want to move here now. By the time Tristan gets here I will control it."

"What about Emma?" Davyd asked drily.

Evan dismissed her with a wave. "She'll come to me when I ask her to. She needs to become a rider first, though." Evan looked up the hill to the new barn. "I see more barns up there, in my mind. Maybe four. That first barn will hold ten horses very comfortably. We'll need to start on the second one soon."

"First Barn will be yours?"

"First Barn. I like that." Evan nodded, thinking. "Might need to let a senior rider like Da have it. I'll be in place for Second Barn. I'll promise the third one to Tristan."

Richard rushed up, a worried look on his face. "Evan? Davyd? A messenger just came up from Tremeirchson. There's trouble in your da's barn. They need you back there as soon as possible."

"Thanks, Richard." Evan curtly dismissed the man.

"That means we fly, Davyd. It's an emergency."

"I can handle flying in an emergency. Whistle that beast in."

Evan did just that, and Clyth responded willingly. Evan leaped aboard and reached a hand down to Davyd. With straps fastened and Evan's helmet securely on Davyd's head, they took off for Tremeirchson.

Evan insisted that his brother's arms be tightly around his waist to aid in the illusion of safety, and Davyd closed his eyes and tried not to grip Evan too tightly. Guiding Clyth to an easy pace, the rhythmic wing strokes gradually relaxed Davyd's arms. He needed to be in control of his emotions when they got there.

It was easier to breathe once Clyth landed and Davyd was able to open his eyes and unclench his arms from Evan's waist. A spurt of pure pride in his accomplishment allowed him to drop from Clyth's back unaided, but he knew riding would never be an activity he pursued willingly. Nonetheless, he couldn't wipe the grin off his face.

"Enjoy that, did you?" Evan asked.

Davyd didn't attempt to correct his impression. Evan would never understand; likely he'd never even try.

Clyth's groom ran up to take the stallion's reins and spoke in a low voice to Evan before leading Clyth away. Evan turned to Davyd with a frown. "Three more of our horses are sick. Da's in the barn. Come on."

The two young men raced to the stall where horrified grooms had gathered. *Not Adain*, prayed

Davyd. *Please, not Adain, not Deryn.*

They were stopped by a grim Morgan leaving the stall, shaking his head. "We've put all three in this stall," he told his sons. "They won't last through tomorrow."

"Deryn?" Davyd asked.

"No, thank Rhiannon. Nor Adain." Morgan turned to Evan. "I don't know whether to tell you to take Clyth and go to High Meadow, or to postpone the move until we are sure none of the others are infected."

"We need to get the healthy horses out," Evan said firmly.

"At what cost? It would only take one, Evan, one with the illness, to wipe out every last horse we tried to save." Morgan's tone was more frustrated than despairing.

"I am taking Clyth to High Meadow, Da, and we leave tonight. The barn will be ready for any you see fit to send, whenever you can. Richard can send messages and supplies back and forth with the villagers who come up to work." In contrast, Evan was confident. And he was right. Davyd found himself nodding in agreement.

Morgan nodded. "In a week we can be sure no more of ours have caught it. I will spread the word to other barns. If they have been free of illness for a week, I will send their healthy ones to you. And we have to get the Rider Ceremony out of the way for those foals. It's early for it, but I don't feel right moving them before they are attached."

Evan headed off to make his preparations.

"This is right up his alley, isn't it?" Morgan asked Davyd. "He seems to thrive on responding to an emergency."

"Sure does. He's always made decisions and assumed people would follow him. And they always have." Davyd chuckled, shaking his head. "I'll have Richard bring up some of the supplies from the storeroom tomorrow for him. There are even a couple of big tents he can use to house grooms until the living quarters are ready."

"You're a good organizer, too. *Diolch.*" Morgan looked searchingly at his younger son. "The ground stuff works well for you, doesn't it?"

"It's what I want, Da."

"I saw you come in aboard Clyth." His voice held a question.

"Not my choice. It was necessity."

"*Iawn.*" Morgan looked back at the stall with the sick horses. "I need to give your mother a hand. Look in on Deryn for me?"

"Of course."

Morgan went back inside the stall and Davyd walked down to Deryn's stall. The stallion was restless. Davyd brushed him. The rhythm of grooming lulled both of them.

"That's a good boy. Everything will be all right, Deryn, *del*. Soon you'll be flying up to High Meadow to take over the barn there. You'll love the meadow, and I'll enjoy watching you lead the herd down the valley. Good boy. I flew on Clyth today. Amazing. I can't believe it myself. Sense of urgency, I guess. Don't be getting any ideas, though. I am not available for casual flights. Nothing casual about flying. Not for me, Deryn old boy. Not for me."

Davyd leaned against the stall wall, still holding the

curry comb. Shaking his head in astonishment, he chuckled. One minute he was angry at Evan for playing a trick and making Clyth take off with him aboard. The next minute he was leaping aboard of his own free will. Well, it was good to know he could handle flight if it was enough of an emergency.

Putting the brush away and patting Deryn, he left the stall and headed for the storeroom. He couldn't bear to think of the sick horses. He had to keep busy with something else. Putting boxes aside to be transferred to High Meadow occupied some time, and he realized Robert still owed him some supplies from his last order. He walked up Aer Road to the tavern.

"*Helo*, Robert, you got the rest of my order?"

"Sure do. Wouldn't sell it to anyone else."

They laughed. Not too many villagers were buying supplies in the quantity Davyd was.

"Richard says it's beautiful up there. Might even attract some patrons from Merioneth someday." Robert busied himself wiping a glass.

"I'll be putting together a list of businesses that might want to help start the new village," Davyd told him. "If you know anyone, let me know. Not everyone will be required right away, so if someone wants to come in a year, say, that's fine."

Robert nodded. "*Iawn*. I may have a few ideas."

"What about the mayor? Think he'll be going or staying?" Davyd asked.

"He'll stay. This is his village like I hear High Meadow will be yours," Robert said.

"Oh, I won't be the mayor," Davyd protested.

"Maybe not, but it's your village. That's understood."

Davyd was pleased. This was exactly what he hoped to accomplish. With others of Robert's beliefs, arranging the village would be easy. High Meadow would support its barns more strongly than Tremeirchson ever had. He walked back to the barn with a light step.

Deep in plans for the village of High Meadow, a whisper from the shadows startled Davyd. Emma stepped forward, and the tears streaming down her face shocked him. "*Cariad*?"

"I just heard about your sick horses. Is Adain..." She couldn't continue.

"No, no, not Adain," he hastily assured her, reaching out for her.

She went into his arms and he closed them around her, shutting his eyes with pleasure even though it felt wrong to derive pleasure from another's pain. Emma was warm yet vulnerable in his arms. He firmly believed that was where she belonged, but he'd realized that too late. She loved Evan. But it was never Evan she came to when she was worried. Davyd pushed away that rebellious thought.

"Thanks, I feel better." Emma smiled as she pulled away. "I was so worried, and no one would tell me anything."

He led her into the storeroom, leaving the door open and lighting a candle. It was still dim in there, a refuge. Emma sat on one of the boxes and drew her legs up, sitting on one hip and gathering her skirts around her.

"Did you see Evan?" Emma shook her head. "He's packing to leave tonight, removing Clyth to High Meadow. It has begun."

"It's a sobering thought that we need to leave Tremeirchson in order for Tremeirchson to survive. Why didn't Evan tell me?"

Davyd stumbled a bit with her abrupt switch from the village welfare to her personal angst. He wouldn't tell her that Evan was only concerned for himself and his horse. No, those words would never come from his mouth. She'd have to learn them on her own. He only hoped it would be soon. *Na*, there was no hope for him. Again, Davyd ruthlessly squashed the rebellious thought and answered the woman he loved. "I'm sure he is going to. He has to pack a lot in a hurry. Then he'll come find you, I'm sure."

She looked at him with a strange look, as if she knew better but couldn't find words to say it.

Bootsteps clunked along the walkway outside, and raised voices could be heard further down.

"Clear out everything in the stall," Evan called.

A muffled female response came faintly to the listening ears. "How long do I have?"

"Move faster, groom!" Evan shouted. "I leave within the hour and I *will* have everything I need!"

More boots, this time running. An unfamiliar voice said, "The extra feed you require has been loaded onto Richard's wagon for delivery tomorrow."

"Very good. And my own trunk?" Evan was curt, in a hurry.

"Already there."

"You've done well. Now go make sure supper is on time," Evan snapped.

The boots ran off again.

"You can't go with him, you know. You have a Rider Ceremony to prepare for," Davyd said softly. Best to get her mind on positive things. He couldn't help her reconcile her feelings for Evan, nor did he want to.

She rewarded him with a smile. "When will it be? Has Morgan decided?"

"As soon as possible. We have to get those foals assigned to riders and up to High Meadow. Da said that any horse that is healthy a week from now will make the move."

Emma nodded. "I'd better pack so I am ready at a moment's notice." She turned to go, then hesitated. Looking back over her shoulder, she smiled at Davyd and said, "Thank you. You always know what to say."

Then she was gone.

Davyd was left with a vision he would never forget, burned into his memory, that he could pull out and treasure for eternity. The sight of her, in the doorway to the storeroom, was a portrait of beauty. Backlit by the late afternoon sun, her outline was in sharp silhouette. The flickering candle inside the room threw enough light for him to see her features: the warm smile, the soft dark eyes, the cloud of chestnut hair that he loved. But the highlight of the vision was the sincere emotion that illuminated her expression. Affection, yes. Maybe love. He savored the possibility for a moment before cutting off that line of thought yet again.

Chapter 16: Hidden List

Conflicting emotions swirled through Emma as she walked away from Morgan's barn. Her fists clenched and unclenched at her sides, but a tear slipped down her cheek. How dare Evan think so little of her that he could leave without saying goodbye! But oh, what a relief that Adain was still healthy! Rider Ceremony was within the week. It would be so exciting to finally claim Adain, but she still had to make her father accept that Adain was her choice. A sigh escaped.

The fountain was still dry, but she laid a hand on Aer's stone flank anyway. It felt cool. Her forehead rested on her hand as she mentally reached for the spirit of the stone horse. Calm eluded her. Just when her future with Adain was within reach, the rest of her life spiraled out of control. She'd mentally shut Tristan out of her life only to have Evan welcome him into a place of power in High Meadow. Evan was hers for the taking, all she'd ever wanted, and she'd kissed his brother. Horses were still dying and although they knew how, everyone had a different theory as to who exactly was behind it and what their motives were. Emma headed for home. Her mother had always been her confidante when thoughts grew troubling. No need to change that quite yet.

Emma found Neste in the tiny tack room inside the barn. Mum was absorbed in polishing a bridle, something she did when she needed to escape. Lately the bridles and bits and saddles gleamed. She looked up with a faraway expression that changed when she saw Emma's face.

"Oh, Mum." Emma hadn't meant to run to her mother and cry, but here she was. "Evan's leaving."

"Leaving you, *cariad*?"

"*Na*, leaving for High Meadow today. For good."

Neste frowned. "But isn't that the plan?"

"He didn't say goodbye."

"*Na, na*. He should not have done that. *Mae'n ddrwg gen i, cariad*. I am so sorry."

She started to get up, but Emma shook her head. If her mother hugged her, tears would cascade like a waterfall. Emma swallowed and took a deep breath. "Part of love, I guess, right, Mum?" She tried to smile.

"If he loved you, he'd care about your feelings."

Had Evan ever said he loved her? Suddenly she couldn't remember. The air grew thick around her, and buzzed like she was going to pass out.

"Emma?" Her mother's voice was concerned.

She couldn't talk about this, she realized. "I'm fine," she ground out in a choked voice.

Her mother went back to polishing the bridle,

rubbing it with an oiled cloth. The leather darkened and softened as Neste worked it. An air of expectation wafted over them. Mum was waiting for her to continue. She had to change the subject.

"Padrig's been arrested. Could he really have poisoned the horses?"

Her mother shrugged, and her face was dubious. "Not without Lord Farley's knowledge, and most likely not without his order. They'll never arrest a patron. The mayor will let poor Sorius's memory be tarnished by this, and use Padrig as a scapegoat."

"Why would one of our own patrons want to kill our horses?"

"It had to be a targeted death that got out of control, *cariad*. No one benefits from the deaths we have seen."

Emma nodded. Before she could respond, though, bluster and boots drew both women's attention to the door. Hoel scowled as he burst in holding a small bound book, its leather cover worn. Emma didn't recognize it.

"What is this?" He shoved the book forward, his growl low and furious.

Emma couldn't remember the last time he'd aimed a pleasant word in her direction. She avoided pointing out that it was a book. Her father could read only a few words, and not easily. Her mother kept the records for the barn.

Neste calmly took the book from her husband and opened it. Emma moved to look over her mother's shoulder. Reading came easy to her, and her mother had taught her to keep barn records. At the time, her mum thought it would be the family barn that Emma would help run. Her stomach twisted as she realized her learning would now help Evan in High Meadow.

Hoel paced the tiny office. "A groom brought it to me just now. Found it wedged behind Bryn's water trough."

Bryn was Tristan's horse. Emma peered more closely at the cramped writing. Her mother's finger moved down the page as she read the names listed there. A few of the names were familiar to Emma. They were riders.

"Riders?" Neste asked, looking up at her husband. "Why would Tristan have a list of riders?"

"Keep looking," Hoel demanded. "It was hidden. It can't be good."

Emma's thoughts flew back to yesterday's meeting in the tavern. Maybe this was a list of riders who wanted to join Tristan. Her mother paged through the book. Sure enough, near the back was a plan of exodus to High Meadow. It included Bryn and Mael, but not Lleu. Neste's eyes met Emma's.

"It appears to be a list of riders who support Tristan," she told her husband.

"Support Tristan for what?"

Neste took a deep breath. "*Cariad*, it looks as though Tristan is planning to start a new barn in High Meadow."

For Emma, time slowed to a crawl as she watched her father's face first blanch to the color of Adwen's coat, then slowly suffuse with scarlet anger. Ice settled in her belly. This would make her father even angrier at Evan and High Meadow, and at her.

Hoel resumed pacing, but he didn't shout. Instead, his voice went to a much more dangerous low, cold place. "What is Tristan thinking? He could have had everything, but he's thrown it all away now. He's ruined his future and mine, too. Tristan could've had the barn after my daughter abandoned me." He paused to glare at Emma. "But no, he has to betray me, too."

It was always going to be about him, Emma realized. She stayed silent. Neste, too, seemed to be waiting for Hoel to wind down.

"How long has he been collecting riders?" He glared at Neste, but she shook her head. The lists weren't dated. "Tristan used this to ruin my barn. He will not be a part of what is left. I want him out today. Emma, you cannot have Adain now. You must stay and help me rebuild this barn. Morgan will be able to find another rider for the colt. He'd be glad enough to put Davyd on him. You can ride Bryn until we get a foal on Mael."

Shock kept Emma silent.

"Hoel," Neste began.

"*Na!*" Hoel thundered. "I will not listen to you defend her!"

Emma stood up straight and took a deep breath. She didn't care about Tristan, but she would not allow his deeds to ruin her life. "Da," she said in a controlled tone, hoping she sounded mature. "I am Adain's rider. The ceremony is this week, then I'll be off to High Meadow with the rest of the healthy horses. This is the life I've chosen. . ."

Hoel roared over her, "Since when do you get to choose your life? I need you here in your family's barn!"

Neste tried again. "Hoel! Let her alone!"

Emma's eyes were locked on her father's. He was afraid, she suddenly realized, afraid of losing his barn and afraid of losing her. But he wouldn't ask her to stay, and she couldn't offer. Her future was with Adain. Calm settled over her. She had made her choice, and he would never accept it. There was no point in arguing. *"Mae'n ddrwg gen i, Tad.* I'm so sorry." And for the first time, she actually was.

"It will be all right, *cariad,"* Neste said soothingly. For a minute, Emma wasn't sure if her mum was talking to her father or to her. Then she put a hand on her husband's arm. "We built the barn together. We can rebuild it together."

But the Barn Leader shook off her hand and rounded on her. "I'm too old to start over. It's the next generation's job to continue. I can't do it again, Neste. If I had known that my own flesh and blood would betray me, I couldn't have done it the first time."

"She's her own person, and we need to be proud of that," Neste said.

Hoel ignored her and resumed pacing. "And Tristan. Took him in and trained him. He could have had it all." Hoel threw his hands in the air and stormed from the office.

Emma hoped Tristan was far away.

"What do you know about this?" Neste asked.

Emma took an end of her hair and twisted it between her fingers. "I heard Tristan say something to Evan yesterday about gathering riders, Mum. I really didn't know what he planned." Guilt washed over her.

"It's not like there's much left for him here anyway," Neste said. She sounded sad. "He's ambitious, but so was Hoel when he started." She seemed to come to a decision, and turned to her daughter. "Emma, we need strong leaders if the horses are to thrive in High

Meadow. I know you love Evan, but I'm not convinced he can do it alone. Find Tristan before your father does."

Emma looked at her mother's stricken face, contorted with fear and despair. She nodded and raced from her father's barn. She ran up the dirt lane to Aer Road, the pounding of her booted feet echoing her frantic thoughts. Tristan and Evan were working together to build High Meadow. Her father was going to kill Tristan. And maybe Evan. Tristan betrayed her father so why would the rider be loyal to Evan? Tristan was looking out for himself, but so was she. She was no better than him, maybe worse since she was betraying her own heritage.

A sob broke through her panting and Emma gasped for breath as she ran and cried. She flung her hands up to stone Aer, laying palms flat against the cool smooth flank and hiding her face behind the upswept wing. She fought for control. There was no time to break down now. Furiously wiping her face, Emma forced herself to take long, slow breaths. She had to sort this out later. Now she must find Tristan. At this time of day, Davyd would be in his storeroom. Evan would be with Clyth in High Meadow. She had no idea where Tristan spent his time. One more shaky breath, and Emma headed for the tavern. It was a meeting place, after all, and Robert knew the people of Tremeirchson well. He might have some idea where Tristan was.

She pushed opened the door of the tavern, noticing about half the tables were filled. Business was dropping off. Too many people were leaving town. She pushed away the guilt and approached the bar where Robert was wiping a mug with a sackcloth. Silence crept behind her, until all conversation had stilled and all eyes were on her.

Emma swallowed nervously. Before she could speak to Robert, Jenett appeared out of the kitchen. She spotted Emma right away and came over to her.

Jenett's hips swayed with their normal sashaying walk. Her long dark hair was tied back and topped with a white cap, but it was the glittering green eyes that compelled Emma's gaze. Half the remaining villagers watched as the two young women faced each other.

Emma's emotions were still in turmoil. She wanted to find Tristan, to warn him away from the barn. She had no time for bantering with Jenett about barn politics. "Where's Tristan?" she blurted out.

Jenett's eyes narrowed. "Why?"

"Please, Jenett, my father's looking for him. He's really angry."

"Are you trying to warn him?" Jenett's eyes widened into surprise.

"Yes. You know about the list?" Jenett nodded. "Da found it."

Jenett tore off her apron and tossed it at the tavern keeper. "Sorry, I have to go, Robert!" she shouted as she bolted out the door.

Robert caught the apron and turned to Emma. "What was that about?"

Still conscious of the watching villagers, Emma hesitated. Taking a deep breath, she decided there was no point hiding anything. In days she'd be gone anyway. "My father is upset about Tristan going to High Meadow. Jenett's gone to warn him." There was so much more than that. But it was all she could put into words.

"Common sentiment," Robert said, his eyes flicking over the crowd behind her.

She looked over her shoulder and was stunned by the hostility in the villagers' faces. A table of men near her farmed the village's fields. She recognized two women who took in sewing and had made some of the tunics for her father's barn. Near the kitchen door was a family whose daughter had often stopped Emma in the street and asked longingly about being a groom. These were people she knew.

"None of you are moving to High Meadow?" she ventured.

The room bustled with negative head shaking and hisses. One of the farmers said, "My field is planted, miss. Are we supposed to leave the entire crop and move up the mountain? We don't have time to ready fields there for planting. I'd rather stay here and know I'll eat this winter." His companions muttered agreement.

Emma turned back to Robert with troubled eyes. He patted her hand. "You can't fix the world for everybody, miss. You do what you must. It will turn out all right." She nodded. "Now get yourself out back. Davyd is there loading Richard's wagon for a trip to High Meadow."

Grateful for the excuse, Emma hurried past the dour villagers and escaped out the back door. She closed it behind her and took a deep breath. The sun massaged her body, and she longed to bask in it and forget the world.

"Emma?" Davyd jumped down from the wagon and walked toward her. "What's happened?"

"Oh, Davyd, my father is so angry with Tristan. He found out he's been gathering support among the riders and he feels so betrayed. He left the barn and Mum thinks he went to find Tristan. Jenett is off to warn him."

Davyd put his arm along her shoulders. "Hey, now, it'll be all right. Tristan is supposed to bring some crates of supplies for this load to High Meadow. He'll be here any minute. Why don't you sit here and compose yourself?" He led her to a bench in the sun.

Emma forced herself to breathe calmly and focus on what was most important — riding Adain to High Meadow and making a success of the new town. In order to do that, she needed Evan and Tristan. They both had supporters. If they didn't work together, they risked splitting the herd into two weak factions. The barns of Tremeirchson may not be as unified as Evan liked, but they had all worked to make a success of Tremeirchson as a whole.

She watched Davyd loading the wagon, his arm muscles bulging as he lifted heavy crates and sacks, and slowly relaxed.

A shadow darkened the sun, and she looked up. A big horse circled in to land. Dark against the sun, she didn't recognize it until it was on the ground. Bryn! Jenett had known just where to intercept Tristan, since she was mounted behind him. Emma stood up, but the other three were coming toward her and she waited. Davyd was gesturing to Tristan, saying something about going now.

Tristan looked at Emma. "What do you think? Are you here to stop me?"

"*Na, cariad,*" Jenett said, putting a hand on his arm. "She came to warn you."

"Really." Tristan regarded Emma thoughtfully. She forced herself not to cringe. "I'm going to leave right now, from here, and take Bryn with me. That doesn't bother you?"

She didn't know why she was surprised, because of course he would take Bryn. She lifted her chin and squared her shoulders. "*Na*, it doesn't bother me. You are important to the future of the herd."

"One thing, though, Tristan," Davyd put in.

They all turned to face him. He looked confident and relaxed, in charge, Emma realized. They waited for him to speak.

"In High Meadow there is one barn. What Evan needs most is a strong second in command."

Tristan began to shake his head and mutter.

Davyd continued, ignoring him. "No barn needs two leaders. High Meadow needs strong unified leadership. So go, Tristan, and tell Evan you will be his second in command for First Barn."

"Or what?" Tristan asked. His defiance was slipping, Emma noticed. He realized his precarious position.

Davyd shrugged. "Or we prevent you from leaving now and tell Hoel where he can find his stallion." He nodded to where Richard held Bryn's reins.

Emma wondered how Davyd would stop Tristan. She couldn't help against the strong rider, and Jenett surely wouldn't. Then she saw the steel in Richard's eyes. The door opened and Robert appeared, a similar grim look on his face. She knew they'd won when Tristan's shoulders slumped.

"I know about being second in command," Tristan said. "At least in High Meadow there is an opportunity to lead my own barn. Keep 'em healthy, Davyd, and send 'em soon. I want to break ground on Second Barn as soon as I arrive."

Richard relinquished Bryn's reins at a nod from Davyd, and Tristan swung aboard. He saluted Davyd and pulled Jenett up behind as Bryn leaped for the sky.

Davyd turned to Richard. "Better get on the road. By the time you arrive, no telling what story he will have told Evan."

Richard nodded and climbed aboard the wagon. As Robert reentered the tavern, Richard flicked the reins and his slower, earthbound horses clopped out of the yard.

Emma sighed. "I don't trust him."

"Nor do I." Davyd shook his head. "Whatever he is up to, whoever he is working for, the horses come first. We must get all the healthy horses to High Meadow. When they are safe, we can watch Tristan." He hugged Emma. "Now we just have to get you aboard Adain."

His arms ignited fire within her as she leaned into the hug. All the turmoil of the last few hours dissipated. Evan was safe in High Meadow, and Tristan had agreed not to fight him for leadership. Davyd's supplies were on their way, too, and the tavern would be ready soon. And day after tomorrow, Adain would be hers.

Chapter 17: Patronage

Normally after the closing of the Aerial Games the skies above the village quieted, a bit of a break for man and beast before beginning work for the next year's competition. This year's quiet skies were grim. Davyd didn't think any barn would have enough horses to fill their usual Dance of Welcome, much less compete aggressively in any of the races or dances. How many years would it be until the Games were back to normal? And what would normal look like in High Meadow? One thing was clear. After twenty-seven days of death and despair, he would never take normal for granted again.

Turning his back on the sky, Davyd walked the length of the barn toward his storage room. As he passed Adain's stall, he heard female voices and paused to listen. Not Emma's voice. Curious, he ducked into the stall.

Elen stroked the colt's neck. Standing to one side was an elegantly dressed, short, thick woman. Her layers and layers of fine clothing added to the impression of thickness. Her hair was twisted somehow into an elaborate pile on her head, with decorative trinkets woven into it. The white skin of her arms proved she was not from a barn. This woman spent her life indoors. Lady Margery. She must have brought the answer to his father's letter in person. That was brave, considering the swirling suspicions about her husband.

Elen twisted her hands and shook her head once. "I don't know. I just don't know."

"Problem?" Davyd asked. He watched both women carefully.

Elen turned to greet him with a smile. "*Helo, cariad!* Hasn't Adain grown into a fine colt?"

"Sure has." Davyd kept his eyes on Lady Margery.

"It's a shame that he won't be ridden by a family member," she said through tight lips.

"Yes, it is," Elen agreed slowly.

Davyd laid a hand on his mother's arm. "Emma is like family, Mum. You know she loves Adain. And he loves her. It will be fine."

Elen patted her son's hand and smiled. "So true."

Davyd carefully controlled his features, forming them into a welcoming smile as he bowed over the patroness's proffered hand. "Enchanted, milady."

"Due to my husband's infirmity, I have permanently taken over the barn." Her voice was cold. It gave no indication if the infirmity she mentioned was his longstanding illness or his misadventure with poisoning horses.

"I'm sure you will find all in order, milady," Davyd assured her. "Are you planning to stay for the Rider

Ceremony tomorrow?"

"I might," the ice queen said.

"All four foals are here. Would you like to see them?" Elen asked.

His mother led the patroness out of Adain's stall. Davyd followed them to stalls that housed the foals. They were settling in well to the new barn, and he admired them. Lady Margery peered at them but did not offer an opinion.

"See that big brown colt?" Elen asked, standing in front of the last stall. "He'll be a good distance flyer. Straight and steady for the long races."

"Maybe that filly will be a dancer. Do you like dancers or racers?" She faced her son, not the visitor.

"Mum, what is this about?" he asked carefully, glancing at Lady Margery. She was moving on down the barn, not paying attention.

Elen's cheeks pinkened. "Oh, just making sure, *cariad*. None of these are for you, then?"

Davyd shook his head. "I have enough to do with the village ready to explode."

They hurried to catch up to the patroness. She stopped at the end of the walk and looked out over the empty paddock. "Six horses left, plus the three foals that are not from our barn." It was not a question, so Davyd felt no need to respond, although he cringed at her use of the possessive. "And they will move to High Meadow after the ceremony tomorrow?"

"That is correct, milady," Elen responded. "My older son, Evan, is already in High Meadow, taking charge of First Barn. They have five horses settled in."

Davyd was impressed at the current information.

213

His mother was regaining her grip on reality after Wynne's death. What a relief.

"Evan is eighteen." Again, it was not a question. Elen nodded. "And what is your role, Davyd?"

"I am in charge of the village, milady. We must ensure enough support people and merchants to make this venture successful." Davyd nodded his head in a clipped bow.

"Hmph. And you're sixteen." She clearly knew how old he was. "Do you plan to be mayor of this new town?"

He was beginning to resent her sneering tone. "No, milady. I will only be in charge until proper elections can be held."

Lady Margery nodded. "And you will control the village from behind the scenes." She peered at him with beady black eyes.

Davyd shifted his weight to the other foot, not sure how to respond. It didn't matter, since the patroness was clearly not waiting for approval.

"Thank you for your hospitality, Elen my dear," she said, dismissing his mother. She turned to Davyd. "Will you accompany me on an errand, my boy?"

Gritting his teeth, Davyd forced out, "Of course, milady."

Leaving Elen standing by the barn, Lady Margery led Davyd up Aer Road past the fountain. On the far side of the fountain from the barn, the mayor's house gleamed in the bright spring sun. The patroness headed for it like a hungry colt to a hay bin.

Davyd felt the blood drain from his face. Tremeirchson didn't have a sheriff like most towns. Mayor Reynallt ran both the town and the jail. He didn't like troublemakers, which he seemed to believe all boys were.

Davyd didn't hesitate, though, as they approached the solid oak door and the patroness rapped the knocker. Mayor Reynallt opened the door, his eyes narrowing as he recognized Davyd and widening again at the sight of the imposing patroness. Davyd struggled to hide his own surprise. He didn't remember the mayor being so short.

"Mayor Reynallt, I need to discuss the new town with you." Lady Margery's tone was crisp and businesslike.

"New town?" The mayor sounded confused, but he stepped back as the imposing woman entered the house. He motioned for Davyd to follow.

Reynallt's gray hair was a bit long in back, Davyd noted. The man hitched his hips when he walked, resulting in the exaggerated rolling gait of someone whose knees or hips hurt. He said nothing as he led his visitors into the parlor and waved at tall carved wooden chairs that resembled thrones. The room was quite a bit smaller than the Great Hall at home, Davyd noted as Lady Margery settled herself in the best chair. He sat, and the mayor perched next to him in a matching chair. They faced a fire blazing in a stone hearth. Davyd could see a massive chest with carvings of horses among heavy iron fittings. On the wall was a tapestry that apparently depicted an early Aerial Games. It was a room designed to show that its owner was important.

But the man sitting across from him was old. Reynallt had been mayor forever, a comfortable position in a village not known for strife. As a boy, Davyd had walked cautiously past him since Reynallt inspired fear in young boys. Once Evan had been caught throwing a rock into the fountain and Reynallt had locked him up until Morgan had stormed in to intercede. It hadn't slowed Evan much, but Davyd had feared the mayor for years. As he watched the man's gnarled fingers tap the arm of his chair, he felt the fear dissipate.

"Mayor Reynallt," Davyd began at the ice queen's nod, "this is the patroness of my father's barn, Lady Margery."

The mayor nodded. "Welcome to Tremeirchson, Lady Margery."

"I am here to discuss the venture to High Meadow."

"I'm not sure how much you know, milady," Reynallt began.

She continued as if he hadn't spoken. "You will remain here in Tremeirchson as mayor, I understand." She hesitated briefly and he nodded. "We must ensure a successful start to the new town. I recommend you endorse Davyd as interim mayor of High Meadow."

"Davyd?" He stared at Davyd in consternation, who in turn stared at the patroness. "Milady, he is a bit young..."

"At sixteen I made my first marriage and was expected to run the household of my noble husband. I believe Davyd here has had an acceptable education?"

"I can read and write, milady," Davyd said, still stunned.

Reynallt leaned forward, his eyes drilling Davyd. "You and your brother are capable young men, but inexperienced at running a village. Probably don't even know what's going on here under your nose. You have to weigh what people tell you, Davyd, and pick out the truth. Only then will you make a good leader." He tilted his head toward Davyd for emphasis. "I arrested the poisoner myself with no help from the barns. He had all you barn people crying curse."

Davyd stared. His mind played a picture of Soirus collapsed at Evan's feet, and a tearful Emma telling him of Padrig's arrest. Did he dare point out that a couple of stewards from rival barns had no reason to poison horses?

"And how did this young man poison the entire town, exactly?" Lady Margery asked.

Davyd winced, hoping the mayor wouldn't accuse her husband of ordering it.

"We believe he put something in the cistern and it flowed to the barn that way." The mayor's voice sounded thin and unsure.

"Wouldn't that amount of water have thinned out the poison?" she asked, her tone blunt.

Davyd admired her knowledge of the barns, the town, and the working of the village. She was an intelligent woman and he was glad she appeared to be on his side.

"We hung the poisoner, milady." The mayor's voice was stubborn.

Davyd stifled a gasp. He must have been in High Meadow when the hanging had taken place. It was no use talking to the mayor about this. Answers would be forthcoming from Lady Margery, later. Not from this man, eager only to put it behind him.

In short order, the serving girl arrived with a tray of wine and three fine goblets. She set it down and scurried away, to return with rolls and honey. Lady Margery accepted a cup of wine, but Davyd refused both food and drink. Reynallt tried to start a general conversation once or twice, but Lady Margery simply sipped her wine and gazed into the fire, deep in thought. Davyd wondered what he should do now.

The patroness looked closely at him. Davyd smiled at her and she turned back to the mayor. "So you are prepared to endorse Davyd here as leader of High Meadow?"

"I said no such thing!"

She just waited. Reynallt wilted under her implacable gaze. Davyd forced himself not to fidget.

"All right, I agree," Mayor Reynallt said sullenly.

"It will be posted and proclaimed today, and again at the Rider Ceremony tomorrow," she stated.

Davyd watched Lady Margery spar with Mayor Reynallt. He admired the way she dominated the mayor. Reynallt was all bluster and swagger. He couldn't hold up to the quiet confidence of the patroness. Davyd studied her posture and the way she spoke. He would be this kind of leader.

The mayor nodded, obviously now in a hurry to end the conversation. "Yes, yes, I will see to it, milady."

"Then we will take our leave. Come, Davyd."

She did not wait to be escorted out. Davyd followed, feeling like a leaf caught in a whirlwind.

At the fountain, she pulled up short. "You have something to say," she stated.

Davyd rubbed his neck, unable to meet her glittering eyes. If he was going to accept her patronage, though, he had to know. "Did your lord husband order this poisoning? It doesn't have to go any further, but I have to know."

For a moment something flickered across her face, maybe a warm emotion. It was gone too quickly for Davyd to identify whether it was guilt, compassion, or fear. He waited. After another moment, although her shoulders remained uncowed, she seemed somehow to shrink inside.

"My lord husband is not well," she said in the softest tone Davyd had ever heard from her. "He ordered Soirus to poison the water to Hoel's barn." She made a tortured sound that was probably supposed to be an ironic laugh. "His biggest worry was that Bronwyn would beat Wynne in the Aerial Dances this year. And Bronwyn died before the poison took effect."

"And he poisoned Wynne," Davyd growled.

She actually lowered her eyes. "I could have told him he didn't know enough about those berries. Poison is tricky." Lady Margery stared into the dry fountain as she whispered, "It truly got away from him."

"I'm to believe you were not involved at all?"

The ice queen patroness was back when her eyes met his. "Of course not. I am merely the wife who does everything her lord husband desires. I have no part of his schemes."

Davyd had no immediate answer. He met her gaze, wondering if he could believe her. She was offering to make the move to High Meadow possible. Maybe it was her attempt to make whatever amends could be made. At any rate, it would save the world's winged horses. "What happens to Lord Andrew?" he asked.

Her frozen facade slipped again, real anguish peeking through. "He's an old man, Davyd, punished by his body. My lord husband fancies himself a powerful man, but he has not been so for years. After these deaths kept increasing…" Her voice caught, and she swallowed before continuing. "He suffered an attack of the heart." Hands clasped to her chest. "He survived, but he is incapable of feeding himself. He is trapped in a body that continues to breathe, to see, to hear, but he has trouble making himself understood, and he cannot walk or even sit up alone. In his youth he was powerful. Now he is faded and forgotten. What, really, would further punishment accomplish?"

Davyd thought of Siorus, dead from his master's poison, and Padrig, hung as the scapegoat. This would make matters worse between his father's barn and Hoel's, if those barns were going to continue to exist. High Meadow had to be a coming together. Everyone who made the move to High Meadow had to be committed to making it work. There would be no room for infighting.

"I trust you and your brother to keep my investment secure, Davyd. We will continue to support you in High Meadow and expect to see a good show next year at the Aerial Games." The patroness was back.

"It will be small," he began, half hating himself for not questioning her further.

She waved away his objections. "You will make it work. Now I must be going. I am due back in Merioneth by tomorrow morning. You'd best secure your leadership."

"It was a pleasure, milady, and thank you for your support."

He watched as she crossed the road to a carriage

sitting in the shade of an oak tree behind Robert's tavern. It was clearly an out-of-town conveyance, too fancy for Tremeirchson. The matched gray horses that pulled it were sleek and well-fed, the harness studded with silver medallions. A footman hastened to help her inside, then climbed aboard and they were off. She was not of his world. She wanted him to secure his leadership. He'd better find out who exactly was making the move to High Meadow and who they might support for mayor. He headed for the tavern, seat of Tremeirchson's real power.

It was crowded inside. He entered and stood a moment, scanning the room. Families and groups of men in pairs and threes ate at the tables scattered around the room. The ambiance of the room itself was inviting and warm. The fire burned low in a large stone fireplace. Paintings of famous horses of the past decorated the walls. Davyd noted details he never noticed before, now that the idea of his own tavern was becoming a reality. Heads turned toward him, but faces scowled instead of smiled.

Davyd approached Robert, behind the counter with his head down. The rotund tavern keeper had been his friend as long as he remembered. He and his brother, Richard, were a few years older than Davyd and Evan. They'd been separated growing up by the arrangement of the village. Robert and Richard's father had run the tavern. His boys were expected to learn the business. Davyd and Evan's father ran the barn. They'd been expected to learn that business. It hadn't worked out exactly how anyone had planned.

"What's going on?" he murmured to Robert.

"The town's divided. Some want to be gone, some don't."

"The Rider Ceremony is tomorrow, and we move afterward. What is delaying their decision?"

The tavern keeper shrugged. Davyd peered at the man who would not meet his eyes. "You know I plan to open a tavern in High Meadow, right?" Robert nodded. "I need your expertise. I very much would like you to be my partner in this venture."

Robert nodded again. "I figured you'd ask me, Davyd, and I admit I'm interested. I can move the stock I have in back tomorrow." He hesitated and rubbed the back of his head. "It's expensive, though, to start a business. Especially when the town is remote. We won't be bringing in any money until next year's Aerial Games, if then."

"Our patronage will continue in High Meadow. We will be fine."

"Oh, that's a relief." Robert's face relaxed into a wide smile. "Then I'm your man."

"One more question, Robert. Are you interested in running for mayor of High Meadow? I've just learned that Reynallt will back me for interim mayor, but High Meadow's first mayor will need more experience."

Robert looked pensive. "A partnership, you say. I suspect the town and the tavern both will be run by that partnership. I like the way you think, young man." He poured two mugs of ale to toast their alliance.

A man approached and interrupted their conversation. Davyd recognized the farrier. He looked angry, probably because his business would be affected greatly by this move. He spat at Davyd, "Haven't the barns ruined enough lives? Taking our tavern too?"

"We can't rely on traders to supply water for the whole village until the winter rains. Once some of us leave, it'll be easier for those who stay to bring in fresh water until the poison is gone. I only want the winged horses to survive. It won't be easy on those who go, nor will it be easy for those who stay."

"How will Tremeirchson exist without the money spent by you barn folks?"

Davyd couldn't see who had spoken. "We have a fresh water source up there, closer than Merioneth. If someone takes over Robert's tavern, we can arrange wagonloads of fresh water."

General grumbling sounded a bit more positive. Davyd leaned close to Robert and whispered, "Be ready to leave right after the Rider Ceremony tomorrow."

He left the tavern, relieved that no one else challenged him. At the fountain, he paused next to Aer and thought of Emma. She would have been proud of him today, had she been here to see him. He moved over to brown Ystrad, the nurturing earth god. He ran a finger along the stone carving that imitated the horse's huge feathers. In declining to be a rider, Davyd acknowledged he was an earth person and now he would nurture an entire town. It didn't terrify him quite as much as flying, but it would be a challenge. He'd convinced Robert that he needed him. Now he had to figure out what to do about Emma.

On a Wing and a Dare

Chapter 18: Rider Ceremony

When the sun came up, Emma had already been staring in the oval mirror of her mother's dressing table for what seemed like hours, trying to reconcile what she saw with what she felt on this most important day. Today she would become Adain's rider. The past four weeks had changed her world more than she would have dreamed possible. Now instead of just spending more time in Morgan's barn, she'd be leaving for good. It was her choice, to move away from family to a new barn and a new village. The gold-painted mirror, trimmed with colored glass to resemble jewels, had been her father's gift for her mother's Rider Ceremony. It showed Emma a slightly distorted image of herself, with no great revelation of her soul.

She twisted a blue and silver ribbon between her hands. It had been the first thing she put on this morning, tied into her hair, but she'd ripped it out and sat staring at her reflection ever since. When she was a little girl, she had dreamed of wearing the blue and silver of her father's barn. But she was joining Morgan's barn, and their green and gold seemed foreign. She didn't own anything green and gold except for the bit of ribbon she'd found by the fountain, and no one had thought to bring her the traditional ribbons.

Then another thought struck her. The four foals were to be moved to High Meadow after the ceremony. She would never actually be part of Morgan's barn since she and Adain would join High Meadow's First Barn. Had anyone even chosen colors for it yet?

She pulled her hair back tightly and expertly braided it. Twisting it up onto her head, she wound it all with plain silver ribbon, hoping it would look pretty and still fit under a helmet. Rising and turning to the bed, she brushed the divided skirt of her white linen gown with her hands, smoothing the simple woven fabric that billowed around her legs. If she stood with her feet together, it would look like a normal skirt. When the time came, though, she would be prepared to ride astride. Her mother had embroidered the long sleeves of the gown, making it as special as the occasion. Emma picked up the blue tunic from the bed and pulled it over her head, careful not to disturb her hair. Leaning over, she checked the length and nodded approvingly. Long enough to be proper but short enough to allow her to ride.

The last days had been hideous. Fifteen more horses had died, including two from Morgan's barn and Mael. The mare's death left Hoel's barn echoing, with Lleu alone. With no mare, Hoel could not breed Lleu and rebuild. Emma smoothed the blue and silver ribbon between her fingers, rolling and unrolling it as her thoughts whirled.

Only Morgan's iron control prevented mass exodus.

He insisted that no one leave for High Meadow until they were proven healthy. So they planned for a Rider Ceremony among riders packing to leave the instant they could, grooms burning bodies of horses struck down, and villagers fleeing for either Merioneth or High Meadow. No, no one had taken time to choose colors for the new barn.

The door to Emma's bedroom opened. Neste entered, closing the door softly behind her.

"*Helo, Mam,*" Emma whispered.

"*Bore da, cariad.*" Neste hugged her daughter. "You look beautiful."

Emma looked in the mirror. Obviously Mum didn't see the slightly frantic expression in her eyes, or the dark circles under them.

"I am so proud of you, *cariad*. This is a big day. Don't think about the oddness of the times, but about the promise of the future."

Emma twisted the blue and silver ribbon again. Noticing, her mother said, "*Cariad*, you never need to be embarrassed to wear this. You have more right than most. Wear it openly or wear it hidden, close to your heart."

Emma smiled. "*Diolch, Mam,* I will." She pinned the ribbon inside the bodice of her tunic.

"Your father and I love you. Know that, where ever you go, whatever you do."

"Mum, I'm just going to High Meadow. I'll be back and forth, once this illness clears up. I'll see you often."

Neste's eyes were disbelieving. "I know you believe that now, and I thank you for it. If those plans don't work out, though, it will be all right. You have chosen a life, a good life, and I support you."

It cost her mother a lot to admit that. Her father never would, and his distance would prevent Emma from visiting as much as she might like to. Tears pricked her eyes.

The bedroom door crashed open and Hoel burst in, his eyes flashing. "So you're really going through with this?"

He wasn't yelling, which was worse. This cold, hard tone wasn't one she was used to. "Yes," she said simply.

"You are no longer part of this barn, and you are not to return. You have turned your back on family, on tradition, and on the future chosen for you. Begone."

He would have stormed out then, but Emma was fed up with his constant disapproval. "Begone?" she scoffed. "It's easy to banish me when I have already made the choice to go. I have chosen my life, my horse, and my man on my own, with no help from you. All you have shown me over the last year is disapproval. I nursed your dying horses while you ignored me. Now you think you have the right to banish me?" By the time she finished, she was trembling from anger and sorrow.

"No action done with betrayal in your heart is pure. All year you planned to leave yet you said nothing. Now you abandon us in our worst time. You are no daughter to me."

Inwardly cringing, Emma forced her chin up, staring back at the angry face where her father's loving eyes used to be. "I am Emma. That is enough. The whole village knew about my choice of Adain, and my choice of Evan. Only you couldn't see it, couldn't accept it. I will be content, Da, and hope someday you will allow a visit."

She stood up straight, then, staring at him, and he wilted before her eyes. He stormed out much as he had entered, and she sank weakly against her bed.

"Oh, Emma, *mae'n ddrwg gen i*," her mother cried. "I'm so sorry."

"I was a fool to think I could avoid it. Now it's done, and I feel cleaner." Emma sighed. Cleaner, maybe, but definitely drained. She willed her legs not to wobble as she stood up and spread some cream over the dark circles under her eyes.

"And you've chosen Evan?"

Emma frowned. "I've been dating him for weeks, Mum."

Neste fussed a bit with the ribbon in her daughter's hair. "I thought you liked Davyd, too."

"I do. He's a friend." Emma didn't trust her voice. She knew her mother suspected something because she frowned and peered closer at her daughter.

"A friend?"

Emma turned, and her face crumpled. "Oh, Mum, what should I do? I love Evan, I really do, but I love Davyd, too. Evan is exciting. I feel alive when I am with him, inspired to do anything. But Davyd really cares. He's always there when I need a hug or a kind word."

Neste put her arm around her daughter. "*Cariad*, this is what I will miss the most—being a mother. Follow your heart. Who do you really want to spend time with? You won't need Evan for flight any more, so who do you prefer to spend time with on the ground?"

"Davyd," she whispered.

"Then Davyd it should be. Get ready now, it's

almost time. *Dw i'n dy garu di.*" Her mother kissed her on the forehead and left her alone.

"I love you too, Mum," she whispered. Davyd it should be, she had said. Could it really be so simple?

A scant hour later, she approached Morgan's barn with equal measures of excitement and dread. Owain spotted her and smiled, leading her to an empty stall where three other young people were gathered.

"Lewes and Thomas," Owain said, gesturing to the riders. "And Angharad."

The two young men looked like they were about twelve, although they had to be sixteen. *One of them should be Davyd.* She shook away the traitorous thought. The fourth was a tiny girl who oozed confidence. Emma didn't know any of them, and they seemed too nervous to chat.

Owain returned to lead them to the ceremony. As they walked them down the length of the barn, Emma was surprised by the number of people in attendance. She hadn't thought there were that many people left in village and barn combined. The patrons of both barns were conspicuously absent, but that gave the event a hometown feel.

Adain and the other three foals had been brushed until their coats shined. Iridescent wings caught the spring sunlight, and manes and tails were braided with blue and white ribbon. Morgan stepped forward and formally welcomed them. Someone in the back of the crowd cheered. Grooms stepped forward with loops of blue and white ribbon that they hung over the new riders' necks. Emma straightened it over her bodice, stroking the silky fabric. Next, the grooms formally handed each of them a leather helmet. Emma could see they had been repainted blue and white.

"Blue for the sky above High Meadow and white for the clouds," Morgan announced. "These will be the founding riders of First Barn, the first ones that haven't ridden for a Tremeirchson barn."

Emma hid a smile as Adain nibbled on a ribbon tied to the mane of the horse next to him. Her mind wandered as Morgan intoned the Riders' Creed. She'd heard it before and already lived it.

To put the life of the winged horse above your own. Yeah, she'd done that in the last weeks. She scanned the crowd, knowing Mum would be watching from somewhere. Da would not. She spotted Mum standing with Elen. They were smiling. Maybe they had been friends once, before they got their horses, married men in rival barns, and Mum lost her horse. It had never occurred to Emma to ask.

To preserve the honor of your barn. That had been hard with her father, but then again, she was not a rider in his barn. Just his daughter. It had to be easier to be preserve the honor in a barn you had chosen.

Evan wasn't here. She'd hardly thought about him in the last few days, and she hadn't missed him. He should want to be here and she should want him here more than anyone else.

Movement at the edge of the crowd caught her eye. It was Davyd, waving a blue and white ribbon. She smiled. How sweet of him to have thought of ribbons. Enough had changed with this Rider Ceremony; it was nice to have at least one tradition continue. She waved at him and saw him grin as he waved back. Everyone around her started to move, and Emma was jolted out of her thoughts. Morgan led them to the horses, who were frisky from standing idle. He formally placed the reins in the hands of each rider. When Emma received Adain's reins, she grinned in pleasure. Adain snuffled her hand, looking for treats.

The four new riders mounted their horses, and grooms helped strap them in. Emma put on her helmet, smiling as it fit easily over her braided hair. Thomas and Lewes had no difficulty, but Angharad had to have her mare's groom help with the helmet. Her long, thick blond hair just would not go inside neatly. Emma smiled to herself. Angharad would learn to braid it up soon enough.

Adain flexed his wings, dancing a bit at the unfamiliar weight of the saddle on his back. Emma knew he had been training with weights and harnesses, but not with a person. Still, he trusted her. She swung up into the saddle with confidence. The colt twitched his ears, fluttered his wings, and stood quietly. She stretched out to run her fingers lightly over his wing feathers. Reaching down, she patted Adain's neck. "Next step, flight, Adain *del*," she whispered.

***

Two Davyds watched the Rider Ceremony. One was thrilled with watching Emma achieve her dream. The other needled him with guilt as he watched the incompetently new Thomas mount his horse. Morgan had known better than to break up Emma and Adain, but it was his idea to use complete newcomers for the other three new horses. These riders would have no residual loyalty to barns in Tremeirchson, and be a solid foundation for High Meadow. Emma, of course, was relaxed and confident.

Morgan would lead the four new riders and their mounts to the new village after the ceremony. All of the other riders had verbally agreed to follow, but some of their body language revealed uncertainty. Davyd would rest easy only when they were all safely on their way. His stomach clenched as he considered what Tremeirchson would be like with no winged horses. Luckily, the villagers' wagons were packed and ready to roll immediately after the ceremony. He'd ride up with Robert.

Clearly out of his depth, Lewes was at least trying to become a rider. He held the reins of the chunky brown colt firmly but didn't seem to know what to do next. Angharad was clearly scared of her dainty light yellow mare. Thomas had to have the reins placed in his hand, but then his fingers curled over them. The chocolate brown colt on the the other end snuffled Thomas's hair and the young man's face paled.

"His name is Cyffin," Davyd whispered. "Talk to him." He was much too far away for Thomas to hear, but the new rider had to do well or Davyd would drown in guilt.

Robert had spent most of the last week carting goods up to the tavern in Tremeirchson. The tavern and the inn were the only businesses operational at this point, besides the barn. Food, drink, and a place to sleep—it was enough to begin with. But too many villagers changed their minds on the hour. Those that moved today would form the nucleus of High Meadow. They would be the ones who were committed to its success. They would be the ones who would elect Robert as mayor, the people he and Robert would lead into the future.

Shrieks drew Davyd's attention back to the ceremony. Angharad's vocal chords seemed directly connected to the nervous dancing of her mare. Teleri's ears were back and she tossed her head, flicking her tail and wings in agitation. A groom snapped a lead onto the halter to help Angharad hold her. Davyd shook his head in disgust.

A cheer from the crowd announced the first pair taking flight. Lewes, aboard brown Llyr, followed their rider guide very capably and Davyd added his yells of approval to the noise of the crowd.

Thomas was next. Morgan helped him into the saddle, his posture and gestures revealing he was giving advice. Thomas could probably use it. Cyffin swished his tail and tossed his head, but followed his rider guide easily. Thomas and Cyffin were aloft.

Drama surrounded Angharad. Davyd suspected it always would. Her rider guide took the lead from the groom and spoke softly to Teleri, ignoring the stupid woman on the mare's back. Teleri's ears twisted back and forth, but she followed the voice of experience into the air.

Meanwhile, a radiant Emma was on Adain's back, eagerly awaiting her turn. Morgan mounted Deryn and rode up next to her. A new rider's first flight was always closely supervised by an experienced rider. Davyd grinned at Emma's surprise, glad that his father had decided to honor her this way.

"So does Evan know how you feel about her?" Neste's eyes were on Davyd.

He flushed with embarrassment but couldn't respond honestly. Not with his own mother right there. Finally, he turned his eyes back to the sky and managed to choke out, "We're good friends."

Emma was shocked to see Morgan ride up beside her. He was the most important man in Tremeirchson these days, and he was going to be her guide. She sat up straighter and beamed with pride.

"Emma, it's finally your turn. Are you ready?" Morgan's eyes were dancing.

"I've been ready a long time, *syr*," she said.

He laughed and kicked Deryn into a canter. She was right beside him, glorying in Adain's gait. They leaped for the sky together, and Adain's wings spread instinctively. Powerful strokes brought them easily to altitude. Emma followed Morgan in a series of glorious turns. She let loose a shout of exhilaration and thought she saw Morgan laugh.

It didn't matter. She had come home. This was where she belonged, above the village on Adain. Her heart was full. Then her mind intruded. She should be longing to share this moment with Evan. Or Davyd. She frowned as she remembered her conversation that morning with her mother. Davyd was her ground, but he could never understand the sheer glory of being up here. No, that was not something she could share with Davyd, yet it was all she could share with Evan.

Next to her, Morgan swerved Deryn, tilting the stallion's wings up and down to catch her attention. He used his thumb to point to the ground. Disappointed, she gave him a thumbs up and reined in Adain. She knew she had to be careful not to overfly the young horse.

Looking over at Morgan again, she frowned. He leaned far forward, hunched over Deryn's neck. That wasn't his usual posture. She edged closer to get a better look. Morgan took the reins in one hand and moved slightly, settling himself along Deryn's neck. The empty hand slackened against the horse. Emma signaled Morgan, but his face was turned away from her, helmet resting on Deryn's mane. The stallion flew at a careful pace. He seemed to be balancing the man on his back. Emma suddenly felt the need to land quickly. Something was very wrong.

Chapter 19: A Loss

Watching Emma and Adain soar over Tremeirchson, Davyd forgot his own fear. They were a thing of beauty, clearly meant to be together. When it was time for the brief ceremonial flight to end, the new pairs with their guides circled lower. Emma leaned toward Morgan suddenly, and Adain veered, uncertain. His father lay flat along Deryn's neck. Davyd frowned. Lewes and Llyr landed safely to a smattering of applause from the crowd as Davyd began pushing his way closer to the barn. Thomas and Cyffin weren't quite so smooth but were on the ground by the time Davyd drew near. Deryn still circled above, Emma and Adain close by. Angharad landed Teleri with a great flourish of wings.

As Adain and Deryn spread their wings to brake, Emma caught Davyd's eye and waved him toward her. "Something's wrong!" she called.

Davyd grabbed Deryn's rein and reached for his father. Morgan slid lifelessly out of the saddle. Davyd lowered him to the ground and worked the helmet off his head, tossing the reins to Deryn's groom. Owain took Adain, and Emma knelt by Davyd.

"Is he all right?" She was almost hysterical.

"He's not breathing. Da? *Tad*?" He jostled his father, trying to wake him.

Emma encouraged the crowd to move back, away from where Morgan lay. Davyd watched helplessly as Neste hurried over, poking and prodding his father. She sent a groom racing for her medical kit.

His mother hung over Neste, horror printed on her face. In another moment all the frantic motion ceased and Emma's mum said, "He's gone, Elen, *mae'n ddrwg gen i.*" She put a hand on her friend's shoulder as she mouthed the condolence.

The groom ran up with the kit and handed it to Neste.

Gone? How could his father be gone? "Poison?" he asked Neste.

"*Na*," Neste shook her head. "No humours were present. It was a collapse of the heart. The foxglove might have…" Her voice trailed off as she clutched her kit. "It happened too fast."

At her request, a couple of the riders lifted Morgan's body and carried him into the manor. Muffled scufflings indicated people melting away, sobered by the death of a powerful man.

As he started toward the house, Emma began to follow him, but he stopped her. "Your place is with Adain. You need to get ready for the flight to High Meadow."

"But surely that can wait?" Tears streaked her face.

"*Na*. We have to get the healthy horses out of

Tremeirchson. That, at least, hasn't changed."

He left her in the road and helped his mother across the courtyard.

Inside, his mother crumpled in a chair by the fire. She looked smaller, somehow, shrunken. Davyd stopped in the doorway, stunned. In the kitchen, he could hear the cook humming off-key as she prepared dinner, as yet oblivious to the family's tragedy. The door to the small sickroom was open. His father's body would be in there. He averted his eyes from the consuming blackness of the doorway. Two women, wives of riders, hovered near his mother. They stepped back as he approached her chair.

"Mum?" He put his arm around her.

She sobbed, "Oh, Davyd."

"*Mae'n ddrwg gen i, Mam*, I'm so sorry."

Enfolding her in a hug, he was surprised how frail she felt. But Elen pushed him away and dried her ravaged face. She turned that face away from him and sank deeper into her chair, facing his father's big chair in front of the hearth. The flickering candlelight danced over her face, enhancing the sorrowful shadows, as she stared into the banked fire, clearly watching memories in her mind.

"Mum," he began, then stopped. He went to crouch in front of her and took her hand. "Mum?"

Elen sighed and patted his hand. She took a deep breath and her eyes focused on his.

"*Cariad*," she said in a broken voice that gained strength as she spoke, "you must carry on. I can't do it. I just can't."

"I'll take care of everything, Mum," he promised, wondering what she was referring to—the funeral, the Rider Ceremony, or the move to High Meadow.

His thoughts drifted to the barn where Emma and the other new riders would be getting ready to leave. Someone did need to take charge. Someone needed to make sure the riders who had promised to leave actually went. But High Meadow's barn leader, and his second, were on the receiving end of today's events. They waited in High Meadow for the horses and riders that would save the herd.

Someone needed to lead, but his father was gone. Davyd would have to make this happen himself. He stood up slowly and patted his mother on the shoulder. She stroked his hand gently, smiled crookedly, and turned her attention back to the fire, to the past.

The two women nodded to him. "We'll stay with her," they assured him.

Davyd let himself out the front door and hurried to the barn. He found Emma pacing the walkway outside Adain's stall, still in her ceremonial clothing. The blue and white ribbon was still around her neck, but she had twisted it into a gnarled mess. The other three new riders were nowhere to be seen.

"How is she?" Emma asked, rushing toward him.

"She's with a couple of the other women. Pretty shaken up."

"Oh, shouldn't you stay with her?" Emma's face was stricken.

"Let's get all of you on your way so I can go back upstairs."

But it wasn't that simple. Thomas and Lewes

weren't quite packed, and Angharad had three meltdowns before she finally declared herself ready. Emma, of course, had been ready for days.

Riders who had intended to accompany the four were reluctant now to do so. Davyd tried to point out that nothing had changed. Evan was still in charge of High Meadow's barn, illness still stalked Tremeirchson, and the village was still moving. Older riders who had fooled themselves into thinking they were following Morgan to High Meadow realized their error and temporized.

"It's not that we don't want to go, Davyd," one said. "We just want to pay our respects to your father."

Mutters of agreement rippled through the gathered riders.

He had to go along. Davyd pulled Emma aside just before she mounted Adain. "Tell Evan these riders need a barn leader. Evan must take charge before they decide to follow someone else."

Emma promised to give Evan the message, and finally the four horses were aloft. Only two other riders joined them. Gryffyth had become rider to Adwen, the white mare, just recently. Gwillim had nursed Emyr through the sickness. They were senior riders, experienced, and not from Hoel or Morgan's barns. They were content with their task, leading the way to High Meadow as the sun set over Tremeirchson.

Davyd watched the six horses disappear into the dusk and willed them to hurry, praying Emma would be convincing enough and Evan quickly on his way, somehow understanding the urgency that had begun to plague Davyd. It had taken all afternoon to get the barn settled and the new riders off to Tremeirchson. With trepidation stalking his heart, Davyd trudged wearily home.

***

He opened the door to a flood of color and muted conversation. Flowers of all shapes and sizes covered the Great Hall. The serving girl hurried from kitchen to hall, bringing in platters full of food and taking away empty ones at Neste's direction. The big table groaned with food, and people milled around, trying to help and not knowing what to do. Hoel sat in his father's chair, and riders from a number of barns sat at his feet, hanging on his every word.

Davyd gulped air, trying to breathe through a constricted chest. He felt like an outsider in his own home.

"There you are!" Hoel called to him without getting up. "Got the barn all settled in and the riders off?"

Stunned, Davyd nodded, feeling like he was reporting in to the barn leader. Hoel turned to a rider on his left, dismissing Davyd.

"Where's Mum?" he asked as Neste shoved a plate into his hand.

"Elen's upstairs resting," she murmured.

Davyd slunk into a corner and stirred the food on his plate. The roasted pork and vegetables looked good, but he couldn't eat, staring at Hoel holding court in his rival's home. Finally he found a spot on the table to set his plate and brushed the curls out of his eyes.

No one but him seemed to think it odd that Hoel was so present at Morgan's death. In his mind, Davyd played out a scenario where he stormed over to Hoel and ordered him to leave. Neste, who had tried to help, was helping now, would be offended. The other riders, who were clinging to every word that dripped from the man's mouth, would be angry. Davyd shook his head.

He had to see his mother. Pushing through the crowd, he worked his way across the small room and hurried up the stairs. The fire in the solar had gone out. The curtain to his parents' bedroom was drawn shut. He stepped forward and parted it.

Elen lay on her back, on her side of the bed, as she always had. Morgan's side was empty. The tiny bedroom fire was banked, its orange glow softening the darkness. Davyd let the curtain fall closed behind him and crossed to a straight wooden chair that usually gathered cloaks. He perched on the edge of it and leaned forward. Gently, he laid a hand on the bed. His father's side of the bed was cold. The silk quilt was the finest item his parents owned. His fingers felt rough and clumsy against the rich fabric and fine stitching depicting winged horses in the air. He sat and watched his mother sleep, and the tears finally started streaming down his cheeks.

When he could compose himself, he left his mother with a pat on her hand. Davyd traipsed the upstairs rooms until the candles in the wall sconces burned down to stumps. Finally he went downstairs and braved the darkness of the sickroom.

Carrying one candle, he approached the old bed. He couldn't see the scratches he knew were on the bedposts. The candle illuminated a pale shape, his father's body laid on the bed and covered with a yellowed linen sheet. He looked asleep, and Davyd found himself treading softly to the bedside, as if Da would wake.

The shadows of the candle and the stillness of the night were too much. He fell to his knees and wept. Loss engulfed him, and the tears flowed as his thoughts tumbled. He'd always believed his father's presence was eternal, that he would forever be available to lead, to give advice, to guide. Now Davyd pictured Tremeirchson riders mingling among empty barns, sick and healthy horses stabled together, reckless riders carousing into the night. His personal sense of order had been destroyed, so it was easy to imagine the world order would be, too.

***

Morning found him tired and dreading the day. Evan had not arrived last night, and Davyd must deal with riders and funeral arrangements and his mother's raw emotions. And Hoel. The serving girl had already been in to tend to the fire, and he'd pretended to be asleep. But he couldn't hide here all day. He paced the solar trying to make coherent plans, but his thoughts would not comply. Finally he just brushed his curls out of his face, pushed the curtain aside and walked to his mother's side.

She was rousing but not yet quite awake. The fire in the other room snapped and crackled. Below them, the cook banged pots, a sound he'd always associated with breakfast. Sure enough, the yeasty odor of fresh bread wafted upstairs to tease his nose. Outside the window, the morning was clear, the sky blue. His eyes returned to his mother's face to find her brown eyes intently regarding him.

"*Bore da, Mam,*" he murmured.

She attempted a smile. "Davyd," she whispered, sitting up. "Oh, *cariad.*"

He sat on the bed and reached around her. She leaned into his chest, and they drew comfort from each other for a few long moments. The tears were all cried, and they were too emotionally drained to speak. Yesterday had been hard, and today would be worse.

It fell to Davyd to be stronger. "Get dressed, Mum," he told her. "I will go downstairs and see to…things." She nodded, and he left their rooms.

Downstairs, the mood was subdued. The serving girl and cook were in the midst of preparing an enormous amount of food. He knew people would start to arrive shortly, some to mourn, some to observe, and at least one to take over. He must be in charge by then. Taking a mug of ale and a hunk of warm rye bread slathered with honey, he left the house.

Across the cobblestone yard, the barn was coming to life. Richard was loading his wagon with Owain and Adain's belongings. Davyd could see the young groom running to and fro, gathering last-minute items. Veering in the other direction, Davyd waved at Richard, not wanting to be hit by Owain's enthusiasm.

He skipped Wynne's stall and entered Deryn's. The big stallion munched on the hay in his trough. It was a normal morning around the barn. Davyd sipped his ale and chewed the bread, savoring the sweet stickiness of the honey. Deryn swished his tail and rustled his wings as he ate. Davyd's mind calmed, and he began to sort his priorities. By the time Hoel and Neste appeared, Deryn had finished his breakfast and Davyd was ready.

"How is Elen this morning?" Neste asked as he walked across the yard to greet them.

"She's all right," he said, acknowledging her

concern with a tight smile. "Neste, would you mind supervising the food arrangements while I gather the riders?"

She flicked a glance toward her husband, but answered warmly, "Not at all, Davyd. Don't you worry about anything." She hurried off to the manor.

Davyd turned to Hoel. He refused to let the man fall into the position of leader just because he was an experienced rider. "*Bore da*, Hoel. We need to make an accurate count this morning of how many horses remain in Tremeirchson." He wanted to project confidence, but he didn't dare say "my barn."

Hoel's eyes narrowed a bit, but he replied easily. "I have only Lleu, still healthy." Davyd nodded. "Neste knows where the sick horses are. I'll ask her. Do you want me to count?"

Davyd hesitated. To his relief, his father's remaining two riders came into view, walking toward the barn from their rooms in the manor. Alis and Mared were about the same height and build, both slender and sun-darkened, about Tristan's age.

"*Bore da*," Davyd greeted them.

They returned the greeting and waited, obviously expecting him to direct them. Confidence warmed him. "Would you two help us inventory the remaining horses?" They nodded.

"We can start with our mares. Rhosyn and Rhonwen are hale and hearty this morning," Alis told him with a flirty smile.

Mared was all business. "I remember most of the riders who were planning to go and didn't. I'll have them come here."

"Yes," Davyd agreed. "I want to meet with all riders of healthy horses this morning."

"Let's go then," Hoel said, his lips tight.

Mared and Hoel set off along a lane to the other barns. Davyd and Alis chose another section of barns.

Two hours passed faster than Davyd thought possible. He and Alis trekked up and down barely passable dirt tracks to barns tucked away in the oddest corners. Back at Morgan's barn, she left to check on Rhosyn, and Davyd climbed on the paddock fence. He sat on the top rail and waited. It was another hour before riders began to assemble. He nodded to them but kept silent, allowing them to speculate in murmured conversations as he calculated Richard's time up to High Meadow and back. Evan had better be in that wagon when it returned.

Some of the men and women that gathered at Morgan's paddock were riders without horses, Davyd noted. That made them curious bystanders, nothing more. Hoel and Mared appeared. She joined the growing crowd, and Alis came out of Rhosyn's stall to stand with her friend.

Hoel walked up to Davyd. "In all of Tremeirchson there are sixteen healthy horses," he said in low voice. "Eleven sick."

"Sixteen." Davyd looked up at the empty blue sky. Sixteen winged horses left below skies that had been crowded with them only two weeks ago. He pushed a curl out of his eyes. Eleven sick. He wondered how many would recover, and how well they needed to be before moving. His father had set the precedent of a week. It was all he had to go on.

"Riders!" He raised his voice and they fell silent. They were not welcoming but not hostile. He wasn't, after all, one of them. But he was Morgan's son. "You know that my father planned to move all of the winged horses to High Meadow. Death and disease stalk them here, and it is our sworn duty to protect them. He is no longer here to lead us, but his last wishes are clear. To save the winged herds, we must leave Tremeirchson."

They had seen too many deaths to object. Faint murmurs reached Davyd, but for the most part they watched him silently. A few nodded.

"Please have the sixteen healthy horses here in the paddock immediately after dinner."

He'd let them know he was aware how many horses there were. He'd given them an order. He held his breath. A few men rubbed their necks uncomfortably. Some of the women looked down, hiding their expression behind long hair. Boots scuffed the cobblestones. Davyd waited.

Alis and Mared left the group and headed for the barn. They returned in minutes, each leading a mare that they put into the paddock. Alis went back to the barn and returned with Deryn. Mared slapped Davyd on the back as she resumed her place in the crowd. Alis said loudly, "My Rhosyn will be safe. I guarantee it."

More nods. Davyd began to breathe. The riders drifted away, but he stayed. He watched them go as he watched them come, silently seated above them. Then he went home for dinner.

Neste brought food for him herself. Sliced pork loin

and a chicken leg and fresh biscuits with gravy, beans and peas and a full mug of ale. "*Diolch,*" he thanked her.

"Hoel told me what you said to the riders, Davyd," she said. "Your father would be proud."

"So is Hoel fetching Lleu?"

She laid a hand on his arm. "Everyone has their limits. Hoel will not leave Tremeirchson."

Davyd shook his head. "So how long do we wait for the sick ones to recover?"

"Five will probably be gone by morning." Her voice was flat, but he winced anyway. Five more? "I can watch the remaining six for you."

"Thank you, Neste. You've been very helpful."

"I do this for your mother, Davyd. She once was a dear friend. I hope she will be again."

***

After dinner, Davyd stepped outside. People milled about the yard, and he couldn't see the paddock. Climbing on the paddock fence, he counted, then counted again. Only eleven. Where were the remaining five? He searched the area for Alis or Mared.

"Nicely done, Davyd." Mared materialized at his shoulder, Alis right behind her.

"And the other five? One is Lleu."

She nodded. "Even your father couldn't have convinced them. They've moved into Hoel's barn. Six, including Lleu."

"Six?"

"One of the riders," Alis seemed in a hurry to explain, but then she hesitated. "One insists his horse isn't sick. He moved in with Hoel."

"Well, we'll see," Davyd said. "Meanwhile, we keep

these eleven here and deal with the funeral."

Davyd spent the rest of the afternoon contacting the cleric who lived outside of village up the mountain and arranging for his father's funeral. Rhiannon's spirit clung to the old cleric. He was the most religious person in Tremeirchson, and Morgan deserved the best.

By the time he returned to the village, he had missed supper and night was falling. A wagon stood in front of the barn. Davyd recognized Richard's horses. He hurried to the manor, as eager to bring Evan up to speed as he was to berate him for taking his time.

Chapter 20: Moving Day

The hills sped by underneath them, steepening into the cliffs that would surround their new home. The rush of departure had engulfed Emma, but now they were aloft, each alone with their thoughts, and grief gripped her. As long awaited as her Rider Ceremony had been, and as thrilled as she was to be finally aboard Adain, the events surrounding Morgan's death sobered her. Images of his face haunted her. He'd laughed when he'd seen how surprised she was that he would be her guide. He'd beamed with pride as they flew together. Earlier images appeared of Morgan counseling his riders, sternly rebuking his sons, or lovingly gazing at Elen. She shook away the images but was not surprised to find her cheeks wet with tears. She had lost two fathers, one to angry pride and one to death. The latter she'd never gotten a chance to know, and the former had never tried to really know her.

For early June, the air around Emma was crisp. The thrill of riding Adain hadn't faded, but she was worried about Davyd handling Elen, the funeral, and the barn transition without help. It would be hard for Davyd alone to replace Morgan. She had to get to High Meadow and tell Evan that Davyd needed him.

Not far away, Emma could see Thomas and Lewes looking around, pointing out landmarks to each other. Angharad's earlier confidence returned; she wasn't squealing any more at least. The two older riders leading them, however, were intent on making this a ceremonial procession. That meant slow.

Gryffyth had somehow managed to become rider of Adwen, the white mare that had been offered to Morgan. Emma liked Adwen, but was less thrilled about Gryffyth, whose first horse had died early on. She didn't like Emyr's rider, Gwillim, either. The two men were older, her father's age, and set in their ways. It was a mystery why they had been so quick to volunteer to escort the new riders to High Meadow. They had negative attitudes and complained about everything, but they weren't Morgan's riders, so the barn leader's death hadn't prevented them from making this move now.

She couldn't think that way, Emma realized. Like it or not, these six horses and the five already in place comprised the core of First Barn. They were all High Meadow riders.

Emma sighed as they crossed the last ridge before the valley that contained High Meadow. She recognized this approach. It would take them past the spectacular waterfall, that wonderful source of fresh water that made the new village's existence possible. Gryffyth and Gwillim hovered, allowing Thomas, Lewes, and Angharad to enjoy the view for a minute before continuing.

High Meadow came into view below them, and Emma marveled at the number of tents on the plateau. Tall grass waved from the meadow, welcoming them. She could see two men standing at the cliff edge near the new barn, waiting to greet them. They were very much alike in height and stance, the wind blowing evenly over both. She had no trouble picking out Evan, though her heart fluttered in betrayal. She had been so wrapped up in Davyd and Tremeirchson, she hadn't really thought about Evan beyond giving him Davyd's message.

The other three riders already established in High Meadow hung back, near the barn that seemed to grow out of the hillside. The first few feet of the walls were stone, and above that sheets of leather flapped. Someday the walls would be two and a half stories of wood and clay with a real thatched roof. Someday this would be home.

The six horses landed pretty much at the same time, but Gryffyth and Gwillim were quick to dismount and take up a formal stance near Evan. They turned first to the dainty yellow mare. "Rider Evan *ap* Morgan, I present to you Teleri and Rider Angharad *verch* Matos," Gryffyth intoned.

"Welcome to High Meadow, Rider Angharad," Evan said with a nod.

Angharad looked nervous, and Teleri danced and shied. One of the grooms led Teleri into the barn to get her settled, and Angharad followed, pausing a moment to simper at Tristan. Emma smiled at that, almost wishing Jenett had seen it.

The next horse to be presented was the chocolate brown stallion.

"Rider Evan *ap* Morgan, I present to you Cyffin and Rider Thomas *ap* William."

"Welcome to High Meadow, Rider Thomas."

Emma was proud of Thomas. He was very calm. She saw Evan's eyes narrow, though, and knew he was disappointed that the horse was so dark. Evan wanted to build a herd of light-colored horses.

The other brown stallion was led up next. It was almost her turn, and the urgency to speak to Evan pressed on Emma. Thoughts of Tremeirchson made her eyes well up again, and the unshed tears made it seem as though the entire barn was under water. She must hold off a few more minutes.

"Rider Evan *ap* Morgan, I present to you Llyr and Rider Lewes *ap* John."

"Welcome to High Meadow, Rider Lewes."

Evan barely spared a glance for them, already looking for Emma and Adain as Thomas and Lewes stopped to talk with Tristan.

Gryffyth scowled at Emma's expression before announcing her as he had the others.

"Rider Evan *ap* Morgan, I present to you Adain and Rider Emma *verch* Hoel."

"Welcome to High Meadow, Rider Emma. *Cariad*, what's wrong?"

To her embarrassment, the tears spilled over. A groom took Adain from her. Evan helped her into the barn, taking her to the relative privacy of the area draped off for Clyth's stall.

"I have terrible news." She looked up at him with anguished eyes. "Your father... Morgan was my guide."

She tried a faint smile. Evan squeezed her hand.

"I'm so sorry. *Mae'n ddrwg gen i.* He collapsed after our ride. He's dead, Evan. He was fine while we were flying, really. We came in to land, and he just slid off Deryn and fell right to the ground. Then people swarmed around him and I didn't know what was happening so I dismounted and pushed my way in. Davyd was there, and your father was so pale. Oh, Evan it was awful and I'm so sorry."

Evan's face drained and his mouth fell open. He took Emma in his arms without responding.

"You need to go back to Tremeirchson. Davyd needs you."

"Emma? We must lead the barn," he said softly.

"Which one?" she said, gulping deep breaths to calm her sobs, then wiping her face with her hands.

"Thank you for being the one to tell me."

She nodded again, but didn't meet his eyes. Suddenly Evan was all business. His eyes were far away, calculating which actions were the most pressing.

They left Clyth's stall and found the riders getting to know each other outside. The horses had been introduced to their barn then released to fly in the meadow. Angharad looked worried.

"What if they don't come back?" she asked Tristan as Evan and Emma joined the group.

"They always do," Tristan answered patiently.

Gryffyth already looked irked with Angharad. "New riders are sent to walk 'em down if they don't come back," he said gruffly.

Angharad looked ill.

"My sympathies," Gwillim said to Evan.

"Noted. But no more on that now. We have to

assimilate our new riders."

Gwillim objected, "Your father's death must be discussed. He wasn't just a rider. Wasn't just a barn leader, either. He was the most powerful barn leader in Tremeirchson. His death leaves that end of the moving operation in chaos."

It was a long speech for Gwillim. Evan stared at him. "Davyd is there, and my mother. I won't risk any of our horses returning to Tremeirchson, and Richard isn't due up here with the wagon until tomorrow."

"Tomorrow night, we return," Tristan said.

"Who's in charge here?" Evan said, half teasing, but half angry.

Emma didn't say anything. She was suddenly very much aware of her position as junior rider. A lot needed to be done here, but in Tremeirchson Davyd was fighting for their future. Her father might try to take over the horses remaining in Tremeirchson. He'd probably think it was his right since he'd beaten Morgan by outliving him. She shuddered at the thought. If he kept some horses in Tremeirchson, it would weaken everything Evan was trying to do in High Meadow. That would threaten the integrity of the Aerial Games. Emma knew that the profits from hosting those Games would provide most of High Meadow's income. Patrons might support barns, but the village needed the Games.

On the other hand, her father wouldn't be able to hold an Aerial Games at all with so few horses left in Tremeirchson. Next year would be light enough if all twenty-six horses were in High Meadow. If they didn't all move, no one would be able to have the Games. Her father might consider that an acceptable risk. She just didn't feel she could trust him any more.

She watched Evan directing grooms and riders, feeling detached from reality. This was the beginning of a future she'd wanted for years. It was finally hers, but she wasn't sure she wanted to share it with a man who chose duty over family.

Gryffyth latched onto Angharad and seemed to be filling her head with every concern he could manage. Lewes and Thomas stood a little apart, watching the horses cavort in the meadow, their expressions pleased and proud as they talked with Tristan.

"Our four grooms will come up tomorrow with Richard," Emma said, not looking at Evan. His place was in Tremeirchson with Davyd and Elen even if her father wasn't plotting anything.

"The grooms that are here probably have dinner ready. Let's go inside. They'll whistle the horses in and feed them after we eat."

All ten of his riders followed Evan into the barn where a couple of planks had been nailed together to form a temporary table. The grooms had, indeed, been preparing dinner under Jenett's supervision. The food wasn't fancy, but it was filling. And Jenett was in her element as grooms scurried to do her bidding. For awhile, Emma talked and made plans with her fellow riders, forgetting about Tremeirchson.

Emma didn't have time during the next day to worry about Morgan's death, his family, or the political situation. Richard arrived early with Owain and the other three grooms, trunks for the new riders, and supplies. He was followed by three wagons full of villagers and their lives' belongings. The ensuing flurry of settling in kept everyone busy, and a party atmosphere settled over the village.

Up at the barn, it didn't go so smoothly. First, Gryffyth and Gwillim tried to take over the sleeping area. Evan had to put his foot down and assign rooms. Evan and Tristan, of course, had separate quarters, but the other three original riders were already bunking together. Emma was forced to share with Angharad since there were no other female riders yet. Thomas and Lewes would share, but Gryffyth and Gwillim were furious at the suggestion that they would share.

"I'm senior rider," Gryffyth insisted. "I deserve accommodations that are a cut above these youngsters'."

"We're starting over in High Meadow," Evan declared. "Everyone is equal and everyone is going to pull their weight."

"But son," Gwillim put in, "we have valuable experience to offer."

Emma cringed at his condescending tone. He obviously didn't know Evan well.

Evan jutted his chin toward the older man, and his eyes flashed. "That's *barn leader*," he said in a cold voice. "And everyone will share what they know, no matter where they sleep."

Gryffyth shot a glance at Tristan, and Gwillim continued grumbling, but under his breath while looking at his boots. Tristan met Gryffyth's eyes and stared him down. Emma was relieved that Tristan was clearly supporting Evan.

Next, Angharad, always willing to elevate the

drama, had a meltdown that was a theatrical masterpiece. Emma couldn't help but smile as she watched Angharad perform.

"It's not possible to cram all of my possessions into this diminutive space," she declared, rolling her eyes and waving a hand in front of her face.

"Her trunks set my wagon down on its axles," Richard muttered to Evan.

"He's going back tonight, Angharad," Evan stated. "He can take the leftovers back with him, or you can find someplace in High Meadow to store them. You have half a room."

"I don't need much," Emma whispered, trying to help.

Evan just squeezed her hand and walked away.

Thomas and Lewes managed to disappear with Tristan for most of the afternoon. They didn't return until Angharad was finally settled. Upon arriving, they joined Emma, who was standing on the bluff watching the young horses cavort in the air.

"Where were you two?" Emma asked Thomas and Lewes. "You owe me."

They laughed. "Tristan showed us a great rock near the waterfall where you can sit and watch the horses fly," Lewes told her.

"And the pool under the falls can be made into a very nice swimming area," Thomas added. "May take a lot of work. By strong men. Working alone." He looked up in the air, feigning innocence.

Their joking lightened the darkness that blanketed Emma's heart. She said, "Oh no, you don't! I think Angharad will need to supervise that work."

They groaned good naturedly, and even Emma was smiling when they entered the barn for an early dinner. Tristan caught her elbow as they walked in, allowing the other two riders to go ahead.

"How are things with your father?" he asked in a tone that seemed tinged with genuine concern.

Emma scrutinized his face, wary. This was the man who had tried to elevate his position by courting her, then insulted her when she realized his plan. This was the man who then used a girl hopelessly in love with him to attempt a takeover of a barn he would eventually have gotten anyway. But Tristan really looked concerned. Emma searched his eyes for signs of treachery and found none. "Jenett seems happy here."

He nodded. "Em, look at her." He nodded toward the table groaning with food. Jenett efficiently dispatched grooms to fetch food and drink, and she arranged it all. "She makes me feel alive. And look at all this." His arm swept wide to encompass the large tented barn. "Being a part of this has made me feel needed, more than your father ever did." His eyes came back to hers. "So how is it with you and him?"

Meeting his eyes, impressed with his words, Emma admitted, "It isn't. As far as he's concerned, he no longer has a daughter." She lightly laid her fingertips on his arm. "Or a son."

Tristan squeezed her arm. "I hope it will hurt less in the next days as you find a place here."

"Thank you, Tristan."

She watched him walk toward the food table, more than a little taken aback by the change in him. He took Jenett's hand and kissed it. The girl actually blushed.

High Meadow meant all kinds of change, Emma marveled as Tristan went to join Evan at the head table.

She caught Evan glaring at her as she took a seat with Thomas and Lewes, but he was surrounded by Tristan, Richard and the construction crew. The morning had flown by, and Emma felt guilty that Davyd's urgent request had been so easily forgotten. It wasn't time to suddenly insist they leave, not now. After dinner would have to be soon enough.

Finally, the dinner was done and Richard prepared to leave High Meadow with Evan as a passenger. Evan sat on the wagon seat next to Richard and looked down at Emma.

"It may take a day or two to straighten things out in Tremeirchson," he warned Emma. "Tristan is in charge." He regarded Gryffyth and Gwillim, loitering by the barn, with a nod and a frown.

"Evan? I'd really like to be there for Morgan." She wrapped her arms around herself as Tremeirchson and Davyd and Morgan's death converged on her. Guilt and loss made her feel sick and embarrassed by her earlier banter with the other riders. "Please," she implored him.

"Come on up," he said, making a quick decision.

Before he could rethink it, she leaped aboard and climbed into the back of the wagon. The pair of horses pulling the wagon were ponderous as they moved slowly out of village. How much more wonderful it was to fly! And faster.

On a Wing and a Dare

Chapter 21: Succession

Davyd hovered in the doorway of the manor for a moment as he tried to control surges of relief and anger. Evan and Emma sat at the table with Elen and Neste. The remains of a simple meal lay before them. Emma sat next to her mother, and Neste's hand kept returning to alight briefly on her daughter's arm. Elen spoke softly to Evan, but she seemed stronger than she had that morning. He joined them at the table.

"Welcome to Tremeirchson." He was not able to control the sarcastic tone.

"We came as soon as we could get away," Evan said.

Davyd picked up a chicken leg to gnaw but said nothing. Neste prattled on about the funeral arrangements. He wondered if she'd told Emma what Hoel was up to. Nothing to be done about it yet. His father took priority.

Davyd and Evan checked on the horses in the paddock after supper. Evan recognized some of them, mentally tabulating missing riders. "The strongest are here," he told his brother. "What's the plan for the rest?"

Davyd felt incredulous pleasure spread inside him. Evan was deferring to him in a matter of horses? "First we conduct Da's funeral. Then we regroup."

The sun sank over the barns as the brothers watched Deryn, Rhosyn, and Rhonwen mingle with their eight new stable mates.

All day people had gathered in the Great Hall of the manor house, and the cook and serving girl were hard pressed to keep platters of food coming. Morgan's body had been dressed and prepared in the small sick room. This was where Elen had said goodbye to her life's partner, and where Neste had helped her wrap the body in a white embroidered shroud. At sundown, two riders carried the body to a waiting cart. The cleric led the procession out of the village and up a narrow, well-traveled dirt road to the blackened top of a small hill. Morgan's body, his performing costumes, and his favorite boots were piled on a bier and set aflame.

Flames were passion, or so Davyd had been taught. Aer and Alon and Ystrad blended to temper the fire while you lived. Then in death, passion consumed, finally burning free of any need to hold back. Davyd hoped his father was flying high amidst his dreams. He took a deep breath and turned back to the people gathered on the hilltop. Elen shrunk in on herself as he watched, leaning on Evan. His brother stood ramrod straight, eyes alight as the cleric's chanting faded into the night.

It was full dark by the time the torch lit procession

returned to Tremeirchson, the mourners had gone home, and Elen was tucked up in bed.

Emotionally spent, Davyd walked up to the dry fountain. The quarter moon spilled enough light to bathe the center of town in patterns of pale and dark. Davyd leaned his head against Ystrad's flank and felt some of the tension drain out of his shoulders. Only then did he hear the faint murmurings. Two people sat opposite him on the fountain rim under Aer's rearing hooves. He recognized Emma right away, and Evan a moment later. Feeling sick, he slipped into Ystrad's shadow and leaned toward them. He heard Emma ask a question.

"Of course you are part of my future," Evan responded. "We need to sort out this move to High Meadow and probably break ground for Second Barn. Then we can plan."

Davyd's world tilted dangerously, but he was frozen in place. Was Evan saying he planned to marry Emma someday?

"Oh, Evan," she hesitated. Davyd thought she sounded unsure, but maybe that was just wishful thinking.

Evan's head bent toward hers. Davyd thought he saw Emma pull away slightly before the kiss.

"We'll talk more about this when we return to High Meadow," Evan told her. "Coming? Mum has a room for you at the manor."

"I know, thanks. My mum told me before she went home to her husband." She paused. "I'll just sit here a bit. It's warm and quiet."

"Okay then, sleep well." Evan walked away, his boots loud on the cobbles.

Davyd drew a ragged breath. How could he watch them forever, every day, every holiday, through marriage and the birth of their children? *Na.* He had to be sure that she really wanted Evan and not him. He must tell her how he felt.

He walked around the fountain, aware that he was appearing out of nowhere. She looked up at him, the pale moon washing her face to nuances of white. He took her hand.

"You are Aer," he told her. "Like the magnificent stallion, you are full of dreams. I, on the other hand, am Ystrad, the earth, practical and grounded. Ystrad can nurture the dreams of Aer, but you know what? He has dreams of his own." Davyd took her other hand in his. "*Cariad,* I have loved you my entire life." His eyes searched every shadow in her face, his ears strained for every inflection in her voice.

"Oh, Davyd. . ." She started to smile, but he watched in horror as her eyes welled up and a tear trickled down her face.

She was crying? Because he loved her? Confused, he pulled back and broke eye contact. She mumbled something that sounded like weak protest. Maybe she wanted him to leave. He brushed his curls out of his face, frustration elevating his panic. He'd laid open his heart and she'd just said his name. Nothing else. Suddenly he had to be gone, out of sight, to hide until she left for High Meadow. It was the only way he could possibly salvage any dignity at all.

He stood up, muttered something about seeing to

the horses, and returned to the barn without looking back.

Emma sat motionless on the fountain rim, twin trails of teardrops marring her stricken face, as she tried to understand what had happened. Her evening started with a romantic moonlit walk. Evan held her hand and kissed her in Aer's shadow. But it hadn't felt romantic. Then Davyd had taken her hand and told her he loved her. She should have thrown her arms around him and told him she loved him, too. She'd been so surprised. And now it might be too late. He would think she didn't feel the same way. He would think she loved Evan.

The tears dried up and numbness spread over her. She got up, moving automatically, and wandered back to Morgan's barn. No, Davyd's barn. No, Evan's barn. It didn't matter since tomorrow it would be empty. Her emotions, encased in a thick fog of denial, seemed distant. It didn't hurt there, and it didn't require difficult decisions.

She let herself into the manor house and slipped down the wing opposite the kitchen. A half dozen rooms along the front of the house faced the half dozen rooms along the back. The hallway was narrow, the wooden floor bare. Emma slipped past two closed doors to the room Neste said had been made up for her.

The oak door creaked as she shut it behind her. A single candle burned low in its holder on the bedside table. The bed invited her into a warm sanctuary. She tugged off her tunic and gown and, wearing only her shift, crawled between linen sheets, pulling the blanket over her head for protection. The strange house was silent around her.

Her mother had not been surprised that Emma did not want to go home with her. "It would probably be best," she'd admitted, "for you to stay here."

Emma had no intention of stepping backwards into her father's barn, so she was pleased her mother agreed. It did hurt, though, that her mother was caught in the middle.

She turned over, the straw mattress rustling beneath her, and snuggled into the pillow.

Fairly certain there was no way she could convince her father to leave Tremeirchson with Lleu, she must help Davyd and Evan convince the rest of the riders to go. And there was that rider who insisted his horse wasn't sick. He had put the horse in her father's barn. Emma lay in the half-world between sleep and wakefulness when anything seemed possible. She envisioned Tremeirchson empty of winged horses except for Lleu. Her father and Lleu, alone and wasting away, unable to build a future.

She flung herself on her back, suddenly sweating, and pushed the blanket down to her waist. The cooler air of the dark room wafted over her. Clenching her eyes shut, she willed her mind away from her father.

A future in High Meadow with Evan would allow her to focus on flying Adain. Her days would be full of practice for the Aerial Games, barn politics, and being with Evan. She'd never have to think about a household or a family. That wasn't what she wanted.

She turned back over to her stomach and pulled the

blanket over her now-chilled shoulders.

Davyd offered balance. She'd have to give up some of her devotion to the air, but she'd have his love. They could share a good life and raise a family. They would be part of the village and the barn. And she loved him. Settling into dreams of a new world, she finally slept.

Her eyes opened on a new day. After such a restless night, Emma did not feel refreshed. At least today would be decisive. Whatever happened today would determine High Meadow's future. She allowed herself to feel hopeful. Dawn's promise lingered as she shook out the rumpled gown she'd worn the day before and pulled it over her head. She ran her fingers through her hair, hoping it was at least decent, and took a deep breath as she left the room.

In the Great Hall, leftover meat pie and a pitcher of warmed wine sat on the table. Emma could hear the serving girl and cook bantering in the kitchen, but only Davyd and Elen were at the table. She cut a piece of the meat pie and poured a mug of wine, choosing to take a seat across the table from Davyd so she would not have to sit next to him. Then she had to choose where to look, since her eyes wanted to focus only on him but her mind wanted to be elsewhere. She had to talk to him, alone.

Elen prattled a bit about the barn and the boys growing up. Emma put in a word, an affirmative sound, or a nod, but couldn't relax.

"Did you sleep all right last night?" Davyd asked her.

She had to look at him and pretend she couldn't

read the question beneath the question. *No, your declaration of love kept me up all night.* "As well as could be expected in a strange bed."   She smiled, feeling her lips spread wider than the coy smile she had planned.

He smiled back until he, too, was widely grinning.

Elen seemed oblivious. She asked, "So are you staying around or heading back up to High Meadow today, Emma?"

The question washed the smile from her face, and from Davyd's, too. *I never want to leave your son's side. This son, Davyd.* "I'm not really sure, Elen," she answered, speaking loudly over her clamoring heart.

Davyd excused himself and vanished out the main door. The cook beckoned to Elen from the kitchen door, and she left to deal with the staff. Sitting alone at the big table, Emma stared into the fire and tried to make plans for the day.

Her father would cause trouble. That was for sure, no matter how much her mother tried to guide him. She ate a few bites of a meat pie, considering how to help. If her father saw her, his fury would cloud his judgment even further. Emma decided to steer clear of her father.

Evan and Davyd would be getting the healthy horses ready to leave for High Meadow. Last night Evan had told her about Davyd's attempts to secure their father's barn. He'd sounded somewhat critical, but Emma had been impressed and silently cheered for Davyd's leadership. It was vital that the other riders see Evan as the leader they needed. She could show them she followed Evan.

But somehow today she would have to put into words what her half-asleep mind and heart had told her.

She had to tell Davyd she loved him, not Evan. Maybe she should tell Evan first. Her fingers tapped nervously on the table. She picked up the mug to still them and took a few sips. It seemed selfish somehow to put her feelings on par with moving the horses to High Meadow.

Still without a firm course of action, she picked up her mug, refilled it with the warm restorative wine, and ventured outside.

The day had moved on much further than she had thought. Midmorning, she estimated by the amount of activity around the barn. Wagons rumbled past, some loaded but some empty. Riders hurried back and forth, clearly on important errands. Alis and Mared were helping to load one wagon with what appeared to be their horses' gear. Emma could see no sign of her parents, nor of Elen. Evan and Davyd leaned on the paddock fence, where it appeared the eleven healthy horses were still enclosed.

They looked up as she approached. Evan's smile was quicker than his kiss, cold on her cheek. Davyd smiled, but his eyes didn't meet hers.

"*Bore da,*" she said to Evan, her eyes on his brother.

Davyd mumbled something about seeing to loading the wagon and walked away. Emma sighed, an exasperated exhalation. Evan's first words to her were, "So, you ready to take a load of supplies up to High Meadow for me?"

Irritated, Emma snapped, "Do I work for you now?"

"Actually, you do," Evan reminded her with a

frown. "Adain belongs to my barn and you belong to Adain."

"So you don't need my help here." It wasn't a question and she didn't expect an answer. Still troubled by her sleep-eluding thoughts of the night before, she asked, "What do you see for us?"

"You'll take all the supplies up to High Meadow while Davyd and I prepare to move the rest of the horses."

That wasn't what she meant. She searched his eyes for something more than business. Had it ever been there or had she been a fool?

She turned away from him and walked away from the barn, up to the fountain, aware he followed. Ystrad, the earth horse, baked in the morning June sunshine while Aer was on the shady side. Laying a hand on Ystrad's flank she tried to feel Davyd's love. Evan may want her in his future, but he had never said he loved her. She continued around the fountain and stopped in front of Alon, the water horse. Water people would go with the flow, follow Evan's plans no matter where they led. She couldn't do that.

She completed her circuit of the fountain and Evan gave her an amused look.

"Come on, don't be mad. You may be a junior rider in my barn, but I rely on you for more than that. I can't be seen to lean on you too much, but when I'm leading First Barn you will be there with me. You do understand that I can't show favoritism, right?"

Emma wrinkled her brow and peered at him, her thoughts awhirl. He wanted her to give him advice secretly? "Are you ashamed of me?"

Evan laughed. "Of course not. But I have to keep control until Tristan is safely established in Second Barn. I'm going to have to make nice with everybody."

"I loved you, you know," Emma murmured, wondering if he would hear the past tense.

Evan had already turned back to the barn. "Yeah, me too," he tossed over his shoulder.

Dissatisfied, Emma followed him back to the storeroom. She was disappointed when she didn't see Davyd. Evan tossed boxes off his brother's neatly stacked shelves.

"Evan, we can't do this."

"Do what?" He was genuinely confused.

"I may ride for First Barn, but I am not going to be your girlfriend."

He stopped rearranging boxes and stared at her. "Where did that come from?"

"Too much is happening, Evan. I need a fresh start." Lame, lame, lame, her brain taunted her.

His eyes narrowed, but before he could respond Richard drove up in the wagon. He came into the storeroom and began loading boxes. Emma and Evan remained eye-locked for another full moment before Evan pulled away and brushed past her.

"*Helo*," he greeted Richard. "Emma will go with this shipment to High Meadow."

Richard glanced at the boxes and nodded. Turning to Emma, he asked, "Ready to leave in an hour?"

Emma looked at Evan. He was totally absorbed in the stored supplies. She wanted to talk to Davyd before they left. "Sure," she told Richard.

The rest of the hour sped by, filled with wagon

273

packing and list checking, but Davyd had disappeared. Finally Richard climbed onto the driver's seat and picked up the reins. He lifted his eyebrows at Emma as she hesitated and turned to Evan.

"Tell Davyd. . ."

"Yeah, I'll tell him you went back to High Meadow." Evan waved a hand, dismissing her and encouraging her to get in the wagon at the same time.

Frustrated, she climbed onto the high seat. When she looked up, she saw Davyd coming toward them. Her heart leaped and she opened her mouth to call to him. Evan's voice chilled her.

"My girl's taking the supplies up to High Meadow," he told Davyd. Emma cringed at the anger in his tone when he said *my girl*.

Davyd's face fell even as his eyes sought hers. Richard clucked to the horses and the wagon pulled away. Emma only had time to call Davyd's name and wave. Then Richard turned the corner and she couldn't see the brothers any more.

She slumped in her seat. Davyd would think she'd chosen Evan. He would think she didn't even want to talk to him. If only she could jump out of this wagon and run back! But Evan was sneaky. He was probably already filling Davyd's head with insinuations.

Emma took a deep breath. She may be a High Meadow rider, but she was not Evan's property. Friends were still hers to choose, and she chose Davyd. "Richard, I forgot something. I'll just run and get it, all right?"

The wagon driver nodded and pulled up the team of horses. Emma was off the seat and running back down the road before he had time to say anything. Evan had already disappeared, but Davyd stood in the road, staring in the direction she'd gone. He didn't move as she ran up, breathless, but a smile lightened his eyes.

"Oh, Davyd," she panted. "I couldn't leave without telling you..."

"I love you," he said, and she wasn't sure if he was finishing her sentence or speaking for himself.

"*Dw i'n dy garu di*," she whispered it in Welsh, and he bent his head toward hers.

All the troubles of the world vanished as he kissed her. She kissed him back, then pulled away and smiled. She hadn't seen him so happy in a long time. Hand in hand, he walked her back to Richard's wagon. Before lifting her onto the seat, he kissed her again. When the team resumed its journey, Richard was smiling, too, but Emma pretended not to notice.

On a Wing and a Dare

Chapter 22: Tremeirchson

After they'd gone, Davyd looked over the paddock, not really believing what he saw. Eleven healthy horses left in Tremeirchson. Plus the six at Hoel's barn, of course. He'd heard riders talking about moving today, but resistant mutters among them persisted. This wasn't going to go smoothly. Eleven horses.

Emma had left for High Meadow and he already missed her. At least he knew she was his, and that promise made him smile in spite of the grimness surrounding his father's death and the riders' stubbornness.

Evan approached, walking toward Davyd from one of the barns where the sick horses were confined. "Couple more gone," he reported. "At least they're dying more slowly."

One of the morning's dead had been the stall mate of the horse that had been moved to Hoel's barn. His rider had insisted it was well. Now its stall mate was dead. Was the other horse showing fever? It already may be too late to save them all. Time to get out of the village.

And that reminded him of last night, after Emma

had cried when he told her he loved her. Returning to the house, Davyd had looked around the room, noticing the wall sconces filled with new candles, the tapestries still on the walls, and the trunks closed tight. His mother hadn't started packing. Most villagers that were moving to Tremeirchson had left already, and barn people were going tomorrow. Elen wasn't a rider any more, but she was more than a villager.

"Mum? Why aren't you packed?"

The serving girl put the laden dinner plates on the table and scurried back to the kitchen.

"I'm not going," Elen had said firmly.

"What?"

"What is there for me in High Meadow? Wynne is gone, and I'm to watch other horses fly all around me? Morgan is gone, and I'm to watch someone else lead his riders? *Na*, I am content here. This is my place."

Davyd mentally reviewed the crowded conditions at First Barn and shook his head. There was no place for her there. And she was right. There was no place for her in the village yet either.

"We'll visit you, Mum. We will." His voice was anguished. The words sounded weak.

"I know it, *cariad*." She had patted his hand, but her tone implied she knew they would be too busy.

Today Davyd wondered how long it would be before he stopped feeling guilty about allowing his mother to stay here alone. He scanned the paddock for Deryn. The big stallion seemed crowded in the paddock with ten other horses, wings and tails aflutter. He moved around the fence to where he could talk to his father's mount.

"Deryn, *del*," he murmured, a hand on the warm neck. "Everything's changed for you, hasn't it? You were the barn leader's stallion, now you're riderless. We'll get you a rider, *del*, and a new stall. Wait 'til you see the meadow, Deryn. Fabulous place to fly."

Davyd knew a rider for Deryn was not a pressing issue, but he couldn't help wondering who they could possibly put on his father's horse. They'd been a great team. But Evan would need Deryn in the air come next year's Aerial Games. At least he was confident his brother wouldn't try to put him aboard the big stallion.

He looked up Aer Road toward the fountain. Tremeirchson was quiet. Very few people were around. Davyd shook his head, not understanding why his mother would stay. Nothing would be here when the horses, the riders, the grooms, and all their families were gone.

Unlike the rest of Tremeirchson, the barns were a flurry of activity. Davyd went to find Evan, who was directing the removal of bodies from a barn.

"How many, Evan?"

"Six, and four more will be gone by nightfall according to Neste."

Davyd nodded. That left only the one that had moved to Hoel's barn. "Come on, the riders are waiting for us in the paddock."

Deryn stood alone among the other ten horses and their riders. Not all of them were saddled. Frowning, Davyd waited for Evan to speak.

"Riders, your horses are the last healthy beasts in

Tremeirchson. To save them we must leave now." His ringing voice radiated confidence.

"Evan, we appreciate what you are trying to do," a female rider said.

Davyd peered, but did not recognize the petite brunette.

She continued, "We have discussed the situation among ourselves and it's fair to say we don't agree. A couple are ready to go with you. Some are still not sure. I, for one, will stay in Tremeirchson. I have good friends who have lost mounts and need my support."

Davyd shook his head. She must be an earth person, channeling her nurturing spirit toward her friends. Normally that would be wonderful, but these were far from normal times.

"Your duty is to your own mount," Evan said firmly.

"Are you saying my horse is neglected?"

Davyd interrupted. "Moving to a new village is a huge decision. I respect your right to stay." In a low voice, he muttered to Evan, "We can send those who are ready now and take the rest as soon as we can."

Evan nodded and began moving through the group, ascertaining which were ready. He was grim when he returned to where Davyd waited.

"Three."

"Three?" Davyd asked. "We have to convince seven?"

Evan shook his head. "The two near the back are nervous, acting odd. Watch them."

Davyd picked out the riders his brother meant, and moved to where he could observe them without appearing to. The riders were, indeed, nervous. Hand gestures fluttered, voices were high pitched. Their horses, too, shifted weight from side to side.

Alis and Mared came up with another female rider Davyd didn't recognize. All three were helmeted and ready to go.

"We'll be off. I'll tell them to expect you soon with the rest of Tremeirchson's herd," Alis said to Evan.

"We'll be there," Evan promised.

The rest of the riders stood by as the three horses took off and headed into the mountains. Davyd watched the group on the ground until their eyes turned from the sky to his brother.

"What now, rider?" one asked.

"First, your horses. Put feed down for them and fill the trough in the paddock with water from the barrel. Then we meet."

Evan waited while the riders cared for the horses milling in the paddock. Davyd took care of Deryn, but watched how the other riders interacted with each other. They had to focus on getting these seven out of the village. Four men and three women stood in a loose group, no obvious alliances other than the two Tristan had picked out. Davyd recognized none of them.

"You all have different reasons for staying. I don't care what they are. It's really an easy matter. You either agree to go with me to High Meadow, or we wait here until all your horses die. Could be a matter of days, could be weeks."

Davyd cringed at Evan's harsh tone, and saw the same two riders that had been acting strangely earlier burst into animated discussion with each other.

"It's not that simple, Rider Evan."

The petite brunette again. Evan waited. She wilted under his gaze and subsided.

"You are to return to your horses and stay there. Your grooms are welcome to move around and acquire whatever you need."

The riders left, muttering unhappily.

Davyd stopped the two riders, the last to leave. "So what's going on?" One of them started to object, but Davyd held up his hand. "What's going on?" he repeated.

Heads bowed, eyes on the ground, they muttered and stalled. Davyd and Evan waited. Finally, one spoke up. "My horse was stabled near Elwyn. He's the one who's supposed to be well and moved to Hoel's barn. He didn't eat yesterday, and I hear Lleu didn't eat this morning. I didn't want to tell anyone."

"They're all gonna die," the other rider said in a grim voice.

"Oh, Rhiannon," Davyd breathed. Six more to fall sick and die because of one rider's stupid decision. He looked over the small herd of horses in the paddock, then back at the pair before him.

The riders shuffled their feet nervously. The taller one glared until the short round one haltingly admitted, "My horse had diarrea this morning. I didn't want to tell anyone."

Davyd dropped his voice to icy calm. Good men and women, responsible riders, had lost their horses, yet these morons still had mounts. "Do you realize you have exposed all the horses to this illness?"

Evan could barely contain his fury. "If the three that

just left carry this illness to High Meadow, you may well have wiped out every winged horse in existence."

"Are you going to lock us up?"

Evan looked daggers at the man. "What more can you do? You've already threatened everything I've worked my entire life for. I recommend you stay out of my sight, though, or I may have to kill you."

His tone must have convinced them. They scampered away.

Davyd undertook a sweep of empty barns in Tremeirchson to keep his mind busy. Making sure no one was hiding a sick horse was critical. He found nothing, but left Hoel's barn for last.

Hoel sat outside the barn, on a bench Davyd didn't remember being there.

"Rider Hoel. I hear Lleu's not eating."

"You come to gloat, Davyd? Stealing my daughter was not enough?"

Davyd fought down his natural reaction to this man who could so easily boil his temper. In a forced casual voice, he said, "Your daughter rides for Evan." His tone conveyed a deeper meaning.

"And Lleu is ill."

Davyd nodded.

Hoel indicated the barn. "It truly is a curse, after all." He'd aged greatly in the last twenty-four hours. He looked old and tired now, not a powerful barn leader and certainly no threat to High Meadow.

"Will he recover?" Davyd asked simply.

"Neste doesn't know," he said bleakly.

"I'm sorry," he told Hoel.

"Leave me, Davyd, *bachgen*."

Davyd complied, returning to his father's barn and the seven remaining healthy horses in Tremeirchson. He stabled each of them in a stall of their own in his family's barn, returning Deryn to his own stall. He relit fresh buckets of thyme, and opened a barrel of water from High Meadow. He was keeping busy. None of it would matter if they all died.

For two days, Davyd cared for Deryn while Evan met individually with the grooms, then with the riders, careful to keep his distance. Only riders could visit the horses, and only their own horse. No one would go from stall to stall and risk spreading illness. Even so, Davyd wasn't surprised when the two riders' mounts started fevers. The other riders panicked, then, but Evan was adamant. If the illness had not already spread to High Meadow, he was not about to bring it there. They would wait a week. Any horse who was not dead would move to High Meadow then.

On the third day, the first horse died. Villagers that were still in Tremeirchson avoided the death vigil at Morgan's barn. Even Elen stayed away, and Davyd didn't go to see her. Asking anyone to witness this was inhumane. Neste stayed away, too, but he knew she was holding her own death vigil at Hoel's barn.

By the fourth day, the other horse had died and the remaining riders were clamoring to leave. Davyd thought it was ironic that now they all wanted to go. If every infected horse in village had died, he told the others, then it wouldn't hurt to wait out the week. They had to be absolutely sure that no sickness was transported to High Meadow. That afternoon Richard drove up in the wagon with five barrels of fresh water. He refused to leave the wagon, so Davyd and Evan unloaded the barrels themselves. At least Richard was able to confirm that all of High Meadow's horses remained well.

The morning of the fifth day dawned, and only three of the remaining four riders appeared for their morning meeting. Davyd sought out the fourth, who was weeping over a feverish horse. He kept his distance and grimly returned to Deryn.

During the night, the remaining four horses began to show symptoms. The sixth day brought chaos as angry riders tried to blame Evan, who could do nothing for them. He barricaded himself and Davyd in with Deryn, desperately feeding the horse and checking his temperature. Deryn ate until he was stuffed then slept all afternoon.

Davyd thought of his mother, and hoped she wasn't worrying about them. Emma would be worried, too.

"I hope Emma isn't being tormented by Gryffyth and Gwillim. They can be a bit imperious."

Startled by his brother's thoughts also being on Emma, Davyd responded, "She'll do what is best for Adain."

"Adain is her one true love," Evan responded.

"Adain? Not you?" He couldn't quite pull off a teasing tone, but he had to know if Emma had spoken to Evan.

Evan waited a long minute. Deryn shifted his

weight with a rustling of feathers. Outside the stall, all was quiet. "I don't have time for love right now. She understands."

Davyd wasn't sure about that, but he didn't know how to respond. The conversation subsided as the two men were overcome with physical and emotional exhaustion.

When the seventh day drew to a close, Davyd cracked open the stall door to a violent orange sky with clouds purpling as the sun streaked for the horizon. Evan walked the length of the barn, checking every echoing stall. People saw him, and gathered in quiet groups, watching. Some wore accusing looks, some angry, some were just numb. They had no friends left in this village, Davyd realized.

One of the riders stepped forward, his face drawn. "They're all dead," he said dully.

"*Mae'n ddrwg gen i,*" Davyd said. "I am truly sorry."

Stretching cramped legs, he walked down the lane to Hoel's barn. One of the smaller barns was empty, its door hanging open on a loose hinge as if it had been abandoned decades ago instead of days. Hoel sat on the same bench as the previous week, his face pale. This time Neste sat with him, her knuckles white where she clutched her husband's hand. She shook her head as Davyd tilted his head and raised his eyebrows in unspoken query. Hoel didn't react at all.

Davyd entered the barn. Nothing was as deafening as silence in a place that once held commotion. His boots thundered as he walked the length of the barn. Lleu's body still lay in his stall, alone. No other stalls were occupied. The presence of the dead weighed heavily, suffocating him. He left without a word to any, living or dead.

He returned to Morgan's barn. It would never be Davyd's barn, or Evan's barn. It would never again be a barn. A few people skulked in the shadows, but no one came near. Evan led Deryn from his stall. Frisky from inaction, Deryn danced and tossed his head. The sun shone off his healthy coat and sparkled off his wings. The stallion's ringing neigh echoed off Tremeirchson's empty barns. The exuberant show of life did little to stave off the gloom settling over the village.

"Catch a ride up with Richard," Evan told Davyd.

He mounted and galloped down Aer Road, leaping into the air over the fountain. As the last rays of sunshine gilded both stone and feathered wings, Evan rode Tremeirchson's last winged horse out of the village.

Thundering hooves, at odds with the serenity of Deryn's flight, drew the attention of the gathered people. Sweated horses drawing a fancy carriage pulled up in the courtyard. Before the driver could hop down and open the door, it swung open. Lord Farley climbed out and scanned the hovering groups of people.

Davyd stepped forward, not bothering with a welcoming smile. "Lord Farley."

The patron peered at him. "Who are you? Where's Morgan?"

"*Syr*, I am his son, Davyd. Morgan is no longer the leader of this barn. He's gone, *syr*."

"Gone? Who leads?"

A young boy, face red with effort, dragged a huge

ledger out of the carriage and stood behind the lord. Padrig's replacement. Davyd could think of no reason to be civil to this man and before his sense of duty told him otherwise, he said, "Lord Farley, there are no more winged horses in Tremeirchson. They are all dead or gone to High Meadow, where Lady Margery is patroness to the town and First Barn."

With a nod, Davyd walked past the gaping lord to Robert, waiting with his wagon near the manor door. Davyd considered going inside to take leave of his mother, but he'd really already done that. He climbed up beside Robert. "On to High Meadow," he said. Robert flapped the reins and called to his horses, urging them out into the line of wagons beginning to move out of town. No one looked back.

Chapter 23: The Future

A year later, Emma readied Adain for their first Aerial Games. First Barn was complete now, all mortared stone topped with timbered walls, perched proudly on the hillside above the town. Adain stood patiently in his stall while Owain curried him. Emma braided blue and white ribbon into his mane and thought of Wynne. One year and so much tragedy since that terrifying flight on Wynne.

"I've got this, Emma," Owain said. "Go outside and enjoy the morning."

"Thanks, Owain." Emma gave him a warm smile before leaving Adain in his capable hands.

She walked through First Barn, buzzing with activity as riders and grooms prepared for the Dance of Welcome. It still gave Emma a thrill to see every horse glossy with health, every wing shining, every eye bright. The barn boasted three pregnant mares, the future of High Meadow.

Outside, the wind was warm for early spring, especially in the mountains. Next to First Barn and slightly below it, the first rows of stone outlined Second

Barn, which would be completed during the summer. In the town below, tents were still more common than permanent homes. All of the villagers' energy had gone into completing High Meadow Inn, the tavern next to it, and a row of three shops, all overlooking the meadow below the plateau. Emma could see visitors leaning out the windows of the inn, and taking their ale on the tavern's courtyard, watching the sky. The blacksmith and the baker were busy in their new shops, as were the carpenter and mason, who temporarily shared one facility. Word had reached them from Davyd that no one from Tremeirchson had come for the Games, but Main Street, in front of the shops, was crowded with people from Merioneth and beyond.

Restless, Emma paced the cliff edge. Today was bigger than the Aerial Games that would launch High Meadow to the world. It was more important than Adain's first efforts in a coordinated aerial dance. After today's Dance of Welcome, today she would be married. A delighted smile spread across her face, pushing the nerves aside. She peered toward the tavern, hoping to catch a glimpse of the groom.

Evan's voice rang out behind her, calling the riders to assemble, and she hurried back to Adain. No time now for pondering the future or thinking about nerves. She swung aboard Adain as he shook out his wings and stamped his foot.

Aboard Clyth, Evan was the perfect barn leader, with Tristan, aboard Bryn, beside him. Alis and Mared flanked the leaders, Rhosyn and Rhonwyn tossing their heads in perfect time. Emma and Adain took their place in the middle of the formation with the other youngsters.

Thomas and Cyffin were becoming a strong team, and Lewes had greatly improved aboard Llyr. Angharad squealed as Teleri danced. Emma rolled her eyes and Thomas chuckled. Gwillim and Gryffyth, mounted on Emyr and Adwen, came next. Four more riders and their mounts arranged themselves around the edges. Emma saw Evan's face flinch as Deryn was led from the barn. It had been his decision to put Catrin on his father's stallion, but it must look odd to see her there. Catrin's broken leg had healed well. On the surface, anyway, she seemed to be over the accident last year that had taken her mare's life.

The trumpets blared the familiar fanfare and the fifteen horses took to the sky. Emma was sure hers were not the only damp eyes. High Meadow's first Aerial Games, but so many favorites were missing. The brilliant blue sky would set off the horses, though, and each one had its moment of splendor before they arranged themselves for the Dance of Welcome. The crowd erupted into cheers as the band began to play.

Emma and Adain swooped and swirled in the simple pattern Evan had worked out. The horses had never flown in formation together, and aerial precision took more than a few months to perfect. This simple dance was symbolic, though, a statement that High Meadow's winged horses were alive and well. A final flourish of wings, and the horses circled in to land.

Below, the people cheered the Dance of Welcome and crowded into the tavern for a noon meal.

At First Barn, the horses landed and riders

dismounted. Evan was in his glory, accepting congratulations from fawning grooms and riders alike. Tristan stood at his side with Jenett beside him. Emma turned her back on her barn mates and started down the hillside to the tavern, where Davyd and Robert, High Meadow's new mayor, would be regaling the crowd with town plans.

Her heart thumped from more than the downhill walk. She had scant hours until her wedding. Positive she was making the right decision, Emma nonetheless had to force herself to take deep, calm breaths.

"Emma! Wait, I'm coming, too!" Jenett hurried up behind her. "Can't have you getting ready for this big day all alone!"

Emma laughed, but the other girl's words stung like darts. Her mother should be here, but she had chosen to stay in Tremeirchson with Hoel, whom Emma had not called 'Da' since the morning of her Rider Ceremony. Davyd's mother wouldn't be here either. Elen had broken off contact with her sons, as most of Tremeirchson had pulled away from High Meadow.

"Have you heard that in Tremeirchson they blame us for taking all the winged horses away?" she asked Jenett.

"I know." If Jenett was surprised where Emma's thoughts were this morning, she did not show it. "It's not even been a full year and no one remembers the true story."

"I do," Emma said. "I'll remember."

"Me too."

The girls continued in silence until they neared the tavern. Emma's face lit up when she saw the leaded glass windows. They'd arrived from Merioneth yesterday.

Davyd and Robert had worked all night to have them in place today. She was excited to see how nice they looked.

Jenett pulled her past the tavern. "*Na*, you can't go in and see him. Bad luck! Come on!"

They continued to the High Meadow Inn. Jenett stopped long enough to order hot water and a meal before they slipped up the kitchen stairs. Jenett's room was so disarrayed it looked as though ten women lived there. It was still better than Emma's room in the barn, shared with Angharad.

A serving girl brought up two buckets of hot water and dumped them into a two big basins. Jenett handed a washcloth to Emma, who stripped off her riding clothes and set about removing the smell of sweat and horse from her skin. Jenett poured lavender scent into the water, and Emma let the warm lavender tease her nose as Jenett's chatter teased her ears.

Glowing from a brisk towel dry, Emma stepped into her shift. She sat on a stool as Jenett worked on her hair, combing and brushing and pinning. Emma closed her eyes and allowed the tugging and twisting to lull her. When it stopped, she opened her eyes and looked into Jenett's hand mirror. Her long chestnut hair had been arranged around her head like a crown. A dainty wreath of meadow flowers would be pinned there later.

"Ohhhh," she breathed softly. "You made it look beautiful, Jenett."

The other girl didn't answer. She carefully lifted the creamy satin gown over Emma's head.

Emma felt it settled into place with a cool swoosh of fabric. The sleeves were belled wide at the wrist, hanging almost to her knees. The bodice laced up from the waist to a modest square neckline. The edges of sleeve, neck, and hem were thickly decorated with gold braid and embroidery.

"Oh, you look like a princess," Jenett said.

"I feel like one," Emma smiled.

Jenett helped her into the white lace-up shoes that matched the satin of the dress, and she was ready. While Jenett dressed, Emma stood at the window and looked out over the meadow. The land dropped away from the plateau that housed the town so that the meadow proper was quite a ways below them. Horses flew, a few with riders, just playing in the air. Emma realized this was the first day in the last year she had gone all morning without seeing Davyd. In just a little while, she'd be with him forever.

Supremely relieved that Robert had forced him out of the tavern, Davyd ran to the little house that he would share with Emma after their wedding that afternoon. It was the last site that was still in town before you headed up the track to the barn. Constructed of stone, it was little more than a kitchen, hall, and sleeping room, but it was a beginning. And it would be theirs.

He changed quickly into the new clothes Lady Margery had provided. At first, he'd been reluctant. She'd tried to tell him that the wedding was symbolic of High Meadow's future, and that the town's leading man and the barn's leading woman had to be suitably attired. Davyd and Emma had no way to acquire appropriate clothing themselves, so they'd agreed. Lady Margery had hugged them, betraying that she cared for them.

Now he put on the fine black silk shirt and thick woolen doublet, fingering the laces and stitching. They were excellent garments and made him feel like a prince. There was no time to dawdle, though. He hurried to put on the black pants and boots that completed the outfit and hoped Emma liked her dress.

It wasn't long before he was outside again, and Robert pulled up in the wagon.

"Climb on up here, if you can," he told Davyd. "I promised your lady I'd deliver you clean and on time."

Davyd laughed and jumped into the wagon. The horses pulled it down Main Street past the shops, the tavern, and the inn. Beyond the inn was a slight rise wreathed in short spring grass. As the legal representative of High Meadow, Robert would perform the ceremony. They had only to wait for Emma. And the guests, of course.

Lady Margery was the first to arrive. Clad simply, for her, in a maroon gown, she was accompanied by a lad that Davyd assumed was her new steward. After their conversation a year ago about the poisoning, he'd never asked her again about her husband. In August, she'd told Davyd that her husband was undertaking a pilgrimage to a holy city in the east, to pray for a cure. Accompanied by a retinue of servants and traveling in a litter, he'd be gone a year. She'd not spoken of him again.

Her visits to High Meadow stopped over the winter, when the mountains became too cold for travel. In spring, though, she'd been there often enough to stake her claim to town and barn. Davyd knew that Tristan would use this Aerial Games to court patrons for Second Barn. They had to have competition. Lady Margery knew it, too.

"Ah, you look splendid, Davyd," she said.

He leaned in to kiss her on the cheek. "Thank you for everything," he whispered into her ear.

She protested it was nothing but smiled and flushed like a girl.

The guests arrived, and happy chatter wafted over Davyd and Robert as they stood apart. Then the back door of the inn opened, and Jenett led Emma into view. Davyd couldn't tell if his heart had stopped or it was beating too fast to count the beats. She was a princess, and she was to be his. Evan and Tristan stepped up to stand with him as Jenett and Emma joined them.

The mountain breeze swirled through the town. It cooled the spectators and lifted the wings of the horses in flight. Teasing its way through doorways and windows, it tickled townspeople's noses as if counting those that belonged. On the very tip of the plateau, the breeze split around Davyd and Emma, standing with clasped hands. It twirled her skirts and tossed his curls before plunging over the edge and sweeping down a valley where not a single nimberry bush grew.

Davyd didn't notice.

Emma's hair, topped with a wreath of bluebells, milkwort, buttercups, and the tiny white bedstraw flowers, gleamed in the late afternoon sun. He clasped both of her hands in his, wondering if the glorious promise of their future shone as brightly from his own eyes as it did from hers.

Emma squeezed his hands. "I love you," she

whispered.

"I love you, too," he said.

The rest of the ceremony was just for show. The important words had been said.

On a Wing and a Dare

Appendix A: Welsh Pronunciation

Welsh	Pronunciation	English
ap	ap	son of
bachgen	BAHKgen	little boy
bore da	BORe daH	good morning
cariad	CARRYad	darling
cer o'ma	KER o ma	get away
del	dehl	pretty, love
diolch	deeOLKH	thanks
diolch yn fawr iawn	uhn vowrr yown	thanks a lot
Dolydd Uchel	doLEETH ixel	High Meadow
dydd da	DEETH daH	good day
dw i'n dy garu di	doo een duh GARee dee	I love you
helo	heLO	hello
hwyl	hooil	goodbye
iawn	yown	okay
mae'n ddrwg gen i	MINE drewg gen ee	I'm sorry
mam	maam	mom
na	nah	no
na drueni	nah dreeENee	a real shame
syr	sir	sir
tad	tad	father
tew	too	fatso
verch	ferk	daughter of

On a Wing and a Dare

Appendix B: List of Characters

In Morgan's Barn (colors: green and gold)
People:

    Alis: rides Rhosyn

    Ana: groom to Clyth

    Davyd: 16, son of Morgan & Elen, not yet rider

    Delana: groom to Hefin

    Elen: wife of Morgan, mother of Davyd & Evan, rider of the mare Wynne

    Evan: 18, son of Morgan & Elen, rider of the stallion Clyth

    Mared: rides Rhonwyn

    Morgan: Barn Leader, husband of Elen, father of Davyd & Evan, rides the stallion Deryn

    Owain: young groom to Adain

Horses:

    Adain: pale brown colt of Wynne by Deryn, groom is Owain

    Clyth: tan stallion, rider is Evan, groom is Ana

    Deryn: brown stallion, rider is Morgan

    Hefin: chocolate brown colt, groom is Delana

    Rhosyn: bay mare, rider is Alis

    Rhonwyn: chestnut mare, rider is Mared

    Wynne: white mare; rider is Elen

In Hoel's barn (colors blue and silver):
People:

    Catrin: rider of Bronwyn

    Elynor: rider of Mael

Emma: 16, daughter of Hoel and Neste
Hoel: Barn Leader, husband of Neste, father of
    Emma, rider of Lleu
Neste: wife of Hoel, mother of Emma, former
    rider of Llawen
Tristan: 20, rider of Bryn
Horses:
    Bryn: black stallion, rider is Tristan
    Gareth: stallion
    Gwen: pregnant mare
    Llawen: deceased brown mare, rider was Neste
    Mael: brown mare, rider is Elynor
    Pedr: black colt
    Rhys: colt
In High Meadow:
People
    Angharad: rider of Teleri
    Gryffyth: older rider of Adwen
    Gwillim: older rider of Emyr
    Lewes: rider of Llyr
    Thomas: rider of Cyffin
Horses
    Adwen: white mare, rider is Gryffyth
    Cyffin: chocolate brown stallion, rider is
        Thomas
    Emyr: light brown stallion, rider is Gwillim
    Llyr: brown stallion, rider is Lewes
    Teleri: dainty light mare, rider is Angharad
In Tremeirchson:
    Jennett: waitress with a crush on Tristan

John: Barn Leader of a smaller barn
Kenn: the apothecary
Ranald: the tailor
Reynallt: mayor of Tremeirchson
Richard: road builder, Robert's brother
Robert: tavern keeper, Richard's brother
In Merioneth:
Lady Margery: patroness of Morgan's barn
Lord Farley: patron of Hoel's barn
Padrig: Lord Farley's steward
Soirus: Lady Margery's steward

On a Wing and a Dare

Appendix C: How it All Began

The waves of Cardigan Bay crashed against the desolate shore. Far above, fog fingers traced cliffs that were old when Cunedda and his sons first came to the land of Gwynedd. Below the shrouded heights but above the foaming surf, the mountains cradled valleys carpeted in grass first greened by the spring rains, then browned by the summer heat. Massive oak trees dotted the undulating hillsides, and reddish cliffs encircled it all.

Nomadic warriors came searching for a pass through the mountains, which they did not find. One of their chieftains must have watched a stallion gallop down the valley and leap into flight, and maybe his gasp startled the horse as it spread powerful wings, cowing the man in the downdraft. The men stayed with the winged horses, and both species thrived. The sons and daughters of the chieftain and colts and fillies of the stallion enfolded their lives with each other, with the valley, and with Gwynedd.

Wars came as they do wherever men linger, but conflict remained distant from the Welsh mountain valley and Tremeirchson, its village. Messengers and refugees came from strongholds of Celts and Saxons and Romans. Some stayed. The herds of winged horses were ridden to war when battles came near enough, but they sickened when ridden too far from their home. As the centuries passed, so did the men. Their languages changed, as did their weapons and clothing and castles.

Finally a time came when the Romans were only a memory and their forts crumbling stone. Peace spread across the Welsh countryside. The winged horses, their herds reduced by contact with men, existed only in Tremeirchson where each horse was assigned a groom and rider to nurture and protect it. In this time of tranquility, the battle god Aeron's hold over men was weakened. The people of Tremeirchson honored the powerful Rhiannon, goddess of horses and fertility, who taught them to balance the forces within themselves. Minor gods revealed themselves as winged horses and followed Rhiannon on her white mare. Aer, the silver, controlled men's dreams. Ystrad, the brown, nurtured their bodies and minds. Alon, the midnight blue, unleashed their whims. Rhiannon's underworld fire kept them from destroying each other.

The need for skilled warfare dissipated, and the people grew restless. The riders in Tremeirchson developed the Aerial Games, a tournament in the air. Each year the Aerial Games showcased the agility, speed, and endurance of the village's unique creatures. Spectators and patrons journeyed from the lowlands for the festival. Some of Tremeirchson's barns were small, but the more powerful ones boasted ten winged horses. Different clans vied for the support of wealthy lords from down the mountain. These patrons made it possible for the riders and grooms of Tremeirchson's elite barns to focus on the training and breeding of their winged horses. The lords chose to support winners, of course, and rivalries sprang up between barns. Traditions grew up around the barns and the Games, becoming the backbone of Tremeirchson's daily life. Sons and daughters of riders followed their parents into the sky, and barn leaders dealt autonomously with their horses and riders.

About the Author

Linda Ulleseit was born and raised in Saratoga, California, and has taught elementary school in San Jose since 1996. When not writing, she enjoys cooking, cross-stitching, reading, and spending time with her family. Her favorite subject is writing, and her students get a lot of practice scribbling stories and essays. Someday Linda hopes to see books written by former students alongside hers in bookstores. *On a Wing and a Dare* is her first novel.

For more information about the author and her books:

http://ulleseit.wordpress.com

For more information about the Flying Horse books:

http://flyinghorsebooks.wordpress.com

Follow **Flying Horse Books** on Facebook!

Excerpt from the sequel to ON A WING AND A DARE, coming 2013

In the Winds of Danger

Chapter 1: Nia

"If you refuse now, they will say you lacked courage," Tristan told her.

Lips clenching in response to her barn leader's words, Nia kicked her horse into motion. *Lacked courage?* How could he say that to her? It wasn't Tristan the Oh So Magnificent that was aboard a winged horse suited up for the world's first aerial joust. Nia kept the lance upright in her right hand, as she'd been told, concentrating on balancing the lance so its very length wouldn't bring it crashing down around her horse's ears. She'd never played at jousting like the boys she'd grown up with. Riding, yes, and flying, but not jousting. No one in High Meadow jousted! Not until today.

She urged Eira into a canter, the winged horse gathering speed as Nia tested her balance with the extra weight of armor and lance. She could feel the horse's muscles bunch beneath her legs as the chestnut mare galloped off the edge of the cliff, powerful downstrokes of her huge wings lifting her into the sky as the ground fell away. Her mane, perfectly matching the silky brown of her coat, whipped in the breeze. Nia watched Eira's ears. They'd go back flat against her head if the mare was overburdened. So far, the horse didn't seem to notice her rider's added pounds.

"Madness, madness, madness," Nia muttered in time with the mare's wingstrokes.

Inhaling deeply, a breath meant to be calming, Nia leaned forward and patted the mare's neck, warm but not yet damp with sweat. A few tendrils of mane blew across her face. The gray Welsh skies were empty this morning. Usually they were full of horses by now, stretching their wings and racing above the meadow, but today First Barn's herd was still in their stalls. Eira stretched her wing feathers to catch the slightest breeze, soaring into the morning. The usual mist clung to the mountains, drifting through the high valleys like a soft caress. The cool air wriggled its way into the unfamiliar helmet, and Nia was glad she hadn't yet pulled the face shield down.

Below, the village of High Meadow stretched before them. More than the usual number of villagers had gathered in the courtyard of the tavern, their eyes glued to the sky. Nia directed Eira to tip a wing to them. Her heart lightened, unable to remain heavy aboard this magnificent creature, the envy of all who were grounded.

But maybe they weren't so envious on this particular morning.

She angled Eira to face her opponent, basking in the response of the mare as she tightened into the turn. Eira was an aerial dancer, known for agility more than speed. Facing them across the meadow was a familiar stallion. Deryn was thickly built, more like the destriers used on the ground. His rider was also familiar.

"He chose Catrin?" Nia whispered, stunned at this

proof that Second Barn's leader may be nearly as mad as her own. Catrin had lost her first winged mare in an accident almost five years ago that caused them both to fall from the sky. Now she rode Deryn, the stallion that once belonged to her barn leader's father.

High Meadow's two barns were thriving, a testament to the leadership of Tristan and Evan. But no one could lead a barn without the patronage of a wealthy lowlander. Lady Margery, of Merioneth, was First Barn's patroness. Second Barn's patron remained a mystery to everyone but Evan, the barn leader. Evan and Tristan had worked together to build High Meadow's herd from almost nothing. Lately though their agreement seemed to be cracking. Tristan had lost his vision. Instead of leading, he followed Evan, and sometimes Evan needed to be questioned. Like when he wanted to joust in the air.

There was no use second-guessing Tristan's decision. Nia reached up with her left hand and clanged the helmet's face shield into place. She instantly hated the reduced field of vision, even though she only needed to see straight ahead. Grasping the amulet around her neck for a moment, she muttered a hasty invocation to Rhiannon, the horse goddess.

14129813R00172

Printed in Great Britain
by Amazon.co.uk, Ltd.,
Marston Gate.